Indian Summer

Richard Neer

A Riley King Mystery

~~~~~~~~~~~

other books by this author:

FM, The Rise and Fall of Rock Radio

Something of the Night

The Master Builders
~~~~~~~~~~~

I love you the best.

Better than all the rest...

Indian Summer

The Doors

Morrison Hotel 1970

ONE

"**I** have to tell you Rick, this is a first for me."

I left plenty of space in that declaration, hoping that my friend Rick Stone would be curious enough to engage. He'd been mostly silent for the first part of our journey, not sleeping exactly, but not showing signs of sentient life either.

"Feels like the first time," he sang, off key.

"Foreigner lyrics? Don't you ever stop with the classic rock references, Stone?" I said.

Stone gazed out of the passenger window of my Audi A5, perusing the South Carolina countryside. We were hurrying safely, cruise control set at 75, trying to stay in the fast lane of I-77 South with little success. Cars with Florida and Georgia tags were flying by us like Usain Bolt in a footrace with Bartolo Colon.

"I guess a friend in need...." I continued, praying he'd break up my choppy monologue with at least a pithy comment or two, perhaps even some enlightenment as to why we were traveling so far on such a vague mission. Stone probably figured I'd ask too many questions if he opened that door even a little, and that I wouldn't be satisfied with his answers. But hell, if your best friend is a detective, don't you have to expect he'll ask a lot of nosy questions?

My work was falling into desuetude. The last major case I had handled was the latest in a string of unsatisfactory endings. It had been months since I had engaged in any sleuthing that couldn't be handled with a few keystrokes. I suspected that this journey was a trumped up attempt by Stone to get me back on the horse. Although I appreciated the sentiment, any revival of my career would have to spring up organically, not through a well meaning friend's intervention.

"So Ricky, explain to me why we're driving two hundred and fifty miles to see your old boss? I mean, I've met with clients outside the office before, but never this far away. And not to seem too mercenary about it, but we haven't even discussed whether this is a paying job or not."

"I thought you were doing well, Riles. If money is tight, let me pay for gas. What does this pig get anyway, 20-25 miles a gallon?"

Riley King and Associates, (the sole associate being my Golden Retriever, Bosco) is keeping me as busy as I want to be these days. When Stone said he needed my help with an old friend, I agreed, trusting his judgment although suspicious of his motives. But on this sunny autumn morning, his silence was undermining my faith.

"Rick, give me a hint about what I'm walking into. All you said was that Ted McCarver was in a bad way and would I help. Next thing I know we're cruising down to Hilton Head to an address you punched into my nav system while I went for the doughnuts. Did you save me any of the old-fashioneds, by the way?"

Almost on cue, the female computer voice I've dubbed Maggie spoke from my dashboard.

"Prepare to exit to I-26 in two miles on the left."

I'd actually heard more from Maggie than I had from Stone for the last hundred miles. Bosco, lolling about in the back seat, occasionally poked his nose in my ear to let me know he was watching the road conscientiously in case any squirrels or birds happened by that needed his attention.

I was starting to get annoyed. "Look, I don't want to be a pain in the ass, but give me *something*, man."

I am used to uncooperative witnesses; I'd spent ten of my early years with the FBI.

Stone said, "Riley, McCarver didn't tell me much. He asked that I bring you down to the island, but to let him explain the situation, which he said was rather complicated. That's about it."

"Nice try, Rick but I've heard your radio show. You don't let people off the hook that easily."

"This isn't my radio show. It's a friend this time. Well … a friend and a mentor, someone I owe a lot to."

Rick Stone is a popular radio personality on WJOK out of Toms River, New Jersey. A fifty thousand watt FM station with a signal that stretches from Manhattan to Philly, it's a potent sports talk presence that can be heard by thirty million people. Ted McCarver had been Rick's boss for a long time before retiring a few years back and retreating to what I assumed was our destination. I'd only been to Hilton Head once, on a case that ended up netting me my current live-in. Going back there isn't exactly my idea of tough duty. The island is beautiful, populated with beaches, golf courses, and natural areas, each more scenic than the next.

But I hate walking into any situation involving important work unprepared. This last minute trip had already caused a potential headache. I usually don't bring Bosco along on business, but my girlfriend was away and I couldn't arrange last minute boarding.

"Stone, come on. I know you know more than you're letting on."

"All right, Torquemada, I'll give you some background, that's the best I can do. When I left the corps, I got a gig at a little rock station in upstate New York, near Woodstock and that was where I met McCarver. He owned the place and did almost everything himself: general manager, sales manager, program director and the morning show. Sixteen hour days. Then his folks died and left him some bread so he bought WJOK on the cheap. It was a dinky daytime FM station, but Ted petitioned the FCC for a bigger stick and turned it into the monster it is today. And every step of the way, I followed. *I put my back into my living*."

"Thanks, Baba O'Reilly. That's a nice little Horatio Alger story, but what does this have to do with us now?"

"Getting to that. As many years as we worked together, I never really felt that I knew him in terms of his private life. He never really talked about that stuff. You know, like you and me, we go out drinking and by the end of the night, I know more about you than I care to."

"Same here, d'Artagnan. Braggadocio about your swordsmanship with barely-legals is getting old," I said.

"Touché. But my point is, all the time McCarver and I spent together, he never talked about anything other than business or sports. Nothing about his personal life."

I said, "I always had the feeling he was gay. Maybe never came to grips with it. I met him quite a few times and I liked him. But I did notice he'd always have a different hot lady on his arm. Ah, not to shock you, buddy, in my profession, well, let's just say I sometimes come in contact with the local working girls and they were usually his companions."

"Hookers? *Take a walk on the wild side.* You never told me that."

"I didn't think telling you that your boss was using an escort service was something that you needed to know. I just filed it away. In case he fired you or something."

"Nice! Blackmail to get my job back? You'd do that?"

"Who'd buy me drinks if you were suddenly unemployed? I always thought it was kind of weird, him with hookers. He's a fine looking man. Tall, rapier slim. Great head of hair. Dresses nicer than Pat Riley. Intelligent. Wealthy. He'd be a catch for any woman unless, of course, he isn't interested."

We took the exit for I-26 East, an unremarkable stretch that would lead us toward Charleston or eventually I-95 to Savannah. Bosco leaned forward toward the front seat. Stone tossed him a Milk-Bone from the stash I keep in the glove box. After loudly chewing it to bits, he nestled down for a nap. Bosco, that is.

Stone was processing my theory slowly. "Huh. I suppose it's possible that he was in the closet all these years, but I never picked up on that. All the time I knew him, I never saw him with a guy. He never came on to me, ever."

"Can't blame him there."

"Funny man," he said. "But why would he hide it, in this day and age, when so many gays are out? Even in sports talk, which is pretty macho, I can't think that anyone at WJOK would give a shit. And the Jersey shore? Asbury Park has a gay mayor who makes no secret of the fact that he wants it to become another Fire Island."

We passed by a tall billboard for an adult superstore, stacked with a sign for Chick-fil-A, a company owned by a man so religious they are closed on the Sabbath. I had to laugh at the juxtaposition. South Carolina is perhaps the reddest of all states, but hey, a place stocking good sex toys and XXX videos? Long as it's not open on Sundays.

I said, "Regardless, Stoney, we're getting off track here. Or do you think that now he's retired, he's acted on some of the things he repressed all those years and it's gotten him into trouble."

"Possibly. He said since he'd sold the station, he has a lot of money and a lot of time and he isn't sure what to do with either. Sounds like a guy wondering what's next."

"How old is he?"

“Pushing 70. Saw him about a year ago. Still looks great, and far as I know, in fine health. Could pass for late fifties.”

“And he specifically asked for me?”

“Yep. Asked if I still was in touch with my detective friend, Riley King. Asked for you by name.”

“Well, no offense, if he needs my services, why are you along? Certainly not for the company.”

“Rarse, pal.” Stone had picked up this vulgar Jamaican expression reading Ian Fleming, and used it frequently with me. “He did say that this was a personal matter, and that he’d feel more comfortable with someone he knows as well as me in the room. I don’t know, maybe he wants your hand in marriage and needs my blessing.”

“Bosco, bite the man in the passenger seat. He is no longer daddy’s friend.”

My golden retriever didn’t stir, undoubtedly dreaming of chasing whooping cranes and seagulls on the beach if Maggie had let on to him where we were going.

TWO

It's an unforgettable sight driving over the J. Wilton Graves Bridge on Route 278 approaching Hilton Head. Splayed before you on the right is Calibogue Sound, on the left, the Port Royal inlet and Intracoastal Waterway. Directly ahead are marshes and wetlands scattered about until the land mass becomes solid and the compact barrier island begins. On the far side of the causeway, somehow the air seems fresher, the breeze friendlier and unspoken promises await.

Once on the island, Maggie guided us toward our destination, which is fortunate, because unfamiliar visitors are befuddled by the island-wide statutes regarding signage. The town fathers decided long ago that markers be kept unobtrusive. Signs are required to blend in with the landscape and thus are almost camouflaged --- colors favor natural earth tones and are extremely easy to miss. Combined with the fact that massive conifers and palm trees line the parkways and commerce is set back out of sight, the island is nearly impossible to navigate for the uninitiated.

On the plus side, you'll never see a more elegant Dunkin' Donuts facade, although I'd imagine that most connoisseurs of this fine pastry and coffee establishment do not enjoy equal expertise when it comes to architecture. I hit Maggie's location mark button as we passed the shop, knowing that without her reminders, I'd have a hard time re-discovering the site of these essential foodstuffs.

The nav system indicated a left turn into a development called Palmetto Dunes. We followed a narrow roadway through copses of pines and oaks dripping with Spanish moss until we reached a small guard station. My previous visit to the island had made me aware that almost every housing enclave is restricted. The only way an outsider is allowed passage is by express permission of the person they were visiting. Luckily, most of the plantations now provide an uncomplicated method to grant that authorization online.

Once we passed through the main gate, Maggie told us it was only a half mile until we reached our destination.

"Wow. I knew Ted did well when he sold the station, but there must be serious bucks in this place," Stone said as we pulled up to the ultra modern structure that McCarver called home.

"Yeah, if we had my builder friend Derek Davis with us, I bet even he'd be impressed. The ocean is just over those dunes. The view here is must be spectacular."

"The house doesn't look gi-normous though, Riles. Very spacious but some of the others we saw on the way in make this one look tiny. I suppose a single guy in his sixties doesn't need a mansion."

I said, "I don't know. Hef is in his eighties. Look what he has."

We made our way toward the entry, which was up one flight. FEMA regulations regarding flood insurance require buildings in certain zones to be elevated lest another Sandy comes through, although tucked away Hilton Head hasn't experienced a tropical storm of note in decades. Longitudinally, it is as far west as Pittsburgh, Pennsylvania.

Upon reaching the front door, an envelope bearing Stone's name was taped under the knocker. "What the hell is this? Is your friend sending us on a treasure hunt?" I said.

"He knew we were coming. I told him around one or so. Let me see what this is," Stone said, tearing the envelope open.

Had an appointment I couldn't postpone so I took the liberty of booking you a flexible tee time at HarbourTown. In the likelihood that you didn't bring your clubs, they've set aside some demo sets for you to chose from. You mentioned that you might have to bring King's dog. You'll find a small fenced in area around back where he'll be comfortable. I've left out a water bowl and there is a nice shady spot where he can rest. After your round, I'd be pleased if you'd join me for dinner. Just call when you're finished and I'll text you the details. By the by, your money is no good here, I've taken care of everything. Enjoy the golf.

Ted

Stone passed the letter my way. The missive was printed on elegant parchment stationery bearing Ted's initials. Why did he go to such lengths to play the gracious host, even including Bosco in his hospitality, when he couldn't bother to be there?

As if reading my thoughts, Stone said, "That's Ted. Thinks of everything. I don't think I ever met a man so, uh, detail oriented."

I said, "I think the word you're looking for is anal. Hey, much as I can't hazard a guess as to why he couldn't be here in person, HarbourTown is a terrific place to while away the afternoon. That's the course the pros play after the Masters every year, with the lighthouse in the background on eighteen. Two rounds, clubs, forecaddies. Had to set him back a grand."

"Depending on what he wants you to do, Riles, that's a nice down payment, at least. Feels like we're getting a taste of how the one per cent live. It's like *The Great Gatsby* or something."

"I suppose you can look at it that way. To me it feels more like *Dracula*. Maybe that's McCarver's problem. He can only see us after dark. Perhaps he wasn't a vampire when you knew him, but he's since been infected."

Stone played along. "Oh, come on. That's a bunch of supernatural rubbish."

"Supernatural, perhaps. Rubbish? Perhaps not," I did my best Bela Lugosi. "But it is kind of like *Dracula*. This mysterious, wealthy aristocrat summons us for reasons unknown, is not physically present when we first arrive at his formidable castle, joining us only after sundown. Next thing you know, we'll be eating insects and laughing maniacally. Hahnhehnmha."

"Halloween is a few weeks away, asshole. Okay, let's tend to Bosco and head out to HarbourTown. If this is a spider trapping flies, you have to admit, the web is first class."

THREE

The less said about the golf, the better. The HarbourTown Links are scenic, immaculately kept and very tricky. It emphasizes precision placement of every tee shot and approach. You can hit what you think is a booming drive into a tight fairway, only to find that a giant tree blocks your path to the green. The pros can work the ball every which way so it doesn't hinder them much, but at my level, I just advance the ball to a safe area and hope to get up and down. The forecaddie gave us tips which would have been helpful had I the skill to execute his suggestions.

Stone shot his normal 76, including a birdie on the signature eighteenth and would have been up for playing another nine had darkness not encroached. I was cranky (score undisclosed) at my futility and was happy to return to McCarver's lair, take care of Bosco's needs and head out to dinner, where we might finally discover what the hell we'd driven down here for.

Dusk made our journey back difficult, because most of the plantations don't believe in street lighting either. It served to make me appreciate Maggie more.

"Maybe Ted will hook us up with golf again tomorrow," Stone said as we blindly followed Maggie's directions.

"Ricky, I came here to help a friend. Much as I like golf, this wasn't in the plan."

"Riles, you really need to learn to go with the flow. You just had an experience that would normally set you back five hundred beans, and you're complaining. Of course, if I shanked it around like you did today, I might not be eager to revisit the scene of the crime either."

Another reason for my crankiness was that Stone, for months, would not let up on the ass-whupping he'd just given me on the links. Besides, I was concerned for Bosco. He was left in a strange place, his dinner was late --- currently in my trunk instead of his tummy. If I wondered what the hell was going on, I can only imagine his confusion. Unless of course, Stone had taught him how to *go with the flow*.

We pulled into Ted's cobblestone drive where another car sat, a battered ten year old Nissan, not the type of conveyance I'd expect a wealthy bachelor like Ted to be cruising around in. When we knocked on the door, it wasn't our host who answered, but a middle aged and dare I say, a generously proportioned Latina greeted us.

"You must be Mr. Stone and King. Welcome, gentlemen. Your doggie is in the kitchen. The poor boy was starving. I hope you don't mind, I boiled some chicken and rice for him and he wolfed it down."

Stone smiled. "I'm sorry ma'am, you are?"

"I am Anna. I tend to Mr. Ted's house. I come twice a week to clean and I come to be of service whenever. He told me yesterday that there might be a dog who needed looking after so here I am."

Anna spoke excellent English and in another setting would be called a personal assistant. She wore mom jeans, a brightly colored tee shirt and sandals. She waved us in and Bosco, hearing the door, came bounding out to say hello, and *where the hell were you?*

"Down boy. Well I must say, you do excellent work," I said. "This place is straight out of Architectural Digest."

Anna said, "Gracias, but it's not me. Don't tell Mr. Ted, but he really doesn't need me to come in and clean. He keeps his house very nice. I do a little mopping and light dusting and watch telenovelas. He sometimes ask me to prepare meals and leave them in the fridge when he doesn't have time to cook, which he does better than me."

I said. "I'm sure he's a gourmet chef in addition to his other talents. Is Ted here now?"

"Oh no, he wanted me to be here to welcome you and take care of this handsome animal. He left this and said to give it to you as soon as you arrived."

She held out an envelope, identical to the one taped to the front door when we first arrived. Stone was fussing over Bosco, so I intercepted it.

The unsealed note was again printed on his distinctive parchment stationery. Ted wrote that he hoped we enjoyed the golf and upon freshening up, would we meet him at his favorite restaurant, an address on New Orleans Road, not far from here? He'd made reservations for eight thirty, but to call the maître'd if we'd be late or wanted to arrive early.

"Thank you, Anna. Will you be staying here after we leave to take care of the dog? His name is Bosco, by the way."

"Bosco. I like that name. No, I have my children to go to. Mr. Ted told me that you'd be going out to dinner. He said leave your dog in the family room. Your rooms are upstairs. I will take you there now if you like."

The inside of the house was airy and well appointed. I found it strange that someone would allow a dog he didn't know to run free in his house. Bosco, while teething in his younger days, had ruined a nice oriental carpet, a crime he hadn't committed in years. But how could McCarver trust that my pup was so well trained?

"Anna, before we go upstairs, could I trouble you for a glass of water, or diet Coke if you have it?"

"Certainly. We have diet Coke. Anything for you, sir?" she asked Stone, who shook his head. Anna bustled off to the kitchen with Bosco close behind, no doubt thinking that more boiled chicken awaited. *Some loyal pal he is when food is involved.*

I really wasn't thirsty but needed to talk to Stone. "You're not laughing at my vampire theory now, are you, pal?"

He raised one eyebrow, Spock-like. "Fascinating. It's almost like Ted is ducking us. I mean, when he called, there was a sense of urgency, like he'd really like us to come down as soon as we could. It's weird that we've been here six hours and haven't seen him yet."

"Well, it's dark now so I expect we'll see him soon."

"Funny. Though Anna doesn't strike me as one of those nymphets that Vlad kept around the castle. You okay with leaving the dog?"

"As long as he has water and something to chew, he's used to being alone. I brought some toys for him in the car. He's very adaptable to new situations, so he's cool."

"If only his owner was the same."

Anna returned with my drink and we followed her up the wide staircase to our rooms. Alas, none of the Count's Ladies of the Night were hovering around to attend us.

FOUR

We got to the restaurant on New Orleans Road a few minutes early. It was a charming little place; years ago someone had taken a spacious ranch house down to the studs and reconfigured it into a cozy bistro. They had been careful not to overstuff it with too many tables. The menu boasted that every dish was prepared to order with fresh ingredients, so please enjoy your unhurried dining experience. A nice way of warning you that you can expect your food forty five minutes to an hour after you order it.

The maître'd, decked out in a splendid tux, squired us to our table. He explained that Mr. McCarver was not present as yet but had ordered a bottle of wine to be sent to our table upon our arrival.

I said, "This puts my mind at ease a little. At least Ted won't appear through the fog and tell us that he never drinks....wine."

"The Count offered Renfield wine but didn't partake himself, remember? Let's drop the Transylvania shtick, okay? I've known this guy for a long time."

I said, "Centuries, perhaps? All right, just going for a little comic relief."

"Why comic relief? The only tragedy we experienced today was your golf game."

"Hey, I think that's our man checking in now. You were right, he still looks great."

McCarver strolled in as if he owned the place. We later discovered our impression was correct --- he did have a substantial stake. (Bad choice of words, no more Dracula jokes). Stone and I were wearing casual slacks and long sleeve rugby shirts. McCarver was nattily turned out in a dark worsted suit, white shirt and crimson tie.

Given the casual nature of Hilton Head, his attire seemed a bit over the top, although I've always believed that it's better to be overdressed than underdressed. You can always shed a jacket and loosen a tie, but if you're wearing shorts and sandals to a classy place, there's not much you can do. I'd once been invited to 21 in New York and was required to don a loud jacket and tie that they kept for Neanderthals like me. It actually made me look worse and stand out more, which I guess was their point.

"Stone. King. Wonderful to see you. And thanks so much for coming. I can promise you a meal you won't soon forget," McCarver said, extending a hand to us both.

I'd forgotten how impressive his voice was. It was deep and modulated, letter perfect articulation without sounding artificial. It was a voice of authority, whether he was talking something trivial like sports or as significant as quantum physics, his sonorous tone projected knowledge regardless of his actual words.

For a man approaching seventy, McCarver looked amazing. His full head of silver hair was swept back from his forehead, longish but not inappropriately so. Perfect whitened teeth, his own. Blue-grey eyes and a strong jaw that had yet to blur into his neck. He reminded me of a younger Christopher Plummer, at around the age the veteran actor played Mike Wallace in *The Insider*, with Crowe and Pacino.

I couldn't avoid the obvious. "I was beginning to wonder if we were on a wild goose chase, Ted. We missed you at the house."

He tilted his head deferentially. "My apologies. I'm afraid I have a Saturday afternoon appointment that I just can't break." He didn't elaborate.

Stone mumbled some compliments on Ted's appearance which he took with humility. The only anomaly I noted was how pale his skin was, given the prevalence of so many outdoor activities in this favorable climate. Unless, of course, he only came out at night. Sorry, can't help it.

The waiter brought over the wine and Ted assumed the tasting duties, swirling it in his glass and sniffing critically before granting his approval. "I've ordered two bottles for tonight," he said. "Silver Oak cabernet. This first, 1991, I consider superior. I would have preferred both be of this vintage, but our wine steward informed me we are still searching for more, it's that rare. I hope you won't be too disappointed in the second bottle. Silver Oak 2000. It's lacking some of the subtle notes of the earlier vintage, but a nice finish nonetheless"

He was barking up the wrong tree with us. Although we enjoy wine, anything past fifteen dollars is wasted on our inexpert palates. I had a feeling that these cabs retailed for many multiples of that, especially given the markups levied in fine restaurants. The wine was very nice, but any observations I might make would only reveal my ignorance.

"So Ted, we're here to help," I said. I tried to keep impatience from showing too much. I should just enjoy the night of fine wine and cuisine and worry about the job later.

"And I am grateful. But there's no need to plunge right into my little issue now. Let's catch up a bit first. The night is young and we can talk serious matters over brandy and cigars at the house afterwards. Rick, I haven't seen you in at least a year. Riley, even longer than that."

Stone agreed. "Yep, last time was at that new media convention down in Atlanta last summer. And I think Riles hasn't seen you since you sold WJOK," Stone said.

"Do you miss it, Ted?" I said, finally encouraging the small talk.

His manner was relaxed --- there was no sign of any distress weighing on him. Stone and he went on with their shop talk. I was observing Ted for a tell, any indication of his troubles, but he seemed cheerfully engaged and sharp.

He said, "Not really. I got out at the right time. No offense Rick, but radio is in real trouble. Stations are worth half of what they were when I sold. Music radio is dying; I don't expect it will be around in ten years. And the bad news for talk is that ratings are down dramatically across the country. AM in particular. I can hear your show now that the station streams. You sound good. They treating you well?"

"Not bad. The great thing is that they let me work from wherever I want now. I've got a Shure RE20 microphone and a Comrex Access, and it sounds just like I'm in the Toms River studio when I'm six hundred miles away."

The meal was superb. A lot of French names that my rudimentary language skills couldn't begin to translate, but Ted took the time to explain the essence of each course, including how it was prepared and what our options were. He was solicitous of our tastes and made his suggestions on what he had gleaned were our preferences. He achieved a perfect score on that count.

As he had recommended earlier, we followed him home for brandy and cigars. Ted was driving a late model Jag, and we were happy to track his taillights through the darkness. When we got near his house, the lights, both interior and exterior, came alive and the place was as illuminated as the Statue of Liberty. There must be an app for that, although I'm sure Bosco was unimpressed.

I don't indulge in cigar smoking and have never understood its appeal. However, Stone was a connoisseur of the evil weed and was mightily impressed by the Cubans that Ted proffered.

I watched them go through their puffy rituals, hoping that McCarver would finally deem it time to reveal why he summoned us. Alas, Stone and McCarver seemed perfectly content to wrap themselves in a smoky euphoria while I stroked Bosco's ears and tried to shield his delicate snout from the leafy bouquet.

"So Rick, are you still seeing Lisa Tillman?" Ted asked.

"Nope." His year with Lisa was still a sore point with him, proof that he and Ted had never discussed personal matters. She had dumped Rick unceremoniously when she hooked up with a television producer who could advance her career.

"She was a beautiful lady. I remember traffic stopped whenever she'd come up to the station to visit you."

Stone was handling this a lot better than I'd expected. When Lisa left him the first time, he'd sunk into a six months long depression when I actually feared that he'd drink himself to death. And it was only the near death experience he'd had after being shot that made him appreciate his life. He'd taken bullets intended for me. We'd been best friends before he performed that heroic act, but since that day, the bond was indissoluble.

Stone sighed. "Well Ted, beauty isn't everything. As old Imus used to say, 'no matter how hot some chick is, there is always some guy who got tired of fucking her.'"

"He said this off-the-air, I hope," McCarver said, laughing.

"Yeah, he's not that far gone yet. But no, since Lisa, women are strictly recreational for me. I'll take my pleasure as it comes."

He was telling the truth. He'd developed a pretty cynical attitude toward the opposite sex after Lisa. He had been convinced that she was THE one. Fifteen years younger than he, she was gorgeous, a football sideline reporter who loved sports. She had a degree from Wake Forest and was a scratch golfer. As I describe her now, it does seem like every man's dream mate.

But she was an unrelenting careerist who would use anyone she could to climb the ladder, and Stone turned out to be one of the lower rungs.

McCarver blew out a cloud of smoke and savored the fragrance. "How about you, King? Still not married?"

I was restless, not eager to play true confessions with Ted. The drive, golf and meal had made me drowsy and I wasn't sure I'd even be up for hearing Ted's problem if and when he got around to it.

"I'm living with a lady now. Charlene Jones."

"That name sounds familiar. Oh yes, the country singer. Is that her?"

I nodded. "The very one."

Ted said, "She played here recently. Every year, Darius Rucker does a charity golf tournament and last time, she was the entertainment. Lovely girl, very talented. How did you meet her?"

"Long story. Hey Ted, I'm pretty beat. I'm about ready to turn in, if you don't mind."

I was again thinking he'd want to at least give me a clue as to why we were here but he didn't take the hint.

He merely said, "No problem. Anna has prepared your room. Does the dog stay with you?"

"At home, he pretty much stays wherever he wants, don't you, boy? I'll keep him with me. That way if he wants to go out in the middle of the night, he won't be scratching on anyone else's door."

"Sleep well, King. Rick, another brandy?"

"I'm up for it. And another cigar if you're not too tired, Ted."

I don't know where Stone found his second wind, maybe the adrenaline of seeing his old mentor. Sleeping part of the way on the ride down didn't hurt. Bosco followed me up the stairs. Each of the four pleasantly furnished guest rooms had its own bath, ample closet space and an inviting bed, overloaded with pillows and matching bolsters. I retreated to the loo to brush my teeth and eliminate some of the wine. When I returned, there was a large Golden Retriever snoozing in the middle of the queen sized bed. I gently tried to move him over and maneuver my way under the covers but Bosco was out cold and didn't help.

It was quiet; I could barely hear a low rumble of voices from downstairs as Stone and McCarver happily chatted the night away. The scent of their cigars wafted upstairs, but it was not altogether unpleasant. I was out in record time.

I awoke to a low growl from Bosco, something he rarely did unless he was having bad doggie dreams. I had no idea if I'd been asleep for ten minutes or ten hours.

"Back to sleep, boy, everything is all right. Daddy's right here," I murmured.

He growled again, louder this time. I forced my eyes open and was stunned to see McCarver, standing in the dim light at the foot of the bed, staring down at me eerily.

FIVE

I rarely feel downright scared. Apprehensive sometimes, when dealing with the occasional dangerous character who can do me harm. But generally, when I'm prepared for trouble, I'm able to channel anxiety into action.

This was different. Being awakened from a deep sleep to see a shadowy figure looming over your bed would alarm even the most battle tested veteran. I quickly shifted into a defensive mode as plans and options raced through my brain.

If McCarver intended to attack, he must have a weapon. My Beretta was locked in the car. I always bring it with me on trips, *just in case*, but I never expected to need it this weekend. It certainly wasn't going to help now.

If Ted had gone bat-shit crazy and was contemplating a knife attack, my size and athleticism would prevail. Bosco would assail anyone who tried to attack me. My fears for his safety overrode mine, knowing the damage a knife could do to his small torso.

The other possibility was that this was a seduction. Was that what all those questions regarding women were about? Had I ever given Ted the slightest signal that I would welcome such an advance?

Assessing these possibilities took maybe ten seconds. In that time, McCarver hadn't moved. Then he spoke.

"I'm sorry to intrude so early in the morning. I wanted to talk with you alone and didn't want to include Rick."

Out of the corner of my eye, the red LED indicator on the bedside radio read six thirty. I'd been asleep for seven hours. Older people tend get up early, so this might not unusual for Ted, but I was used to awakening a bit later.

"Why not Rick, Ted? You know him a lot better than you know me."

"I'm afraid this will lead to a rather lengthy conversation. If you want to get dressed and meet me in the kitchen, I have coffee and doughnuts."

No attack. No seduction. Silly paranoid me, with my vampire fantasies.

Ted had said the magic word. Doughnuts. I just hoped that they were from Dunkin' and not the yeast ones so prevalent throughout the South. Although in a pinch on visiting turf, one could do worse than Krispy Kreme.

"Sure, Ted. Let me throw some pants on and take Bosco out. I'll be there in five minutes."

I splashed some water on my face and took the dog out the back door for a quick pee. It was too early for Bosco's breakfast, not that he'd mind gobbling down a meal this early. Problem was, he'd soon forget that he already ate and pester me for another helping at his normal time.

Ted's kitchen was impressive, like the rest of the house. White Poggenpohl cabinets, restaurant quality appliances, granite counters, scrolled wood and leather stools flanking the breakfast bar. None of this mattered to me or Bosco more than the dozen Dunkin' doughnuts that sat on the countertop along with a thermal coffee pot. Kudos to the man who thought of everything.

"Okay, Ted, I'm all ears," I said, savoring the rich brew. I bit into a doughnut; it was still warm. Either a quick burst from the microwave or Ted had ventured out early to procure them fresh from the oven at the shop we'd passed on the way in.

After refilling his own cup, he began. "You asked, why not Stone? I originally thought that his presence would make it easier to tell you my story. But the more time I spent with him, the more I thought it would only make it harder. And given his own situation regarding women, well, let's just say that he'd have a less sympathetic ear."

"Very perceptive of you. He puts up a brave front, but that experience with Lisa Tillman still bothers him. He tends to take it out on the entire gender."

The sun was still over the mid-Atlantic, not due here for at least an hour. The overhead pendant lights made Ted appear smaller and older than he did last night. I felt silly at my earlier apprehension --- he posed no threat.

"The reason I wasn't here to meet you when you arrived is that I've been seeing a therapist. We have a ninety minute session every Saturday afternoon which I consider unbreakable. An hour after that, there's a group that she leads, which I attend more often than not. I started going a couple of years ago. I'll be seventy soon, and I guess I've started to look back at my life and reassess certain things."

"Are you okay health wise, Ted? You're not going to tell me you have something wrong, are you?"

He smiled. "No, nothing like that. My last checkup was clean. No, it's just that I've been attending a lot of funerals these days. Old acquaintances are falling left and right, and I can't tell you how many of them seemed perfectly fine until they just keeled over one day. I'm becoming increasingly conscious of my own mortality, although I try not to dwell on it, it's there."

"I'm not that far away myself. But that doesn't explain why you need a detective."

He took another sip of coffee. The way he paused to savor it seemed like the taste reminded him of something. "I'm not going to therapy because I fear dying. I still think I'll live forever. I kind of feel guilty at these funerals because I keep thinking that I'm happy it isn't me that they're interring. No actually, the reason I started going to see my therapist is pretty basic. It's all about women."

If Ted was about to come out now, it wouldn't change my opinion of him. I've dealt with many gay clients over the years. Maybe some of my experiences could be helpful to Ted if he was having a problem acknowledging who he was.

He continued, "You see, Riley, I was married once. The marriage failed, and it was all my fault."

"It's never that simple."

"In my case, it was. I know that you're aware, I've used the services of prostitutes. I could tell you knew what some of my dates did for a living when you went to charity dinners with Rick up north. You never said anything to anyone and for that I'm grateful."

"Nobody's business. I have to confess though, I did mention it to Stone on the way down when we were trying to figure out why you needed a detective. It always mystified me, Ted. I'm not trying to flatter you, but you're a handsome dude with big time stature. I'd think women would be throwing themselves at you."

"That's not the reason I frequented and still frequent these ladies for hire."

Here it comes. "And your therapist is helping you get in touch with your true self?"

He smiled at the code words behind my mistaken assumption. "It's not what you're thinking. I'm not gay. And I'm not bi-sexual, either. Is that what you thought?"

"Had crossed my mind," I admitted.

"No. My problem is that I've been a total failure with women and the failure is all because of me. So rather than put another woman through my particular brand of slow torture, I've decided that it's better if I just attend to my needs commercially. That way, there is no misunderstanding or chance that I'll destroy anyone else's life because I'm a total loser when it comes to the opposite sex."

At this point, I would have preferred Ted telling me he was gay.

I said, "Wow. And I thought Stone had an attitude. Ted, you're being way too hard on yourself. I've been at those events where you supported charities like homes for abused women, Planned Parenthood and the like."

"Globally, sure, I've supported women's causes with my wallet. But that's in the abstract to me. I've failed at personal relationships, one on one. There have been enough of those defeats to make me certain that it's me, not them. I'm deeply ashamed of my actions toward the few women who've let me into their lives. That's why I'm not fit for any decent woman and that's why I decided years ago the best thing to do is to disqualify myself from any future encounters that could be serious."

Bosco had been lying on the floor under us and somehow a chunk of doughnut slipped out of my hand and landed near his snout. It vanished as quickly as it appeared.

"Ted, I could throw a lot of clichés your way, but I'm sure you've heard them all before."

There was a faint sound of water rushing through the pipes from upstairs. Stone was stirring. Was it the need to pass water several times a night that we men of a certain age are cursed with, or was he rising to start his day? Bosco's ears perked up, then relaxed.

"Riley, I'm sorry for the long preamble, but I felt you needed some background before I tell you how you can help me."

Bosco jumped up and yelped at some movement on the landing above us. It was Stone, ready to take on the day.

He shouted down. "Hey guys, you're up early. Are those doughnuts I see on the counter?"

"They are. And they're waiting for you. Good morning, Rick," Ted said.

Then he turned quietly to me, "We'll talk later. Don't say anything about this to Rick yet. There's a lot more you need to know. And at this point, you're the only one I feel comfortable talking to about this."

SIX

The meticulous genius who always planned several moves ahead had arranged for Anna to arrive right after sun-up to prepare her legendary blueberry pancakes, with freshly ground sausages and rashers of bacon. She even made a plain pancake for Bosco, which he made short work of. Doughnuts and hotcakes were a great start to his day, and come to think of it, ours as well.

After we ate, Anna cleaned up in the kitchen, my dog hovering beneath her in case another pancake might fall his way. The three of us settled in the keeping room where McCarver had lit the gas fireplace, which lacked the smell and crackle of wood but merely took the flick of a remote to ignite. The magnificent ocean views were obscured by what they now call a marine layer. We used to call it fog.

Rick and Ted began talking sports again and I again marveled at how off-topic I'd allowed this weekend to become. I tuned them out and fantasized about Charlene and how good it would be to see her after a two week absence, as she toured the southeast, opening for Dierks and Eric.

McCarver was devoted to accommodating our every need, except when it came to the purpose of our visit. He said, "I have the NFL package so you can watch any game you care to, Rick. I take it you're planning to do the show from King's place in Charlotte tomorrow."

Stone said, "That was my plan. I didn't bring the remote equipment down. Wasn't thinking I'd need it. For futures though, I could always do the show from here. Just need to plan ahead."

"I feel bad that because of me, you probably have a lot of catching up to do. Between the golf and dinner and our late night bull session, you missed a whole day of sports," Ted said.

Stone shrugged. "I can catch up this morning. Spend a couple of hours reading the papers online."

"Hey, I have an idea. Why don't Riley and I leave you alone for a while to do your work. Eliminate distractions."

"Ted, I can always do my homework on the ride back or tonight for that matter. I don't want you and Riles to have to twiddle your thumbs while I read up on some stupid BCS poll."

"I don't mind giving you some time to work by yourself. I always thought you were the most well prepared host on the staff, and I wouldn't want to get in the way of that. Riley, what say we take a walk on the beach and give Rick some space?"

I said, "Not a problem. It might spare me some more of his pithy comments on my golf game and Bosco always appreciates a walk."

Ted had skillfully manipulated Stone, playing on his professionalism. Most of Rick's listeners never considered the behind the scenes work --- programming and sales meetings, phone calls working his sources, and careful attention to the games themselves. I can turn off a lopsided match and do something more productive. Stone has to suffer through every excruciating minute of the local teams' travails. He probably spends two hours in preparation for every hour he's on the air. Fans consider it a dream job --- watching and talking sports for a living --- but there's a lot of drudge work involved. Although, as Stone always says, it beats moving oak furniture.

"Fine with me," Stone said. "*Alone again, naturally*. If you're sure you don't mind, Riles."

"Nope. After all the wine last night and your smelly cigars, a little fresh ocean air will do me good."

We leashed up Bosco, said our thanks and goodbyes to Anna and headed over the dune. The tide was low and the fog was lifting, but it was still too thick to see very far into the water.

The Atlantic beach on Hilton Head Island stretches over twelve miles. McCarver's place is near its midpoint. There are a couple of incursions where tidal pools that are too deep to ford break through the sand, but it is possible to walk for miles without turning around.

"If I know Rick, he'll be tied up for the next two hours," Ted said. "He probably won't even realize how much time has passed until we get back."

"To get someone to go along with you and make him believe that it's for his benefit --- that was smooth. No wonder you've done so well in business."

"Speaking of *business*. Let me make something clear before we start: I am not a charity case. I was lucky with WJOK. I sold it for many millions of dollars. I don't expect a 'friends and family' discount from you. Bill me at your normal rate or at a premium if you feel it's justified. And since this will likely involve travel, please do so first class. As for an advance, just name it and I'll wire it to your account."

Bosco was dragging me all over the place as he started after seagulls, sandpipers and a cocker spaniel that passed by off leash. I tried to keep him under control but a seventy pound willful animal is hard to restrain with all this new temptation in front of him.

Ted watched me struggle with the dog, bemused, but now he was ready to get down to why he had summoned me. "Through my talk therapy, I've come to some realizations about myself. I shared some of them with you earlier. But you see, I *do* want to get better. I want to have a successful relationship with a woman. I want to grow old with a partner. Not alone, or in the company of prostitutes."

"Bosco, heel." My dog was tugging at the leash again and I needed to concentrate. "Sorry, Ted. Have you tried online dating? Church groups. Your club?"

"Attracting women has never been my problem. It's what I do afterwards. Dr. Mills, that's my therapist, has helped me indentify some issues and we're working on fixing them. But some of these can't be resolved just by talk. I need to be proactive."

"I still don't follow what you need from me," I said.

"It's my fault that you're becoming impatient, I know that. But try to understand, I've been contemplating what I'm about to ask you for a very long time. I had misgivings about involving you, being how close you are with Rick and that I've always considered you a friend, if only by proxy. But I came to the conclusion that you were uniquely qualified."

Qualified for what? I wasn't going to ask any more questions. The answers would come in due time or I'd be headed back to Charlotte and Charlene with nothing but a humiliating round of golf and a couple of fine meals to show for it.

At last, he let it out. "I need you to find somebody. Three people, actually."

Finally, something concrete. A mission.

"You see, I carry around a tremendous amount of remorse, which is stymieing me from making progress. After all the therapy, we've narrowed this overriding guilt down to three women I mistreated."

"Ted, sad to say, just about any man at your stage in life has mistreated lots of women. Only three? I'd consider just three a major victory."

"King, I'm not talking minor transgressions here. Not one-nighters or a couple of dates and then not returning calls. That's a normal part of the deal, I get that. Women do that to men too, all the time. I'm talking about abuse."

"Abuse? Physical abuse?"

McCarver stopped walking and stared at the Atlantic. There was a catch in his normally modulated voice.

"No, it only got physical with one of them and I have a feeling she's the one who'll be easiest to deal with."

"So I find these three women. Then what? Deliver a formal apology? And that will ease your mind?"

"No, it's much more than that. I want to give them a million dollars."

SEVEN

"Each?" was my stunned reply.

"Yes."

"So you want me to find three women, hand them a million bucks each, and then you'll be free to pursue love and happiness? And here I was marveling at how you're always the smartest man in the room."

The sun was breaking through the fog and the ocean water was turning from dishwater gray to cobalt blue.

"You're too young to remember, Riley, but there was a TV show in the fifties called *The Millionaire*. This eccentric old fellow, John Beresford Tipton, whose face you never saw on camera, hires a man called Michael Anthony to dispense a cashier's check in the amount of one million dollars to a total stranger. It then followed the recipients' story."

"Why don't you dig up this Michael Anthony dude and have him deliver the check instead of me?" I started to walk away but Bosco pulled me back toward McCarver.

"Hear me out, Riley," he said. It wasn't a tone of voice I'd ever heard from the suave and supremely confident Ted McCarver, not the self-assured baritone I was used to.

"Let me tell you about these women. They could all be dead for all I know and in that case, there may be no redemption for me. But given who they were when I knew them, I'm sure a million dollars would be a godsend. I have no relatives, no children, no heirs. I'm in the process of re-doing my affairs, but bottom line, my money is mostly going to charity. But I'd rather see some of it go to people who I've damaged."

"Reparations. Noble, but misguided."

"I expected some push back from you. But you're my first choice, mainly because I saw how you worked back in Jersey. Stone told me a lot about your investigations. I admired the way you made moral judgments when it came to their resolution. You seem to have a firm sense, or at least one that coincides with mine, on what constitutes justice being served."

If I needed a testimonial for an advertisement, what Ted had just described was pretty much my philosophy these days. Basic detective work involves finding truth. It is fact finding --- separating lies and cover-ups from reality. But I do make judgments and exact punishment or exercise mercy. I've never acted as an executioner --- I don't believe that any man should have that power, even state endorsed actors. But I have punished evil people in ways I deem appropriate. Have I broken the law doing so? It has never been tested and I hope it never will be, but I sleep pretty well at night.

"All right, Ted, I'll listen. No promises."

"That's all I can ask. I said there were three women. Indulge me --- I need this done in a particular order."

We had come to one of the small creeks that intersect the beach. Back in my Georgetown basketball days, I could get a running start and clear the twenty foot chasm with ease. Now any such attempt would result in a cold wet walk back. Bosco has never been an agility dog, and I reckoned his chances of clearing the gully were as bad as mine.

Ted continued. "The first woman. She may prove the toughest to find. You see, I don't even know her name. I think her first name was Mary, but it could have been Maria or Martha."

"Okay. You want to give a million bucks to someone whose name you don't remember?"

"Please listen. It was 1974 or so. I was a salesman for a big radio station in New York. Our station sponsored rock concerts several times a year. One night, we did a show at the Beacon Theater on the upper West Side. I forget who the act was. After the show, well, it was the seventies, and there were groupies. There was a hierarchy, the band got the hottest ones, then the deejays, the roadies, then if there were any left, a lowly sales person might have a shot if he had an extra backstage pass. There was this young girl who was giving me looks, and one thing led to another. I took her back to the station. She was really into radio and wanted to see what a big time New York station looked like. She said she was eighteen and she looked it. Anyway, we wound up having sex on the couch in the sales office at two in the morning."

"Let me guess, she wasn't eighteen."

"That's only part of it. After that night, I felt guilty about what had happened. It was just quick and meaningless sex and it wasn't even good. So when she showed up at some other venues, I pretended not to know her. She seemed stoned all the time and I wasn't sure she even remembered me. Flash forward almost twenty years. My first big ratings book at WJOK. New Jersey magazine did a huge feature on the station, pictures, interviews, everything. They made me out to be some bloody genius or something."

"I remember that story. You guys were giving slick handouts for years."

"It really helped establish us with some of the big agencies. Anyway, a couple of weeks after the article, I got this letter at the station. It was from her. She saw the story and wanted me to know that all those years later, she recognized me as the man who had raped her when she was fifteen."

"Raped? Fifteen?"

"I was shocked. She described the night in question so I knew it was her but it was like Roshamon. My recollection was totally different. She claimed I forced her to have sex and that she was a virgin at the time. Claimed it messed her up big time but she had finally overcome the trauma and now was the program director of some station out on the island. But she wanted me to know the hell I had put her through."

"Did you try to contact her?"

"No. I talked to an attorney and he told me that in New York, there is no statute of limitations so I was in danger of being prosecuted but proof would be hard to establish. He said that it was possible that she would try to blackmail me and that if she did, we should discuss options. Paying her off or denying the whole incident --- you're familiar with this stuff. But I never heard from her again."

"But fifteen? From what I know of the law, it's not a legal excuse to claim you thought she was older. But I understand how, at the time, you didn't intend to have sex with a minor. So, if you don't think you raped her, why give her a million dollars?"

"Whether I did or not, her recollection of that night scarred her permanently. The letter was very painful to read. And did I rape her? If she was fifteen, it was technically statutory since the age of consent is seventeen. We're talking forty years ago. Things were different then. 'No' didn't mean 'no' like it does now that we're more enlightened. 'No' meant it was time to try another tactic."

I said. "Now it sounds like you're not a hundred per cent convinced that you didn't force yourself on her."

"There's no way of knowing for sure, is there? I don't think even drunk that I'd be capable of that. Whatever did happen that night, I'm ashamed of it. After we had sex, I dumped her out at the subway. If it truly was her first time, can you imagine how painful that must have been? I want to know what became of her and if she went on to recover and overcome what she thinks I did. And I'm lucky to be in a position to help her, regardless of whether my recollection or hers is accurate."

He shivered, as if icy fingers had clasped his heart. "Either way, she was my victim, I want to help her and if the money doesn't do it, I'll do whatever it takes."

I wasn't sure how I felt. On one hand, I don't think money could begin to make up for the psychological damage caused by raping a fifteen year old virgin. However, I could not believe that even a forty years younger incarnation of McCarver would force himself on an underage girl. The fact that he wanted to do the right thing now made me think that although he acted with bad judgment, it was not with evil intent. But would giving away a million dollars truly assuage his guilt?

"Ted, I'll do this on one condition. I want you to put me in touch with your therapist and grant her permission to tell me everything. No secrets. I need to know if this quest you're on meets with her approval and it can really help you. And if re-opening this chapter with your so-called victim may do more harm to her than good. If she's on board and makes sense to me, I'll do it. I'll try to keep an open mind, but I've got to tell you going in, I think it's crazy."

EIGHT

Doctor Jacqueline Mills was an attractive fiftyish woman who did everything in her power to hide her good looks. To wit, she wore a shapeless floral print granny dress, flat hiking boots, and oversized horn rimmed glasses. She pulled her unwashed hair back severely and did nothing to enhance its mousy color. Sharp eyed detective that I am, I could overlook these attempts at camouflage and envision the lust worthy creature lurking beneath the surface. Those fake TV makeover shows would have a field day with this woman. A little polish and she could look like Julia Roberts.

Dr. Mills wasn't available Sunday and didn't normally see patients until the afternoon the next day. Ted had somehow arranged for me to spend sixty minutes with her at ten Monday morning, either incentivizing her financially or just appealing to her therapeutic instincts.

The next problem was getting Stone to a place where he could do his mid morning program on WJOK if we stayed over Sunday night. Again McCarver worked his magic: he located a small radio station in Bluffton that had remote facilities compatible with WJOK and after a brief chat with the chief engineer, Stone was sharing his scathing critique of the Jets' latest loss with his New Jersey audience.

Mills worked out of a nondescript office on the second floor of a commercial building on Main Street.

Hilton Head didn't have a main street which bisected the island. Main Street was neither Main nor a street, but rather a series of outdoor strip malls. Apartments and offices rose over main level shops that sold ice cream, memorabilia, art, and antiques, punctuated by higher end restaurants and glorified diners. My builder friend Derek Davis had lost a fortune trying to re-create something similar but more modern in North Carolina.

Mills' office was in one of the plazas designed for professionals; it shared a floor with a real estate firm, an architect and a cosmetic dentist. Her space was spare but served its purpose. There were several comfortably worn wing chairs that could be arranged in a group setting or more intimately if the session was to be one on one.

"So, may I call you Jacqueline or Jackie?" I asked, after shaking her rather cold and dry hand.

"I prefer we keep this formal, Mr. King. Doctor Mills, if you don't mind."

No warm and fuzzies here. "Okay, Doctor. As you wish."

"I must say this is the most unusual request I've ever had from a patient. Mr. McCarver said that I was to be completely open with you regarding his sessions. He was quite insistent; normally it's the other way around with my patients."

"Bully for him. Are you aware that he wishes to gift a million dollars to three women in his life that he considers his victims? Is that okay with you?"

"Mr. King, I'm in favor of anything that will help a patient. I'm sure you know that if you succeed in spending three million of his dollars plus your fees, he'll still be a very wealthy man who will want for nothing if he lives to be a hundred."

I steepled my fingers and leaned forward in the leather chair. "Was this your idea or his? The reparations."

"Oh, completely his. I believe in discovering the experiences that shape our personality and resolving them through talk therapy. Once the source of some of these psychological scars can be identified, then true healing can begin."

"I'm curious as to how you came up with these three. I mean, a man of his age growing up when he did must have had many female friends."

"Oh, he did. He was quite adept at sowing the wild oats, so to speak."

"So again, why these three?"

"Actually his problems with women, like so many others, start with 'mommy issues' as the armchair folks call them. His father was absent most of the time --- he was a successful pharmaceutical magnate who traveled frequently. I sense he was a good father when he was available, but that wasn't often. His mother was left to raise Ted, their only child. She did the best she could, but she was a hard case. She was always bickering with her husband. Even though they were quite wealthy, it was never enough. She would always find someone in their orbit who was more successful and belittled him for not topping them."

"Did she have a career of her own?"

"No, and that's where Ted's problems stem. He saw his father work tirelessly and his mother did nothing but complain and cast him as a failure. She nagged young Ted like she rode his father. Nothing the boy did was up to her standards even though he was a high achiever in school. So to reduce this to its simplest terms, Ted resented women because he saw them as leeches, sucking off their mates' success and reflected glory while doing nothing to earn it on their own."

"That's strange because I knew him at WJOK and he had a female sales manager, promotions manager and he employed a lot of other very sharp ladies."

"In business, he had no problem working with accomplished women where he was clearly the boss. Take Donald Trump as an example. He's apparently appointed lots of women to big positions in his companies, but look who he dates and marries: Supermodels. Likewise in Ted's relationships, he gravitates to women he can control who aren't his equal intellectually. Where he could be the opposite of his father who was dominated by this one tough woman. With me so far?"

"So he liked working with powerful women he could boss around. And it came to personal relationships, he liked to be on top as well."

"That's a rather crude way to put it. He made sure that whoever he got involved with, he always had the edge. Women he had power over. He never became interested in someone he considered an equal, at least initially. And when two of the women he wants you to find rebelled, he couldn't handle it. It brought back bad memories of his parents."

This was a lot to digest. But it made sense now that Ted used hookers. They could be hired and dismissed at his whim. "And his parents aren't alive today, are they?"

"No, they died in a private plane crash that his father was piloting. They left him a good sum of money, which he invested wisely and multiplied tenfold."

I said, "He's a great businessman, no doubt. But he still seems afraid to trust himself in a relationship because of what happened with these three women. I don't know about the other two yet, but we might be talking rape with the first. How do you ever get over that, from either side?"

"This is the hard part. Ted did rape that girl in a legal sense, all those years ago. She was fifteen, unable to give consent. And back then, he wanted what he wanted and didn't take no for an answer. Lucky for him, with his looks and charm, he didn't hear no very often. Don't get me wrong, I don't think Ted is a serial rapist. I think when he got that letter years ago, it truly shocked him. But..."

She paused and it seemed as if she wasn't sure how to proceed. I waited for her to find the *precise* words she sought.

I said, "Doctor, Ted assured me that there would be no secrets, otherwise I wouldn't be involved in this."

"I understand. It's just that Ted should have been arrested for what he did if she had come forward. Can you imagine the fallout now if a high profile executive in media slept with a fifteen year old? He'd never work again. And my fear for him is that he's exposing himself to charges if he admits it now."

"He's retired and it seems he's willing to risk that. What about the girl?"

"There's no way I can know. From what Ted told me about the letter she sent years later, she was successful in her industry. As far as her personal recovery, I can't say. Even though she says it was rape, she may have felt she brought it on herself to an extent. That was a prevailing sentiment with many back then. Hearing Ted admit that he was in the wrong may liberate her from that. Or she may have deeply repressed the incident and reimagining it may be painful. I'd say *that* was unlikely since she was able to address it in the letter. She may resent the offer of money, or welcome it as vindication."

"So it sounds like I can't let him admit what he did, but position it that he is willing to help her based on her perception of what happened that night. That's a thin line but you're right, there could be no actual proof, just two hazy recollections from forty years ago. Unless she saved DNA and even then, I don't know how you prove it came from the particular incident. What do you recommend I do?"

"I can't advise you about that. It may work or it may cause unintended consequences. Ted feels strongly that he needs to do this and even if I do express my disapproval, he'll go forward anyway. And I can tell you likewise, that if you don't do this, Ted will find someone who will. But he thinks you're the perfect candidate for the job. Just understand, this will require skills far beyond detective work."

NINE

Stone and I were back in the Audi again, heading north toward Charlotte. Bosco was asleep in the back seat. Rick had just gotten off the air and was eager to get back to my place, where he planned to do his program tomorrow and then fly back to New Jersey.

"So, good show, Ricky?"

"Always better when the locals lose. Lots of second guessing. Angry fans calling for the players' heads. I have to calm them down, but at least it gives them an outlet to vent."

"Cheaper than a shrink."

"Speaking of which, don't keep me in suspense. What happened with this Doctor Miller?"

"Mills. She said she wanted to dissolve her practice and come to Charlotte with me. Started letting her hair loose and doffing the specs and then she ripped off her clothes. But I told her Charlene wouldn't like that."

"Even your dog wouldn't buy that one, Shank-o-saurus. Come on, tell me this weekend was worth it, other than me kicking your ass at Harbour Town."

"You keep bringing that up and you'll stay in the dark, pal. Ted gave you the bare bones, right? That he wants to lay a million bucks on three women he wronged years ago?"

"Not that I lean that way but --- for a million bucks? He could have his way with me. Yeah, he told me that last night after you went to bed for your much needed beauty rest."

I explained to Rick about the potential rape victim. Ted had given me a flash drive detailing his recollections which he hoped would provide clues on how to find her. He said that he'd already wired a retainer to my account, with instructions that if I needed more, all I had to do was ask.

Stone said, "God, can you imagine that. Some woman that you had a quickie with in the past surfaces and cries rape. I tried to talk Ted out of this. He thought it was consensual at the time. She told him she was eighteen. Why buy her off when she didn't even ask for money?"

"It's part of his rehab. He thinks if he makes it right, he can get on with his life and find a good woman to settle down with. And he feels guilty about ignoring the letter and that fact that he admits he is guilty of statutory rape at the very least, which could have damaged this woman in many ways. He said if the money doesn't help her recovery, he'd be willing to do just about anything."

"Like what, anything?"

"Personal apology. Start a foundation in their name. I almost thought he'd agree to a pound of flesh. Whatever they want."

"I still think that's a lot for what politicians call a *youthful indiscretion.*"

We were on I-95 and my favorite truck stop was not far off. It boasted a Wendy's, Dairy Queen and Dunkin' Donuts, a winning culinary trifecta. Stone had worked through the lunch hour and I was hoping his appetite would trump his eagerness to get back to Charlotte. That way, I could get a Pumpkin Pie Blizzard at DQ while he pigged out at Wendy's. Not exactly the same quality of food McCarver had treated us to, but more in line with our standard fare.

I said, "Youthful indiscretion? Well, if that's all there was, I would agree. But raping a fifteen year old is serious business. Now the two other women --- that's a bit different. One was his ex-wife. They were married for five years, and it ended badly. I haven't read up on all the specifics yet, but I do know he stalked her for months after she split, and she wound up getting a court order to keep him away. She feared for her life."

"Ted? Are we talking about the same guy? When we had a mouse problem at WJOK, he insisted we use humane traps and release them. Ted wouldn't hurt a rodent, much less a woman."

I said, "He admitted doing it and he hates himself for it. And then after the divorce, there was a third woman, who he described as his one true love, even more so than the wife. She was his first attempt at dealing with an equal, not someone he could dominate. They fought constantly. It was only verbal until one time, it became physical. She was taken to the emergency room."

Stone was shocked. "That's incredible. I've known this man for over twenty years. He's the most gentle man I know. In all that time, I've never seen him angry. Never heard him raise his voice even. *A Momentary Lapse of Reason.* Wow."

"You never really know anyone until you live with them, and even then.... Notice how Ted would only allow himself two glasses of wine? Apparently all three incidents happened when he was drinking much heavier than he does now."

Maggie informed us that the exit for the food court was but a couple of miles away.

Stone said, "You know, as half-baked as this million dollar idea is, it does reflect well on who he is today. The fact that he is willing to put out big bucks to make up for some of the bad things he's done, putting his money where his mouth is. Most men would just deny that it ever happened and blow it off. Plus, he confided in us. Stuff that makes him look pretty bad. Takes guts to do that. So his shrink endorses this?"

"Who knows? That's why I never liked the idea of therapy. They always stay non committal. You never know where they stand. They want you to figure it out yourself. So I don't know what she really thinks about this. I'm just afraid that digging all this crap up after all these years may do more harm than good. For both Ted and the women."

Stone said, "Like what's the worst that could happen?"

"Worst is that the first woman can prove he raped her and presses charges and wins. That's almost impossible. Or if he has some hidden agenda that could further harm these women. I'm going on the belief that his motives are pure. I'll play it by ear. He says he trusts my judgment. I have serious doubts about this whole plan and

I told him that. But he's your friend and I want to do right by him if he's leveling with me. I hope his faith in me is justified."

Maggie beeped two quick bursts. "Oh, damn. We need gas and Maggie says there's a truck stop just off the highway. Hungry?"

TEN

At this moment, Charlene Jones was not a happy woman.

We had met under pretty strange circumstances. I didn't tell her at first that I was investigating her husband. She got wise to that little deception early on. I was involved with someone else at the time, but after trying for weeks to resist her charms, I finally gave in.

But the red flags flying around her were larger than Russia's in October. First of all, she *was* married --- to a very bad man. Secondly, she had been an aspiring country singer who had slept around in search of a record deal until her ambition had taken a back seat to wedded bliss. Third, there was no wedded bliss. It was less a marriage than a business arrangement --- she gave him the arm candy he needed to ingratiate himself with Charlotte society. In return, he gave her anything she wanted.

The man she married was formerly a Russian mobster from Brooklyn, although she professed not to be aware of his sordid past. To her credit, when she found out about his less than wholesome present, she backpedaled as fast as her shapely legs could carry her. Her flight became academic a few days later when hubby turned up on their bathroom floor with a .22 caliber slug in his brain.

We had to avoid each other while the cops investigated the murder. But their probe was cursory. They quickly pronounced that Johnny Serpente had been killed by the mob from up North in retaliation for stealing from them in his past life. They took the attitude that he was a low life criminal and that no one would mourn his demise. Charlene sure wasn't in widow's weeds very long.

After a few fits and starts, she moved in with me. Despite my initial misgivings about the drug use and promiscuity of her youth while trying to forge a life as a country music star, I've never been in a more passionate relationship.

With all the legitimate reasons we had not to trust each other, we'd made a pact to stay faithful and not keep secrets. I had kept my end of the bargain. I was pretty sure about her --- there was no tangible evidence that she had strayed, so I took her at her word.

But I now was regretting that I told her about accepting Ted McCarver's case and given her a quick outline of what it was about.

"Riley, how could you? You've taken the case of a serial abuser and rapist, just because he was pals with Stone?"

Fortunately, Stone had flown back to New Jersey earlier that afternoon, just about the time Charlene was returning from her latest set of gigs.

"Charl, I told you, it's complicated. The man is almost seventy years old. He hasn't been with a woman other than a hooker in twenty years."

"That's the argument you think will sway me, sugar? That he hooks up with ho's?"

I wasn't making much headway with my vague explanation of the case. I had skimmed over the details, fearful that her reaction would be just as it was.

I said, "Honey, just hear me out. The man is seeking help, going to therapy. And he's indentified three situations with women in his life that he regrets a great deal. He's been alone for twenty some years because he didn't trust himself not to hurt someone else. And now, he's trying to make amends the best way he knows how."

"By paying them off. Sounds like more prostitution to me."

"He didn't limit it to that. He said he'd do whatever was necessary and even instructed me to make the money anonymous if I thought it best. He gave me that power. I think he's on the up and up."

"You told me yourself this guy is cunning as all get out. What if he's using you to get back at these women for messing with his life? God, there's got to be a song in this somewhere."

"That's you. Always thinking about turning somebody else's woes into a hit for yourself." I smiled as broadly as I could, hoping she'd see that I was only teasing.

"You laugh, but while I was on tour I learned a thing or two, talking to your bud Darius Rucker. He told me that the best songs are the ones that are most honest about pain because they resonate with country folks. If you can take the hurt you've experienced firsthand, and use it to make people feel better about their own hard times, that's what it's all about."

Rucker wasn't really a buddy of mine. I knew a guy who knew a guy who knew Darius, and I'd met the former leader of *Hootie and the Blowfish* a couple of times. We hit it off pretty well one night after a show while overindulging in adult beverages. I know him well enough to have sent him an MP3 of Charlene's work, asking for his opinion. He responded by hiring her to sing backup on a few small dates he was doing to try out new material. From there, he agreed to have her perform a couple of her own songs to warm up the crowd before he came on. Word spread, and now she was doing the same warm up act for Dierks and Keith and Eric and a bunch of other big names. The pay wasn't great, but the exposure was phenomenal and the encouragement she got from country music royalty gave her the hope that she could join them on equal footing someday.

"Char, I was very careful with this. I talked to the man's shrink. I really believe that this is a good man who has made some mistakes in one sector of his life and he sincerely wants to make up for it."

She sang in that honey soaked voice of hers, "And he's buying the stairway---to hea-ven."

Stone wasn't the only one throwing lyrics at me. "You do a country version of that song and this relationship is over. Seriously, I'm on my guard. If I catch anything hinky going on, I'm out of there. You're going to have to trust my judgment here, babe. Kind of like I trust you, on the road with hot dudes like Keith Urban."

"I'm six inches taller than he is."

"Doesn't seem to bother Nicole."

"She is a sweetie. She's been with him on some of these dates. Been nice as pie to me."

"Warding off the competition."

She was wearing jeans and a tight white tee shirt, looking good enough to star in her own video right now. She slid over closer to me on the sofa and tucked her head under my neck, her hands drifting down my stomach.

"Do you really have to go to New York tomorrow, darlin'? I'm going back on the road Friday. Can't you stay 'til then?"

"Duty calls. I've made some appointments already. Got to be out by oh-dark-thirty tomorrow. It's a long drive and I want to beat the traffic."

"In that case, we'd better get you to bed now."

"But it's only seven thirty, Char."

"I didn't say to sleep."

What could I do? Maybe tonight, I could help inspire another country song.

ELEVEN

I'm not a big fan of flying. I was okay with it before 9/11, but since, it's become more trouble than it's worth. Security lines where you have to divest yourself of all your electronic gear, remove your shoes and belt, and arrive at least an hour before boarding causes me to look into alternate means of travel whenever possible.

The most pleasant experiences I've had have been by rail, but alas, it takes thirteen hours to get from Charlotte to New York and the only available train leaves at 5 a.m. And as Harry Chapin sang, "Take the Greyhound, it's a dog of a way to get around."

So I left my warm bed with Charlene at six thirty and hit the road in the Audi. With any luck, I'd reach my destination on Long Island after the area's notorious rush hour let up. The money I saved McCarver by driving instead of flying first class was going toward a splurge on food and lodging: I'd made reservations for two nights at the swanky Garden City Hotel on Long Island.

Charlene would take care of Bosco until she left for the airport Friday, at which time our kindly old neighbor, Mrs. Keegish, would care for him until I got back. I hated to leave Charlene and the dog. Up until McCarver's urgent call, we had planned to spend a couple of days gazing at the fall colors in the mountains near Asheville during long hikes with our canine friend. There were several charming inns and Bed and Breakfasts in the area. Maybe next week.

The sun shone brightly over the Blue Ridge Mountains to my right. I brought an audio book, Reed Farrel Coleman's *Blind Spot* to make the time pass quicker. While listening to James Naughton's narration of the Jesse Stone tale, I thought about Ted's dilemma, Charlene's misgivings and how to approach McCarver's victim once I found her.

Ted, in typical fashion, had prepared a précis containing all the relevant information on the woman. She would be about 55 years old now and he thought her name was Mary. She had a longish surname --- something British sounding. She was a program director of a Long Island radio station in the winter of 1992-3, presumably a rock station. Through an internet search I found no such animal, but I did find a source who could help.

His name was Neal Rossi. He was an associate professor at Adelphi University in Garden City. He had founded the Long Island Radio Hall of Fame as a labor of love, having grown up in the sixties in nearby Roslyn as a fan of rock radio. Every Spring, the Hall inducted new members at a rubber chicken dinner at a local chain restaurant, and Rossi had dreams of creating an actual museum stocked with air checks and memorabilia from the golden days of Long Island radio. So far, the Hall had no brick and mortar presence, merely a website that was updated when Rossi had time. He was always seeking contributions to further his ambitions, but there was scant interest, even among current broadcasters on the Long Island. Most of them saw their jobs as stepping stones to the more prestigious and lucrative New York market, twenty miles to the west.

Rossi had been cooperative when I reached him by phone and agreed to meet me at his campus office. I told him I was working for an anonymous benefactor who might consider a donation if he proved helpful in locating an old friend who had worked on the island. He had a gap in his class schedule and invited me to meet with him then.

After meeting a friend for dinner in New Jersey, the trip over the Cross Bronx to the Throggs Neck Bridge was plagued by only minor delays and those damned potholes that I've forgotten about since I moved to Charlotte. I checked into the renovated Garden City Hotel, and after opening my email, watched a couple of mindless procedurals before drifting off.

Long Island is dark territory to me. I'd been there a couple of times on cases with the feds, but hadn't set foot in Nassau or Suffolk County in at least fifteen years. As I neared Adelphi's campus, I was impressed by the old stately Tudors and Colonials that lined leafy Stewart Avenue. The tall maples and oaks were nearing peak color and the ride was a lovely riot of russet and yellow.

Adelphi's campus is pure Ivy League, although the college itself isn't considered quite at that level. It is largely a commuter school. There are dorms, but not nearly enough to hold the entire enrollment. Tuition is on the steep side; the most successful team sports are soccer and lacrosse.

Rossi was a handsome, lean man, mid fifties I'd guess. He had a smooth, soothing voice that could promote sleep during his duller lectures. Dark curly hair, just a touch of gray. Intense brown eyes, Roman nose and the requisite two days growth that hip men sport these days. I'm not hip.

His office smelled of old books, furniture polish and the clutter of a man too preoccupied with academia to organize his detritus.

“A pleasure, Mr. King. Welcome to Adelphi.”

“Thanks for seeing me on short notice. I’m told you’re the man when it comes to radio on the island.”

“Well, I try to be. We have had quite a few distinguished alums who’ve made their mark. You’ve probably heard of Al Trautwig? Gary Dell’Abate? We’re not quite Syracuse but I’d say we give Fordham a run for its money when it comes to graduates of our communications program who’ve done well.”

“For what it’s worth, I applaud your attitude. We have a nice classical college station down in Charlotte, Davidson actually. But it’s manned by pros. No students on air.”

“Sad. Where will the next generation of talent come from? The internet, I suppose, that’s where we are anyway. I wish I had gotten here in time to keep them from disposing of the tape and record library. What treasures were lost then, we’ll never know. But let me not waste your valuable time. I’m afraid I looked into the situation you described but I’ve come up with very little.”

I wasn’t surprised. I could have gotten the same information or lack thereof from Rossi on the telephone or via email, but I prefer face to face encounters with sources. Although Rossi had no reason that I knew of to conceal anything, he might know something that he didn’t know he knew.

"Well professor, it's a tough nut, I'll grant you. Exactly how many rock stations were on the island in 1993ish?"

"Two main ones. There was WLIR and WBAB. LIR was started as a rock station in 1970. They were the first suburban station in the country that could claim to be free form, although the man who founded it, Michael Harrison, might bristle at that description. They had structure, but the rules were so loose that by today's standards, they'd be considered inconsequential. By the nineties, they had been programmed for years by a man named Denis McNamara, who guided them through their salad days doing what they call Triple A, or adult alternative as WDRE."

"And what about this WBAB?"

"They were a highly structured and very successful AOR station, or album oriented rock. Another case of a long time programmer. Very little turnover there and certainly there was no Mary running that place in 1993."

I looked out his window at the ivy covered brick building across the way. "How about the campus station here, WBAU, is it? No female programmer named Mary? Or anything close?"

"I'm afraid not. There is one possibility I thought of, but I hesitate to send you down a blind alley."

"Blind Alleys 'R Us. That's my job description."

"There was a small time station in Garden City, broadcasting out of the hotel where you're staying. WGCR, Garden City Radio. They lost their license years ago, but I think they were around in 1993. They're kind of off my radar screen because they were low power and they tried a lot of different formats before they went under. But they did play rock music for a while."

"Why did they lose their license?"

"Funny, it's for something that's pretty common these days. They leased out the station. Back when the FCC had real teeth, they insisted that the license holder have complete control over the programming. That didn't preclude blocks of time sold to advertisers for infomercials, but the licensee was responsible for content. Apparently they had sold their entire weekend programming to a Middle Eastern group that was linked to terrorists. A lot of it was Farsi or Urdu or some other language. The owners probably had no idea what went out over their airwaves. The commission was about to pull the license when they went dark on their own. Without the revenue from the Middle Eastern clients, who were apparently paying quite a premium to lease the space, they couldn't stay afloat."

I remembered something from my FBI days --- the first World Trade Center bombing in 1993. I knew we were investigating the brother in law of one of the perps. He had something to do with a syndicated radio show that ran on a couple of stations in the tri-state area. We were afraid the program was being used to pass coded messages to other cells. They eventually cleared the guy --- his biggest issue was marrying the sister of a terrorist.

"Can you point me toward someone who might know?"

He pulled a keyboard drawer from beneath his desk. "I've got a pretty good list of stations on the Island

and who the licensees were. The owner's name was Evan Rogers. Let me check something here." He punched a few keys, fiddled with the mouse and said, "Yes, sir. He's still listed if it's the same guy. He'd have to be in his late seventies now, maybe eighty. Lives in Long Beach. You know where that is?"

"No, but I have a very intelligent nav system."

He gave me an address and phone number. "This may not help. Again, I'd hate to send you on a wild goose chase. This address is about fifteen, maybe twenty miles due south. Might be a total waste of your time."

"Professor, I'm used to that. I drove all the way up from Charlotte to find this lady, and I don't have any other leads so I'll follow this one. Even if this fellow doesn't know directly, he might point me toward someone who does."

"Sorry, I couldn't be of more assistance. You know, I hate to bring this up, but you mentioned on the phone that your client was somewhat of a philanthropist who had an interest in radio. The Hall of Fame is always looking for support."

Aren't we all? McCarver's largesse could be better spent than on a tribute to some minor league local celebrities. Would Rick Stone be likewise immortalized someday? I shuddered at the thought.

"I'll report your interest to him and he'll make the call. It's his money. But thanks for your help, professor. Keep up the good work with the students."

"And good luck to you, finding this woman. I hope she's worth the expense your client has incurred finding her."

If he only knew.

TWELVE

I wasn't looking for trouble. I was polite. I called ahead. It didn't matter. Trouble found me.

Despite what I'd told Rossi, it was a waste of my time to drive all the way to Long Beach if Evan Rogers didn't live there or it was the wrong Evan Rogers. So I called the number Rossi had given me and after four rings, a woman's voice answered.

"Hello, is this the Rogers Residence?" I put on my best radio voice, my McCarver impression.

"It is. Who's calling?" The voice was whiskey-cigarette husky. The late Joan Rivers came to mind.

"My name is Riley King. Is Mr. Rogers available?" And is he wearing a cardigan?

"He's at work. What's this all about?"

"I'm trying to locate someone he employed a while ago. The lady has come into an inheritance and the family has lost track of her. So were re-tracing her employment history in hopes of finding her."

This was close enough to the truth without telling the world that McCarver may have raped a teenager.

"Listen, mister, car salesmen come and go like streetcars. You can't expect my husband to remember them all."

“Car salesman? Forgive me, I thought that this is the Evan Rogers who owned a radio station in Garden City some years back. Have I contacted the wrong party?”

“Oh that. Well, that was a long time ago. Why do you want to know about someone who worked there back then?” There was a suspicious tone in her voice.

“As I said, there’s a decent amount of money involved and the estate would prefer that the government didn’t get it.”

“My husband is at one of his dealerships. I’m not sure which one. Hold on, let me find out.”

The phone clicked loudly in my ear and I wasn’t sure if she had inadvertently cut me off. As annoying as that MUZAK is that businesses play on hold, at least you know that you are still in the queue to be answered by a human eventually. I did a quick search and discovered that Evan Rogers was a major car dealer on the island, owning several franchises stretching from Hempstead to Oceanside.

After a couple of minutes, whiskey voice clicked back on.

“Hello? I’m afraid I forgot your name.”

“It’s King. Riley King, ma’am.” My, I was polite today.

“He’s at the Cadillac dealership in Valley Stream. Near the Sunrise Mall. You know the place?”

“I’m sure I can find it. And he’s there now?

"He'll be expecting you." She hung up before I could ask how the hell he could be expecting me when she claimed to have forgotten my name. Regardless, maybe I had found someone who worked with Mary whatever-her-last-name-was.

Maggie somehow thought that Rogers Cadillac was a POI, or point of interest. I've never been interested in Cadillacs or car dealerships in general, having been screwed around by enough of them in my life. But like Audi and other luxury brands, Caddy dealers now tailor their showrooms to match the cars --- large, posh and overpriced. The service areas boast free wi-fi, coffee and snacks for those who have time to wait for minor service calls.

I parked the A5 out front and walked across the gleaming marble floor toward the pretty receptionist. She looked up at me from her massive mahogany desk, smiling. Checked her fingers, no rings. There was a time when I might have tried to weasel her phone number for a drink later while I was in town on a road trip, but I have been unfailingly loyal to Charlene. I hope that she reciprocates with Dierks and Eric and Keith.

Regardless, I flashed my most devilishly charming smile. "Riley King. I'm here to see Mr. Rogers. I believe his wife called ahead and he expects me."

"Certainly, sir. Please have a seat and I'm sure he'll be out shortly."

I retreated to an oversized velvet sectional that could sleep three in a pinch. The pretty receptionist called what I presumed was Rogers' private office. She frowned, nodded, and waved me back to her desk.

"He's in the service area at the moment. If you'll just go outside that door over there, his assistant will show you back."

My antenna went up. Why the service area? Why wouldn't he just have me wait in the showroom until he could see me in his office? My suspicions were confirmed when a burly man in mechanics' coveralls met me outside the tall glass doors. This was not Mr. Rogers' personal assistant.

"You King?" he asked, gruffly.

"Well, I would have settled for president, but you know the peasants."

He didn't appreciate my wit. These kids today.

"This way," was all he said. A Dale Carnegie course was in order.

He led me into the mammoth service barn. The place was immaculate, with epoxy painted cement floors that bore not a drop of engine oil. All the tools, parts and lubricants were neatly organized along the walls, which were painted a soothing cream color. Not a stain or chip marred their utilitarian simplicity. A far cry from the smelly garage that my mechanic in Charlotte uses to mend the Audi.

My grunty friend was joined by another equally large fellow. "This way," he repeated, pointing to a unmarked steel door on the opposite side of the space. He led the way, while his second in command trailed behind.

This smelled like trouble, but I couldn't imagine why. Other than Professor Rossi, no one could possibly know the reason I was coming. And since my intention was to hand out money to a (maybe) former employee, why the muscle?

Mechanic #1 opened the door and as I anticipated, his cohort shoved me inside. I stumbled into a darkened room whose main feature was a bench in front of a wall of metal lockers. A changing room for the mechanics, perhaps leading to a shower where they could clean up after work.

Both men converged on me, fists at the ready.

“Hey men, is this the way you treat paying customers?” I quipped, trying to keep them off balance with my innate charisma.

It didn’t work. The first one took a wild swing at my gut, which I easily sidestepped while planting my heel in his kneecap. He crumbled to the ground in pain. His buddy dove at me. Again I ducked under his punch and delivered a forearm shiver to the base of his nose. A loud crack signaled its effectiveness and he howled in agony. These were not pros, just big guys who had probably participated in their share of beer fights on Saturday nights and looked dangerous with their bulk and tattoos. They weren’t --- not to me, anyway.

“All right, enough of that.” A voice boomed from the opposite side of the room. I blinked through the low light to see a rotund man in a tan sport jacket holding a gun on me.

“Mr. Rogers, I presume?” I said, not even slightly out of breath.

THIRTEEN

"**G**ive me one reason why I shouldn't put a bullet in you right now," the rotund man said.

"Why *would* you do that? All I wanted was to ask you about someone who may or may not have worked for you over twenty years ago and you threaten me with a gun? And you don't even know who I'm asking about."

He blinked and wasn't sure what to do next, except tighten his grip on the gun.

I had to keep talking, engage him. "Think, man. This is crazy. You're a car dealer. Let's negotiate."

"What's to negotiate? You interested in an Escalade?"

"Okay, we can exchange witticisms all you want but just saying, you might want to take care of your men here."

I pointed to the two big boys who were on the floor in obvious pain. "Get that knee stabilized and that nose looked at. If I misjudged that shot to the face and pushed some of his cartilage into the brain, there might be some danger. Quicker you take care of that the better."

Rogers backed off toward an old fashioned wall phone, picked up the receiver and muttered something, still pointing the gun at me with shaky hands. He gestured toward another doorway, which led to a washroom. Nothing special, just a couple of pedestal sinks, two urinals and some stalls. There was a small tiled shower area with multiple heads across the way.

Rogers followed me in and closed the door behind him. "So you want to negotiate, eh? Let's start with why you're really here, Mr. G-man."

"G-man? I didn't know anybody still used that expression. In any case, it's ex-G-man. I haven't been with the bureau for almost twenty years."

I wasn't too surprised. When you Google Riley King, my website contains a blurb which mentions my time in DC.

He said, "Sure, I know that. But why are you still nosing around about terrorism and WGCR? Why can't anyone leave that alone?"

I finally understood. It had to do with the Trade Center bombing investigation in 1993, the allegations that certain radio stations were collaborating with terrorists. "Evan, put the gun down. I was hired by a man who was a radio station owner like yourself. He's looking for a woman he met years ago who may have worked for you. She claimed she was a program director on a Long Island rock station around 1993 and her name was Mary. That's all."

"Mary Chesterton. Yeah, she worked for me. What of it? She was a good old American girl from Brooklyn. Catholic. Nothing to do with the fatwa."

This was exciting. I finally had a name. If I could convince this oaf not to shoot me, I had something I could work with.

I heard some rumbling in the next room, which I assumed was whoever Rogers had called to attend to his wounded mechanics. The heavyset man was sweating profusely now, looking for a way out.

"Evan, let's go back to your office and you tell me why you'd go to such lengths to avoid a few questions. Maybe I can help. There's something that doesn't make sense here. Tell me your story."

Rogers hesitated, then lowered the gun. It was a .22, not much stopping power. I had one myself and it was great for intimidation purposes against someone who didn't know guns, but not effective against professionals. But from the get-go, it was obvious that Rogers' men weren't pros.

"What about my guys? You hurt them pretty bad."

"They started it. I did the least I could to incapacitate them. For future reference, you might try calling them in *after* you call bullshit on someone, not before."

Now that the immediate threat of the pistol was out of the way, I started thinking more critically. Rogers was no older than me, not seventy or eighty as Rossi had speculated. Twenty years and fifty pounds ago, he probably wasn't a bad looking guy. Thick black hair, slicked back. Regular features, gentle brown eyes. His tan blazer was a couple of sizes too small, it could never be buttoned while on him. If you crossed paths with him on the street, you wouldn't look twice. You'd think he was a nebbish, a car dealer. Which is what he was.

Once in his office, he motioned to a small wooden armchair in front of his desk and I sat. He had a battered grey metal desk and a credenza behind it, which housed his mini-bar. He poured himself a generous dollop of cheap scotch, not bothering to offer me any. I had caught some on his breath earlier, which might explain the extreme of his paranoia.

"All right King, your turn. What about Mary Chesterton? Why the interest?"

"The man who hired me is an older gentleman. He's quite wealthy and more than a little eccentric. Back in the seventies, he knew this Mary Chesterton and she made quite an impression. Well, he has no heirs, and he wants to give her some money. But he knew her forty years ago. Didn't remember her full name, just a few odd facts about her. So he hired me to find her. That's it. Now your turn. Why turn a gun on a total stranger?"

He took a pull on the scotch, drunk neat. "I wasn't going to shoot you. I wanted to scare you, that's all. I was afraid someone hired you to re-open the case and screw us in some civil suit."

"Who could possibly instigate a civil suit? The families of the victims of the first bombing? Even the sleaziest ambulance chaser would have a hard time making that stick. Come on, that can't be it."

He took long drink, draining the glass, and poured himself another. Sighing deeply he said, "I'm not a big fan of the FBI. Those government bastards killed my daddy."

There were and still are some tough guy agents, especially when it comes to terrorist suspects. My guess is that most of my countrymen today really don't mind. But I would be shocked if any of the gung-ho types I knew back then of would roust a natural born American citizen to the extent of killing him. I let the accusation hang and said, "I'm listening."

"I'm Evan Rogers, the second. My dad started selling cars back in the fifties. Built an empire from scratch, became the biggest dealer on the island. Manhattan to Montauk we used to say. I was a typical sixties kid, all rock and roll and revolution. Hated my dad's materialism. Last thing in the world I wanted to do was sell cars."

He took another swallow.

"By the end of the eighties, I was approaching thirty. Never earned a dime on my own. Parties, coke you name it. Finally my dad sat me down and told me I had two months to get my shit together or he'd cut me off completely. Disown me. Said it was time to decide what I was going to do with my life. Even if it wasn't selling cars."

"And how did you respond?"

"I got wind of the fact that a small radio station was going through some hard times and was on the market. I'd grown up listening to Scott Muni, Alison Steele and the like and the idea of my own station was pretty frigging attractive. So I convinced my dad to lend me the money and I took over WGCR."

"Did you actually know anything about the business?"

"No. I was still a naive kid. I hired all my friends at crazy salaries and basically ran the place further into the ground. My dad didn't understand radio either, but he was pouring money in to keep it afloat. After a few months, I could see I needed help. I felt guilty pissing away my dad's money. That's when I hired Mary Chesterton."

"And she had radio background?"

"She claimed to know all those New York jocks I grew up with, told me stories about them. I never really checked. She seemed to know everybody and everything. So I brought her in and she programmed the station for like, six months or so."

"Why such a short time?"

"Problem was, we were still hemorrhaging money. Maybe if I had started with her in the first place, it could have worked but my dad was getting impatient and the losses were mounting. So we took on this clean cut Iranian. The guy was willing to pay us a classical buck to program the station on weekends with their towelhead shit. It was enough to offset the losses during the week. Well, Mary went ballistic. Wouldn't accept the concept of anything less than a pure 24/7 rock station. So she quit."

"Any idea where she went?"

"Oh, yeah. We had been doing some live concert broadcasts at a club in Rockville Centre. After she left us, she worked there for a few years, booking talent. I kept the station going, using some of her systems and programming it myself. With the money from the weekends, we actually were in the black."

"I know some of the rest," I said. "The Trade Center bombings. I was with the FBI then, stationed in Washington. One of the blind sheik's followers had a sister that your *clean cut Iranian guy* was married to. The Philly agent in charge had read too much LeCarre and thought that he was transmitting secret messages to different cells during the show."

Rogers nodded. "So they turned our little radio station over. Grilled the weekend engineers, held them for days, constitutional rights be damned. These were minimum wage kids, just racking tapes, trying to learn radio. They couldn't even understand what was being said. Arabic shit. Feds brought me in, interrogated my dad too. And my dad was the biggest patriot going. Fought in WW2, was gung ho on Vietnam. Lost all respect for the government, the way they treated him."

"So, of course, they found nothing to tie you to any conspiracy."

His voice grew thick. "If it had stopped there, it might have been all right. I mean, we were all scared after that bombing. Little did we know what was in store on 9/11. But after the feds harassed us and cost my dad thousands in legal bills, they turned the FCC on us. Those bastards wouldn't let go. They demanded paperwork, form after form, details on stuff we had no clue about. Even though my dad was no fan of rock and roll, he swore they'd never take the station away from his son. He even had to sell one of his dealerships to pay the bills. By that time, no one would advertise with us. Even though we were cleared, customers thought we were in bed with fucking terrorists. The last straw was when our lawyers told us that our case was hopeless --- that technically they had grounds to take away our license. That night, my father had a stroke and he died a week later."

The man's rage at the government was justified. Taking his anger out on a simple private investigator was irrational, but I had re-opened a wound that would never completely heal.

I said, "I'm ashamed to say that Washington did stuff like that. Scorched earth policy. Sending a message that if you collaborate with terrorists, you're going to get burned. Assholes called people like your dad collateral damage. That's one reason I quit the bureau --- they had no remorse."

"Yeah. So after my dad passed, we shut down the station voluntarily rather than pour more money after a losing cause. The car business got hurt too, but I dedicated my life to rebuilding it and making it bigger and better than ever. In my dad's memory. And I've succeeded. I'm just sorry he's not around to see it."

"Even though it's been over twenty years since I worked for the feds, I apologize. Keep honoring your father's memory, Evan. Sell a million cars."

He extended his hand. "Hey man, even my wife can't mention that radio station, without me seeing red. I can't let it go. I've seen a shrink. didn't help. I feel like it was my bullshit and irresponsibility killed my old man. No matter how many cars I sell will ever make up for that."

"I get it, but you can't take that guilt all on yourself. Hindsight is 20/20 and we've all done stuff we'd never think of doing now we're supposedly older and wiser. Even the feds who went too far were just trying to find out who bombed the Trade Center and make sure it couldn't happen again," I said.

Time to go but there was one more thread I had to pull.

"I almost hate to bring this up after what you've told me, but I don't suppose you'd have a picture of Mary Chesterton?"

"I keep a folder, bottom drawer. Every once in a while if I'm drinking and down, I pull it out and get pissed off all over again."

He pulled a manila file from a drawer and extracted a 5x7 black and white glossy. It was a yellowing print of a much younger and more handsome Rogers with his arm around a pretty young girl in a pantsuit.

Mary Chesterton was real. Now I just had to find her.

FOURTEEN

As I feared, the internet yielded no clues as to Mary's whereabouts. An image search found a couple of shots of her with members of the Allman Brothers and Little Feat, taken at the club where she booked talent. There was nothing about her online at public resources like the DMV or tax records, and my trove of private sites showed bupkes as well. I debated calling my old friend at the FBI, Dan Logan, but decided that burning a favor this early in the process was like a football coach throwing a challenge flag in the first quarter. If I was stymied later on, Dan would be my secret weapon.

The club that Rogers pointed me toward was in Rockville Centre, the next town east on Sunrise Highway. The village was becoming popular for New Yorkers who wanted an urban experience but didn't fancy the congestion of Manhattan. It had a convenient Long Island Railroad station that could put you in midtown in just over a half hour. Not far from the main drag were comfortably sized suburban homes, luxury condos and coops, and affordable rental apartments. The heart of the village was easily reached on foot from all but the most outlying areas, and featured numerous restaurants and shopping opportunities. The schools were highly rated; it seemed a nice place to raise a family.

Morrison's Road House had been a bustling tavern at one time. In the mid-seventies, it was converted to a club modeled after the Bottom Line, the legendary music venue in Greenwich Village. It thrived for a over a decade as the rock culture blossomed on Long Island, but things hadn't been so rosy since the turn of the century.

The proprietor, an aging hippie named Theo Bernstein, had taken desperate measures to keep it afloat. Live professional music was only on weekends now --- during the week, it was karaoke and open mic comedy. Most of the big bands who had made their bones at Morrison's were now either dead, disbanded or too important to play a five hundred seater. There were a few who remained loyal to Bernstein, thankful that he had supported them on the way up. The Allman Brothers had done a benefit for Theo a few years back when the place was on the verge of closing. It sustained them for a while, but it was a far cry from the days when the Rolling Stones played there for three raucous nights as they geared up for a major stadium tour.

Tonight was comedy night, with domestic draft beers for three bucks and ladies admitted free, waiving the ten dollar cover charge. It was just after five and since the club was on my way back to the hotel, I decided to pop in unannounced and see if I could discover more about Mary. I walked past the unattended front door and asked the barkeep if Bernstein was around. He rang back --- didn't even bother to ask who I was or why I needed to see his boss. Quite a different welcome from my last stop.

Bernstein shuffled out from the back room under his own power, but it seemed to take all his strength. He shook my hand weakly and motioned to a round high top, struggling to get his frail body onto the elevated stool.

"Mr. Bernstein. My name is Riley King. I'm a private investigator and I'd like to ask you a few questions." I sketched out my story about Mary's possible inheritance, and he listened with little interest, his mind elsewhere.

The man was dying. His body was skeletal, cancer most likely. His skin had taken on an ashen gray color and his oversized clothes hung loosely. The only thing keeping his trousers up was a belt cinched tightly at the waist. It looked like he had tried to shave recently, but long white hairs sprouted randomly, dotting his harshly creased face.

When I had finished my story, he withdrew a small metal case from his shirt pocket and produced two joints. He offered me one. I declined.

"Medicinal purposes," he said, by way of explanation.

"Understood. In any case, I was hoping that you might know where Mary is these days. How long did she work for you?"

His voice was think and reedy. "She left, what year is it now? Yeah, brother, she's been gone years."

This was depressing. Whether it was the grass, the meds, or just dementia, it didn't seem like Theo would be of much assistance. His physical breakdown directly paralleled the venue's. I imagined in its heyday, the club would have sparkled with energy, when big name artists would perform on its small stage. But now, with the late afternoon sun pouring in through the front showcase windows, neglect from years of deferred maintenance and uncaring sanitary practices prevailed. The interior partitions were painted black, scarred and streaked. Behind the stage was the requisite wall of brick, badly in need of re-pointing.

I could foresee the day when Bernstein finally gave up the fight and his heirs sold to some ambitious restaurateur, who would sink serious money into refurbishing and re-inventing it as a hip eatery, perhaps festooned with posters of its glory days.

"Mr. Bernstein, do you have any idea where Mary might be now?"

"Mary? Who's Mary?"

"Chesterton," I said, knowing my query would be in vain.

"I'm a checkers man myself. Chess was always too complicated. Some great artists on Chess though. All the legendary bluesmen."

He stared into space and took another deep drag. I was beginning to reevaluate my decision not to call Logan, when a stunning woman emerged from the back offices.

"Theo, what are you doing out front?" she chided. "I'm sorry, sir. Kevin, would you help Mr. Bernstein back to his office. Thanks."

She must have been hot stuff in her day. I had her pegged for mid sixties, but her face was still smooth, her long silver hair tied back. She wore a flowing blouse over a floor length dark skirt, barely disguising a remarkably fit body. She introduced herself as Theo's wife, Doris.

"I'm sorry, you are?" she asked.

I told her my name and my story. She lit up when I mentioned Mary.

"Mary. Our Mary. God, we hated to see her leave. She was a godsend, that girl."

"How so?"

"She came to us, oh my, maybe twenty years ago. We were doing live broadcasts with that radio station in Garden City, the one they thought that the Arabs infiltrated. She was working there at the time. She quit over something and their loss was our gain. She knew every rock star on the planet. Within a couple of months, she took over booking for the club and we had a renaissance. It was like the seventies all over again for a while. And the ears on her? My! She had a talent for finding new bands. We used to tease her that she had 45 rpm ears, although I imagine a young man like yourself won't understand the reference."

"You flatter me. I owned a bunch of forty-fives back in the day, but I was always more into albums. Why did she leave here? It seems like this was a perfect gig for her."

"One day a man showed up claiming to be her father. You're not working for his estate, are you?"

"No, I have no idea who her father is. My client is someone who knew her way before she started working here. She made quite an impression on him and he's an older gentleman with no heirs. He'd like to help her out, if she needs it. That's all."

She gave me a long hard stare, as if her deep blue eyes were the ultimate lie detector. Fortunately for me, I was telling the literal truth and she decided to accept it.

"All right, I can't see any harm in it. This happened years ago and I'm sure the father isn't still alive. She was in the back room when the man came in. She saw him but he didn't see her. I'd never seen anyone so frightened. She said she needed to leave right away and that she'd be in touch. That was the last time we saw her."

"She just up and quit after ten years? No forwarding address? What about back pay?"

"About a month later, she did call. She was living with a family out in Huntington. A rock singer, had a few bubblegum hits in the sixties. Played here a bunch of times with a pickup band, doing his songs and a few British Invasion covers. He was only playing music for fun those days. He'd become a builder, one of those rehab guys who restores old homes. When she called, she was living with him and his wife and helping out with the business. We kept in touch, on and off, after that, but I haven't talked with her for a couple of years now. She might still be with them. Or not."

"Can you describe the father?"

"Handsome gent. Tall. Dressed well. Very slender. Gray hair. What you'd call a patrician. Looked like a banker or some kind of businessman."

She had just described Ted McCarver. I needed to call my client.

FIFTEEN

I complain about technology all the time when it doesn't work properly. Or when it works too well and I allow it to do things I should be doing myself. I'm afraid it's making me lazy. I worry about how dependent I've become on my phone and tablet.

But today, technology spared me from making a big mistake and losing a potentially lucrative job. Without my tablet, I would have called McCarver immediately and cursed him out for lying to me. I would have quit looking for Mary Chesterton. But a couple of swishes of a finger brought up a photo of Ted that we'd taken this past weekend. I showed it to Doris Bernstein.

"Is this the man who came looking for Mary?" I asked.

"There's a slight resemblance. It's been many years. Is this a recent picture?"

"Taken a few days ago."

"Then, no, unless he's Dorian Gray. This isn't him. The man who scared Mary was older and much more gaunt. He said that he had been ill. Didn't have long to live and wanted to see his daughter once more before he passed. The man you're showing me looks healthy as a horse."

I knew Ted years ago and he'd never looked emaciated. Slender, but in robust physical condition. I thanked Doris for her time as she gave me the name of the former pop star who had taken Mary in. She also produced a head shot of Mary. She was older than in the one I got from Rogers, still pretty but she didn't do much to enhance her looks to my taste, with punk chopped hair and Goth makeup.

I drove back to the hotel in Garden City and ordered room service. While waiting for dinner, I settled in to do some research on the man who had taken Mary in after she left the club. Bobby "Stonewall" Jackson and the Rebels released their first record a year or so before I was born and continued to turn out semi-hit songs until the psychedelic era gobbled them up.

Even though Charlene is a couple of years younger than I, she is my go-to source for music history. She could probably get a job teaching a college course in pop culture somewhere if touring with the country boys ever gets old for her. Stone is a great resource too, but I wanted to see Charlene and my tablet indicated that she was online and available on Skype. Her image popped up right away.

"Hey sugar, where are you? That light is pretty harsh," she said. "Oh, that's better," after my webcam adjusted the brightness down a couple of stops.

I told her about my day, leaving the fisticuffs out lest she worry about my safety. She was sitting up on our king sized bed, wearing a white tee shirt and little else that I could see.

I said, "You look great as always, hon. How's Bosco?"

She turned her tablet around. Sprawled on my side of the bed with his head on my pillow was a large golden retriever.

"He misses his dad. I miss you too. It's great that you got that woman's name already. When ya coming home?"

"Hopefully over the weekend. I feel like I'm getting close. Actually, I want to take advantage of your musical expertise about a lead I have."

"I'd rather have you take advantage of me another way." She lifted the tee shirt, flashing one perfect breast.

"The NSA boys just got a rare treat. Careful."

"Really?"

"Just kidding. But on to business. What can you tell me about Bobby 'Stonewall' Jackson?"

She whistled softly. "Wow, haven't heard that name in forever. Let's see. Bobby 'Stonewall' Jackson and the Rebels were an English band. They pre-dated the Beatles and the British Invasion. Believe it or not, they tried to hide the fact that they came from Merry Olde. Their first record was out like in early 1963, right before it was cool to be British."

"So if they came along a few months later, they could have been like the Stones or Kinks or Dave Clark Five?"

"I don't think they were that good. Their shtick was to look like Johnny Rebs from the Civil War. At first, it was seen as a cute gimmick but the civil rights movement didn't take too kindly to their Confederate flag logo. They couldn't get arrested after the *Summer of Love,* even though they cut some interesting sides. Robert W. Jackson was what he started callin' himself in the early seventies when he had a bit of a comeback. Sounded hipper than Bobby or Stonewall. He was kind of a singer/songwriter. Think like a less talented James Taylor."

This woman was a virtual encyclopedia of music in addition to being gorgeous. I said, "By 1980, the only references I could find online to his musical career were a few one nighters as a nostalgia act, replaying his old songs with a pickup band. Kind of sad, Charlene."

"This is the business we've chosen." She affected a choked, whispery Brando as Vito Corleone. I'd never heard a woman attempt that impression, and I hoped she wouldn't try it again.

I said, "Well, it seems that Bobby has been doing home restorations on Long Island for the last three decades. *Stonewall Construction.* His website doesn't have any indication that he was a pop star once."

"I guess he wants to be taken seriously as a builder and not some dilettante, dabbling in it as a hobby. Although if he's been in business that long, sugar, he must know what he's doing."

"I expect so. I'll probably meet him tomorrow. Anything I can reference from his musical career that will ingratiate me?"

"The Rebels spent a week as the house band on American Bandstand after their breakout single got to maybe as high as #2 on the charts. *Not like Me*, was what it was called if I recollect. Paul Revere had a big hit song called *Just like Me*. a couple a years later Some thought it was a rip-off of Jackson's song. I bet he's still sensitive about that."

"How do you know all this stuff?"

"Back when I was an idle housewife, I studied pop music history with a passion. I'd go to libraries, music stores, then later the internet, and learned all I could."

"Are we all set with Keegish and Bosco? Are you back Monday for sure?"

"The boy is all taken care of. His food is measured out for a few days, got his toys together and she's a coming to pick him up in the morning. My flight gets in Monday midday. Any chance we can make that Asheville trip next week?"

"I hope so. I'm thinking if I don't hit pay dirt tomorrow, I may never. Who knows, this chick may have split for the Coast or Europe. I'd love to hit the mountains with you next week. I'll definitely try to make that happen. What's the weather like in the Carolinas? Freezing here later."

She flashed me again as if her erect nipples were an indication of how chilly it was. Beats Accuweather radar by a wide margin.

She said, "Getting really cold here tonight too, frost warnings. But by Sunday, back to eighty degrees. Indian Summer. I think it's actually my favorite time of year."

SIXTEEN

I turned in at ten, squelching as best I could fantasies about my next encounter with Charlene. Slept hard until two in the morning when I awoke and had trouble getting back to sleep. When I closed my eyes, I kept visualizing the photos of Mary and the prospect that I might meet her today. How would I play it? I wound up channel surfing the Velocity and History Channels until four, when I finally dozed off. I awoke for good at 7.

I found a diner with wi-fi on Nassau Boulevard, close to Hempstead Turnpike and researched Stonewall Construction while eating a mediocre Western omelet. Two cups of coffee helped me feel human enough to take on the day.

Stonewall's website not only had a marvelous gallery of *before and after* shots, but a webcam trained on Jackson's current project. It was a Victorian in Garden City, minutes from where I was now. The company was small; they took on very few projects and devoted their full resources and attention to each one. They were big on historical accuracy, incorporating state-of-the-art conveniences into noteworthy structures. Jackson's attitude seemed similar to that of my Charlotte builder friend Derek Davis, who refused to use cheap imitation materials, even if it meant losing business.

The website didn't give the street number of the project, but the avenue it was located on was short. The subcontractor trucks in front of the house were a dead giveaway that didn't even begin to tax my deductive powers. I wasn't sure if Jackson would be at the site, but I figured that one of the subs could point me toward him if I played a prospective client.

It was my lucky day. Not only was Robert W. Jackson on site, but he was a pleasant man with an open face and welcoming manner. I introduced myself by name only, throwing in some of Charlene's bon mots to loosen him up. I'd listened to a couple of his songs on YouTube and agreed with her assessment of their virtuosity, but I put aside my critiques and played fanboy.

"So, how did a rock star turn into a builder? That's an interesting career pivot," I said.

"I suppose it's like an athlete, Riley. Unless you're one of the super talented, you're pretty dodgy by thirty five. You never made it to the pros, did you, lad?"

"You recognized the name?"

"I was a Big East fan in the eighties, that conference's heyday. Saint John's, Syracuse, UConn, Seton Hall. Up here in New York, we hated Georgetown. I guess we were jealous because you guys were always so good. But you got knackered senior year, if I'm remembering right, no?"

As the years pass, fewer and fewer people remember my college hoop exploits. It wasn't like I was a star or anything, but I did have a few big games coming off the bench and had my knee not given out in my last year of eligibility, I might have been good enough to play in Europe. My life would have taken a very different course. I rarely watch basketball these days, I suppose to avoid being reminded of what might have been.

I said, "I'm flattered that you remember. Yeah, it was the knee, *always the knee*, as Cosell used to say. But back to you. Why restore old houses?"

"I've always been keen on historic buildings. That's what I was studying in London when the band took off. I never really expected my music career to soar like it did, but for a decade or so, it was a nice ride. Unfortunately, all those stories you hear about record companies ripping off artists are true and it all went pear shaped. After the golden years, I didn't have much to show for it so I needed to follow an honest living."

"You don't seem bitter."

"Wouldn't have traded those years for anything. The tales I could spin for you. Maybe someday we'll have a pint and I'll share a few of them. You live nearby?"

"Actually, I live in Denver, not Colorado, but North Carolina." I was glad that I hadn't created a false pretext for meeting him. He was chatting freely and I didn't feel like I was intruding on his time. Maybe the basketball helped. Or maybe he was just a gregarious guy who liked to talk and he was in a business now where most of his workers spoke little English.

Jackson was a big guy, but he carried the weight well. His online bio put him at 73, and his craggy countenance showed every minute of it. His long white hair was tied back in a ponytail. He was clean shaven other than a soul patch under a mouthful of ragged British teeth. Chiseling a couple of stone off his belly, I could picture him onstage back in the seventies, crooning his folksy dirges to a somnambulant crowd.

There was a small pistol sticking out of his leather tool belt, which hung loosely under his belly. It had a fancy mother of pearl handle and looked to be small caliber.

I said, "That's a pretty gun. I bet there's a story behind it, too."

"It was given to me back in the sixties by an Irish lass who followed my band. Her mother got it from an American GI who said that it was one of General Patton's famed revolvers. I usually don't even keep it loaded, but with all the scavengers around these days, stealing copper and selling it to scrappers by the pound, sometimes it's handy for scaring them off. So what brings you all the way up to these parts, Mr. King? You a scout for a team or something?"

I didn't have the heart to tell him the Patton carried an ivory handled Smith and Wesson Model 27 .357 Magnum. Americans stationed in England would grab cheap knockoffs with fake pearl grips and use them to get laid, claiming they came from the great general's private stash.

"No, I'm a private investigator. And actually, I'm here to see you."

He didn't looked startled. "Crikey. Why would you want to see me? That shite record company finally paying the back royalties they owe?"

He laughed.

I explained that my client was looking for Mary, that she'd made an impression on him way back when. When I brought up her name, his face changed from its naturally jovial state to one of sadness.

"I'm afraid Mary's no longer with us. She's been gone for almost a year now. By her own hand."

The air went out of my lungs. The woman whose life I had been tracing was dead. I needed to know more.

"My client will be devastated. Can you tell me what happened?"

For the first time in our conversation, I sensed there were wheels turning in Jackson's brain. He didn't respond right away. Suicide will do that to friends and family.

"Last year wasn't such a cracking one for me. Lost the wife. Then Mary did what she did. She was never a happy girl. She had some terrible things inflicted on her when she was very young. She was like a daughter to Samantha and me. We took her in at a very low spot in her life. We got her to seek help. She did, but she never really got sorted. To her credit, she made something of herself. She was very good at her job at the club. And when that scene went barmy, she went to night school and took computer courses while she worked with us during the day. She became quite the digital whiz."

"Did she ever marry?"

Again he bit his lip. "No. She was very shirty when it came to men. I don't know if you've seen pictures or anything but she was an attractive lass. Just never could form a relationship. Probably because of those experiences when she was young."

"Any siblings? My client really was insistent that he wanted to help in any way he could. He's quite a wealthy man and I know it would make him feel better. Even if he was too late to help her, I'm sure he'd like to be of service to someone close to her."

"Ah, that's a bit thorny. She has a brother. He's a very private person and has dodgy issues of his own. Given the circumstances, I don't know that it's my place to give out his information."

Jackson was clearly uncomfortable with the turn our conversation had taken. He looked around furtively and barked out a couple of instructions to a plasterer who was restoring an elaborate cornice.

I wasn't sure how far to go with this. If I told McCarver that Mary killed herself, possibly because she had issues at the hands of a man or men when she was young, his guilt would only increase. I could spend more time tracking her brother down, but if he only confirmed Ted's worst fears, my choices weren't appealing.

I could lie to him, say she died of natural causes. I might need to run that by Dr. Mills, although she had a habit of staying neutral on matters like these.

There was a slight chance that the brother would know something that might exonerate Ted, and that's why I decided to cautiously press on.

"Well, Robert, I've taken enough of your time. You're a busy man. But please, do me one favor. From what you've told me, it seems you know how to get in touch with her brother. Please reach out to him and explain the situation. Ask him to call me or meet me somewhere at his convenience. If he doesn't want to do that, I'll honor his wishes and we'll consider the matter closed."

Jackson put his hand to his weathered face, fingers scratching a long white sideburn. "All right, Riley. Give me the name of your client. Not that I don't trust you, but the idea that some old sod who knew Mary forty years ago would go to the expense of hiring you to find her out of the goodness of his heart, well, I'm sure you can see."

Ted had never given me specific instructions about revealing his identity. He trusted me to make the call, saying that he was content to be an anonymous benefactor, if I judged that to be best. My mind quickly reviewed the ledger, whether it was in McCarver's best interests to accede to Jackson's request.

I handed him my card with my cell number and email address. I told him I was at the Garden City Hotel until at least tomorrow. And then I gave him Ted's name.

SEVENTEEN

Jackson promised to call Mary's brother within the hour and report back to me, regardless of the outcome. He had only known her as Chesterton, and said that it was her brother's surname as well.

I've taken extraordinary measures in the past to get crucial information. I could swipe Jackson's phone with some sleight of hand and extract the number. I could follow him around for a couple of days in case if he planned to meet up with this brother. But to what end? Would Mary have told her sibling details about a rape that happened forty years ago? And if so, would she have left some indication the incident bore any responsibility for her final act?

I called Evan Rogers and Mrs. Bernstein as I waited to hear back from Jackson. Neither had ever heard Mary mention a brother but they maintained that they knew little about her life outside of work. No help there.

I was at loose ends. A quick online search of Nassau County's Hall of Records revealed no death certificate under Chesterton. Did Ted really need hard evidence to accept that Mary was gone?

Jackson had told me she'd been in therapy at one point, but he didn't remember the name of her shrink. Since there were tens of thousands of therapists in the metropolitan area, it could take years to track down the right one and then try to convince them to reveal the intimate secrets of a former patient. And again, would it serve any purpose as far as McCarver was concerned?

Stone was about to go on the air for his midday show on WJOK in a few minutes. I called his cell to check in and to hear a familiar voice.

"Hey Riles, what's doing?"

"Nothing much." I gave him a quick rundown of the past forty eight hours. "Unless something breaks with this brother, I figure I'll be heading south later today or first thing tomorrow."

"What are you going to tell McCarver?"

"I have to tell him she's dead, but the next question he'll ask is how it happened. If I tell him it was suicide, it probably will set him back and he'll feel responsible. I can't see it helping."

"Riley, you owe him the truth. You're not his shrink. He paid you to investigate and present your findings. You can't spin this in some half-assed attempt to sooth his conscience."

"This would be a whole lot easier if we didn't know the guy. If this was just some client off the street, I'd just submit a report and that would be it."

"And that's how you have to look at this. Don't let your concern for the guy intervene. Maybe the other two women will be more therapeutic. God, listen to us. We're playing armchair psychologist. I hate it when callers try to psychoanalyze coaches and players based on their own bullshit, and that's what we're doing now. *Games without frontiers.*"

"I guess you're right. I was thinking of calling Doctor Mills and running this by her."

"Couldn't hurt. But I still think you owe him the truth. Look, I'm on the air in five minutes. Call or text me when you know what you're doing. Maybe you can swing by here on your way south. I could ride down with you, maybe do a show or two from your place and fly back."

"Okay. I'll let you know. Have a good show."

I called Jacqueline Mills next, expecting to get a machine, menu, or receptionist. I was shocked that the good doctor herself answered on the second ring. I explained my dilemma and sought her counsel.

"Mr. King," she said in that officious voice of hers. "I've been over this with Ted. He's fully aware that his plan may not work out the way he wants it to. In a perfect world, you would dispense the money and the women would send him sweet letters saying that all is forgiven. We'd be hopelessly naive to expect that outcome, wouldn't you agree? If this woman killed herself recently, I would position it to Ted that events forty years ago most likely weren't directly responsible."

"But don't you people always look for things that happen when we're young as the cause of problems when we're older?"

"Yes, basically. Listen, forty years is a long time. There must have been a lot of life-changing experiences. From what you've told me, this woman sounds like a high functioning bipolar type. Current thinking is that there may be genetic causes or perhaps experiences in very early childhood, not teenage years."

"So is that how Ted will see it?"

"That's my job, not yours. I'll work this through with him. Your job is to present the facts, not shade them with lies or half truths that you think are what he needs to hear. You're just a reporter, not judge and jury."

I could tell her about all the situations where I've had to make those kinds of calls. But this wasn't like any other case I'd handled, and it might be prudent to defer to her judgment. Dealing with three women from decades past --- this was the very definition of random outcome. There was no predicting the result.

"All right, Doc, I hear you. I'll tell Ted the truth and let you take it from there. Thanks for your time."

I rang off and sat in the Audi for a moment. My best course now seemed to be to head for the hotel, check out and have lunch somewhere close by. If I didn't hear from Jackson soon, I'd call him for an update.

I was just pulling into the hotel parking lot when Bluetooth alerted me to an incoming call. Blocked number. I wasn't in the mood for a sales pitch but answered it anyway. Maybe it was an exclusive investment opportunity that was too great to pass up. Not.

"Riley King? Stonewall Jackson. I just got off the phone with Mark Chesterton."

EIGHTEEN

"Thank you for calling, I really appreciate it."

"You may not feel that way when you hear what I have to say."

The call quality was spotty, as if one or both of us were in a bad cell location. "Would you be open to meeting with me somewhere? Anywhere that's convenient for you? I'd really like to hear this face to face, if that's possible."

He said, "To be honest, I didn't really want to make this call and get into a row, but I got the sense that you mean well. I don't know what's to be gained by resurrecting something that happened forty years ago."

"I was hired by Ted McCarver to find Mary. He wanted to try to make things right with her. Whatever it took."

"Yes, well I don't think Mark would be willing to accept anything from that git. Were you aware of what happened with her and McCarver all those years ago?"

"I'm aware of his side of the story, yes."

"So you know that the old sod raped her. That he treated her like a used condom afterwards. That he ignored a pleading, heartfelt letter from her years later."

There wasn't a harsh edge to his voice, just a weariness that sounded like he'd been over all of this before.

I said, "Ted in no way defends his actions back then. He claims that he didn't know Mary was fifteen; he honestly thought she was older. He believed that the sex was consensual, but regrets it, in fact, he regretted it right after it occurred. He was drinking and Mary seemed a little high on something."

"Something *he* gave her."

"He claims that he never gave her anything to eat or drink. Back then, even some of the sealed soft drinks backstage at these concerts were spiked. A lot of bands, maybe not yours, thought it was funny, or that it might help them get lucky later. If she drank anything, even a soda or beer, it's possible that it was tainted. I don't expect she could have known that at the time."

This wasn't going well. I was trying to plead Ted's case instead of what he had tasked me to do. Maybe I still needed to convince myself of his innocence, and that was why I was working so hard to persuade Jackson that Ted wasn't guilty of anything other than thoughtlessness and misplaced libido.

Jackson didn't answer immediately, leading me to believe that he was at least entertaining the possibility that Ted's version was plausible. "He must have known she was a virgin. He was bloody old enough to know that. But again, why throw a spanner in the works? Mary is gone. It's too late."

I said, "Here's where we're at now. Ted has been a very successful businessman. He's retired, on Hilton Head

Island, almost seventy years old. He sincerely regrets that he treated her badly. He gave me carte blanche when it came to deciding what form that assistance may take, financial or otherwise."

Stonewall's voice finally lived up to his name. "To ease his balmy conscience. Well again laddie, it's a bit late for that, isn't it?"

I took one more stab. "While doing my background checks, trying to locate Mary, I discovered that she quit working at Morrison's Road House rather abruptly when a man claiming to be her father showed up."

Silence.

I said, "Is there anything you can tell me about that? She was valued greatly at the club and the owners were pretty upset that she left so suddenly."

"Mary told me about her predator old man and the damage he caused. Do you really need to know the whole skeevy story?"

I took this assignment in hopes that I could vindicate McCarver and help make his remaining years as rewarding as possible. It sounded like Mark Chesterton's story might plunge Ted into a morass of psychotherapy that could eat up a substantial portion of that time.

I said, "I want to know the truth, yes. And Ted wants to know the consequences of his actions."

"The truth is pretty grim. Mary told us that her father abused her, starting at age seven. Sexually. Never penetration, always oral. Her mother had no idea. When Mary finally told her about the man she married, she threw *her* out of the house, not him. Mary had no place to go. That's when she started hanging with rock bands. She was street smart enough to find refuge where she could. It might be in some drummer's hotel room for a while. Backstage at some venue because a roadie agreed not to snitch in exchange for a little blower. She lived by her wits. She couldn't go to uni because her father might find her there so she educated herself --- days in the library or record stores, nights as a rock and roll gypsy --- all this at fourteen. She was scraping by until she met your man McCarver. Despite all her travels, she didn't even know what so-called normal shagging was, it was all of the oral variety. So when McCarver forced himself on her, she went wonky."

I have heard some horrific stories. But the depravity that Jackson had portrayed in the last sixty seconds made me sick. A father, so perverse. A mother so insensitive. A child, cast out like yesterday's rubbish. Charlene had told me some of the appalling things that men had done to her as she tried to forge a career in music. But even her drama paled by comparison.

Stonewall Jackson went on. "She could never have a real relationship with a man. She sussed them all as exploitive monsters."

"But there were men who really did care for her. I talked to them. Evan Rogers, Theo Bernstein, and you yourself. They gave her opportunities and she ran with it."

"Some detective you are. Rogers and Bernstein were trying to snog her every time their wives were out of sight. They were total shites. I'd like to think I was the only one who wanted nothing in return. I tried to be the good father she never had. All I asked was for her to earn her keep by working for me in the rehab business. I gave her room and board and a decent rate. We had no kids of our own. I guess she was sort of a surrogate daughter."

"So why did she decide to end it all when she was in a nurturing situation? From what you've told me, she finally got to the best place she could be."

He said, "She's in the best place she can be now. She's at peace."

"Do you know what happened to her father? Is he still alive?"

"I saw his obituary a few years ago. The rotten sod died of cancer, hopefully slow and painfully."

"He told Doris Bernstein that he wanted peace of mind and his daughter's forgiveness before he died," I said.

It sounded like Jackson spat on the ground. "Mary would never give him that satisfaction, just like she won't be bought off by your McCarver. So tell him to keep his bung. He had a chance when Mary wrote him that letter. She was about to lose her radio job. He was doing brill, a recommendation from him would have helped her career a great deal."

"He didn't know what to make of that letter. He was worried about being blackmailed and his attorney advised him not to respond," I said.

"She landed on her feet at the club, no thanks to that whinge. He ignored her letter like he blew her off the few times their paths crossed after the rape. That would have been the time to reach out to her. Tell him to bugger off, will you? This man is a wolf in sheep's clothing, whatever he tells you, mate. If you're really the stand up bloke you claim to be, you should dump this cheeky son of a bitch now. Before he ensnares you deeper into his blinkered web."

NINETEEN

I stayed at Stone's house in Mantoloking that Friday night and we lit out for Charlotte early the next morning. Rick and I took our time driving back, stopping for food and gas twice. The temperature warmed the further south we traveled --- by the time we pulled into my place just before sundown, it had risen to a toasty 82 degrees. We ordered a pizza, watched a Cumberbatch Sherlock and hit the hay early.

I called Ted before retiring and told him I had news best delivered in person. He said he would fly up the next morning if that worked for me. I said it did and he told me he'd be there by nine a.m. and that he'd bring breakfast. He hung up before I could decline the offer.

McCarver wasn't wearing a suit (surprise!) when he arrived shortly before nine, but even his casual attire was elegance personified. Sharply creased tweed slacks, a scarlet Ralph Lauren turtleneck adorned with polo ponies, and slip on moccasins from Brioni. He greeted us as if he hadn't a care in the world.

"Great to see you fellows, twice in one week. Anna sent some French Toast. Hope it survived the trip intact."

He produced a silver thermal bag that smelled fantastic and transported enough breakfast to feed six hungry detectives.

"You didn't need to trouble her, Ted," Stone said.

"Coffee's in the carafe," I said.

Ted was eager to get down to it. "I must say, you work fast, Riley. I wasn't expecting you to turn up anything this soon. Why wouldn't you tell me what you found when you called?"

Informing someone of a death by telephone, email, or Twitter as some do today is not my style.

"Yeah, well it's complicated, Ted. Sit down and I'll give you the news. Before we eat?"

"Now is fine with me."

"As you know, I drove up to Long Island and found the station that Mary worked at in 1993. I located the owner, who's now in the car business. He gave me her last name and her next stop, a club in Rockville Centre. After that, she worked for a builder who used to be a musician. He was the one who told me that Mary took her own life last year."

"My God." Ted seemed honestly shaken by the news.

"Mary had a brother who told this builder, man named Stonewall Jackson, that their father molested Mary at a very young age. She was already pretty messed up when you met her."

McCarver was still reeling. "Did this brother know about what happened with me? Does he believe I raped her?"

"He thinks that you slipped her a date rape drug or something, and that's why she went along with it. I told him about how bands often spiked the backstage food and drink. Even though he had to already know that from his musician days, I don't think that he accepted that explanation. In any case Ted, she *was* fifteen at the time."

He shifted uneasily in his chair. "As I remember, God, I can't believe I'm saying this. It was awkward. It was rushed. I finished very quickly. She didn't move much. So what I did that night might have led to her suicide."

Stone had remained silent through all of this. I'd never seen Ted lose his composure and it was unsettling to witness. Rick gently put his hand on his shoulder. "Ted, it happened forty years ago."

"I know." McCarver pulled a linen handkerchief from his breast pocket. His eyes were pleading for the answers and absolution no one could give.

I was sympathetic. "We've all had one night stands. We don't call again for lot of different reasons. Ted, you had the misfortune of encountering a young girl who was already on a bad road. But I think the time to have cleared this up was when you got that letter from her. Her brother thinks she was reaching out to you to help her, since her station was about to go under. If you had responded then, her memories of that night might have been altered. But it hurt that you didn't answer."

"I see that now. I wish I had responded. Instead, I gave it to a lawyer and it got lost in the shuffle. The station was just starting to make it big, and those were heady days. I'm afraid I didn't spend much time thinking about it back then, after she never followed up on that first letter."

Stone said, "I suppose the advice you got from the lawyer was technically in your best interests, given what you knew at the time. Had you made contact with her, for all he knew, she may have been trying to blackmail you. You know how lawyers think. They protect the client at all costs and don't consider the costs to their adversaries. That's what they're paid to do."

Ted slowly shook his head. "So damned self centered. As if my reputation was more valuable than that girl's life."

I couldn't let him wallow in this. "A lot of things destroyed her life before and after you knew her. If she had a more normal childhood, she probably doesn't wind up backstage servicing rock stars. She went to therapy later in life but it didn't prevent what happened. I'm not saying you were right messing with a fifteen year old, but you didn't start that train rolling."

"None of that helps that poor woman now. I realized all of this much too late. I have to live with that."

This was Dr. Mills territory. I said, "Ted, you have someone you're paying to help you work these things out. Talk to her; there's nothing you can do for Mary Chesterton now. If you want me to drop it this whole thing, I will. I'm good with whatever you decide."

TWENTY

Exactly a week before, I was walking with Ted on the shores of the Atlantic Ocean, talking about his problems with women. Today, we were hiking along the edge of a considerably smaller body of water, the manmade Lake Norman, which resided less than a decent sand wedge from my back porch.

The other difference was that Bosco was not with us. Mrs. Keegish spends Sunday mornings in church (I don't want to know what she does on Saturday nights), so I couldn't pick him up until later this afternoon.

Stone had to watch the woeful Jets and Giants go through their weekly ritual of discovering new ways to lose football games. Since I'm not addicted to this form of misery, Ted suggested we leave Stone to his curses for a while and enjoy the warm Indian Summer weather.

Unlike the wide Hilton Head sand beaches, the lake is mostly contained by rip-rap rocks that developers put down to protect the shoreline if the water was to rise considerably above its normal limits. This really constitutes *belt and suspenders*, since the Cowan's Ford Dam at the bottom of the lake regulates the water levels and that nothing short of Noah's Flood could cause a breach. I was more nervous about the nuclear power station directly behind the dam, but the low electric rates it provides assuages the nearby residents' fears.

We picked our way along a narrow trail bordering the water. "Riley, I guess I'm experiencing what the military calls *mission creep* now. What I mean is that I'm beginning to agree with you that my initial plan to give away a million dollars was foolhardy. Maybe that old TV show is emblazoned on my memory stronger than I realized. Money isn't going to buy me peace of mind when it comes to these women. I know that now."

I missed the distraction Bosco could provide at these moments. I could laugh with Ted at how my dog would react to the gaggle of geese swimming thirty feet offshore. As soon as this walk was over, I'd head right to Keegish and get Bosco back and overfeed him with dog cookies.

I said, "Don't worry about me. If you want to drop it all, you owe me nothing, just expenses, which won't amount to much."

"Thanks, but I *do* want to move forward. I'm just saying I want to take the million dollars out of the equation as a starting point. I mean, if money is necessary, the sky's the limit. But let's not make that the first gambit. I can see how it might come off as trying to buy my way out. The next woman I want you to locate is my ex-wife. Back at the house, I have all the pertinent information on her."

"Of course you do."

"Let me finish, please. I know I seem a bit obsessive but this is important to me. You shouldn't have a very hard time finding her. I need you to convey my feelings to her as accurately as possible or best case, open the door so that I can do it myself."

"Why do you need me to carry your message in the first place? I can locate her and you could approach her yourself. Wouldn't that work better?"

"She has a restraining order against me. She got it after we split. I'm not sure there is a limit to its length and I doubt there's any record of it available to find out."

What the hell was I getting myself into now? Normal gumshoe work doesn't involve delivering messages to ex-wives. They have lawyers for that. Perry Mason never asked Paul Drake to send love notes to Della Street. Speaking of TV shows, I was beginning to feel more like *Ray Donovan*, the Hollywood fixer played by Liev Schrieber, who takes care of dirty business for his clients with no limits as to what the job entails. Dangerous ground on which I don't wish to tread.

"May I ask, what specifically caused the restraining order? You mentioned it briefly in the first file you gave me, but there weren't many details."

"I'll tell you before I fly out tonight. But suffice to say, I deserved it."

TWENTY ONE

We came back to the house after picking up Bosco and joined Stone. Despite doing everything in their power to give the game away, the New York Jets eked out a close victory against the equally woeful Tampa Bay Bucs.

"When are you headed back to New Jersey, Rick?" Ted asked after the final gun sounded.

"Nothing firm. I mainly came down to keep Riles company on the drive. Haven't booked a flight back yet but I have a pilot friend at Charlotte/Douglas who tips me off on last minute deals. Usually Tuesday afternoon, I can hop a flight back for a buck fifty."

"I can offer you a better deal than that. I need to get up north for a couple of days on some business this week. Since my plane is already here, I could run you up with me tonight and you could work from the studio tomorrow. If you think that Riley can manage by himself for a couple of days, that is," McCarver said.

I was a bit surprised at how calm he was now, mere hours after receiving the disturbing news about Mary Chesterton. I guess some people are better at compartmentalizing than others, or maybe some people are sociopaths who can't feign empathy for long.

"Won't be a problem on my end," I said. "Since I was gone most of the week, I have some catching up to do.

Charlene's due back tomorrow afternoon. And Bosco is better company than either of you."

The dog's ears picked up at the mention of his name. When he saw that there was no cookie being offered, he plopped back down on one of the six dog beds we have strewn around the premises.

"What are you flying these days, Ted?" Stone asked.

"I've got a Socata TBM850. Cruises at 320 knots. We'd be at MJC Monmouth in around two hours give or take."

"When are you flying back south?"

"I only need a day or so up there. I might call a friend or two for dinner. Probably hit Hilton Head HDX by Tuesday evening."

"Sounds like a plan."

My head was spinning with all this airport alphabet soup. Ted looked at me and shrugged his shoulders. "Let's see, I flew into Statesville Regional, SVH in. It's only about 30 minutes from here. I can get her topped off with a phone call. We can be wheels up within an hour or whenever you're ready."

Stone usually travels light. He keeps some essentials here, clothes and toiletries, in case his stays unexpectedly become extended. He disappeared into the guest room to pack up, and I used the opportunity to ask Ted more about his ex.

"You know me by now, Riley," he said. "Always prepared. Everything you need to know is in the file I brought with me. Names, dates, and a list of my negative interactions with her, at least the major ones. What I'd like you to do, in a nutshell, is find her, convey my apologies and find out if there is anything I can do to meet with her and apologize in person. If she needs money, I'll be happy to provide. You don't have to be specific as to the amount."

"What do you think her reaction will be when I tell her I'm working for you?"

"Like I said, we parted on very bad terms. She may still harbor some bad feelings. But it's been almost thirty years. Maybe time heals all wounds or wounds all heels, I don't know." Again, his levity after digesting the news I'd given him earlier was out of place and disturbing.

"So you think finding her will be easy. Why?"

"She was a singer. Then she started touring with national companies of Broadway musicals. She was using my last name then as Gretchen McCarver. She went off the radar years ago. Maybe she changed it, got married, I don't know. Somebody we both knew thought she was writing children's books at some point, using a pen name."

I said, "All right, we'll be in touch, but depending on where she is, I may not be able to see her right away. I promised Charlene a few days away and for the sake of *my* relationship, I can't keep putting it off."

He smiled at that. "If only I had had that attitude. I might still be married."

TWENTY TWO

After Stone and McCarver left, I opened the file Ted had provided. Everything was precisely organized. He listed dates, places, and notable incidents. Everything was set down in chronological order from the time he met Gretchen to their last contact.

On the face of it, locating her seemed as simple as McCarver had suggested. She was a singer who had toured with several national theatre companies in the eighties. I was tempted to call my FBI pal Dan Logan, whose knowledge of everything Broadway is encyclopedic, but again, I hate to burn up favors with him on things I can do myself with a little effort.

At least some of Gretchen McCarver's road shows must have been sanctioned by the unions who govern such endeavors, and it took me no time to hack into the database for Actor's Equity and SAG/AFTRA. She had indeed been active thirty years ago, touring as Aldonza/Dulcinea in *Man of La Mancha*, Nelly Forbush in *South Pacific*, a variety of female roles in *A Christmas Carol* and a few minor parts in some Sondheim offerings. Her head shot displayed a generically attractive blonde.

In the late eighties, the trail grew cold. She would have been in her forties by then, and I've heard numerous actresses' laments that if they aren't firmly established by that age, they have little hope of success. It was a business that truly favors the young, especially if you are female. Even the few minor credits she had on television dried up.

I tried accessing both unions' pension fund. They were locked behind firewalls that even my advantaged inquiries couldn't penetrate. I took a bit of comfort in that, despite it making my job more difficult.

The most current lead Ted had given me was the notion that she was now writing children's books under a *nom de plume*. I had a great source for that, but it took me an hour and two single malts to summon up the will to make the call.

Jaime Johansen and I had been in a relationship. She was fifteen years my junior and we spent a great year together. During that time, she and I had found the man responsible for her mother's death. It was the same man who had shot Stone, when my friend had intercepted bullets intended for Jaime and me.

A few months after that drama ended, I moved south to Charlotte. Despite my best efforts, there was no way I could convince Jaime to come with me. The literary agency she had inherited upon her mother's passing demanded her presence in New York, or so she believed. We visited each other every few weeks after I left, but time and absence caused doubts to seep in. The final straw was Charlene.

I had taken her in to keep her safe from a dangerous husband. Nothing physical, although I was sorely tempted. Her husband's death a few days later made big news in Charlotte. That's how Jaime found out about our cohabitation arrangement. I had been reluctant to tell her, afraid of her reaction. But by not letting her know upfront, she took it as a serious breach of trust. My attempts at an explanation after the fact were unconvincing once she saw a picture of Charlene. She said she needed time to process it all and she would call when ready. She implored me not to reach out to her first.

It had been over six months since then and I took her silence as an indication that she had moved on and it was time for me to do likewise. I needed to tell her that Charlene and I were now shacking up for real, even though it seemed that she had passed the point of caring.

I still care for Jaime but I don't see a way for us to be together, given our career circumstances. I didn't want to break my vow to let her initiate contact, but asking for her help with Gretchen McCarver presented an excuse to talk. I'd let her take it from there.

"Jaime, it's me. How are you?"

"I'm doing well, Riley. You?" There was nothing in her voice that gave me the impression she was happy to hear from me, or that she was angry I had breached our agreement.

"Not bad. Look, I know you needed some time. I'm calling for a favor, some help on a case. We can keep this strictly business if you're still not ready to talk."

A beat. "What do you need?"

"I'm trying to locate a writer. Her name *was* Gretchen McCarver, but she now writes children's books, we think, under a different name."

"And why do you need to find her?"

"I'm working for her former husband. They divorced years ago and he feels bad about the way it ended. He wants to apologize for his role in the breakup and offer her financial help if she needs it. She'd be around sixty nine now."

"And this wouldn't be a pretense so they could get back together?"

Jaime was too smart not to know her question cut both ways. I wondered if her phrasing was intentional. I played along as if I hadn't picked up on the irony.

I said, "No, I don't think so. The man is in therapy, and he wants to make amends for the harm he may have caused."

"Sounds like a twelve step program. Is he an addict of some kind?"

Never having addiction problems of my own, I am only vaguely aware of the twelve step program and that the need to make amends was one of its tenets. I'd ask Mills about it tomorrow and see if that's where Ted's million dollar folly gestated.

"I don't think so, Jaime. He's just getting up there in age and reassessing some of his past failures. He's very wealthy and he wants to do the right thing by those he hurt. I can tell you that this woman isn't the only one he's reaching out to."

"We don't handle kiddies' books but we have someone in the agency who used to. You need this right away?"

"If it's not an imposition. I mean, I'm trying to find her through other means as well, but I thought that this would be something you could do pretty easily. If not, I don't want to trouble you."

How sterile I sounded. I might as well be talking to a stranger behind the counter at the DMV, instead of a woman I'd been in love with once, and maybe still was.

"Let me see if she's at home now. She knows the kids' book business inside out. Get me whatever else you know about this woman."

I emailed her a photo and all the vitals I had. She said that she'd call right back, whether her associate was available or not. Give her a few minutes.

I realized that I'd been shaking the whole time I'd been speaking to her. Was I afraid that she might put a permanent end to our story, or worse, that she wanted it to continue? I'd been honest with Charlene about Jaime in that we had come to an uncertain finale. I poured my third Glenfiddich of the evening.

Jaime was back to me within twenty minutes. "You got lucky, Riles. Turns out your lady pitched my associate to represent her a few years back. She was self publishing at the time and wanted to see if her stuff could pass muster with a big company. They met in person a couple of times and the picture you sent clinched it."

"Do you have an address?"

"I do. Turns out that in addition to writing a book every year, she runs a small bed and breakfast in Wintergreen, Virginia. Apparently, it's a little town near Charlottesville, where you grew up. She's writing under the name Rebecca Hunter."

She gave me an address and a phone number that she said was a few years old and might no longer be valid.

I thanked her and waited for her to ask about where things now stood with us. She wasn't about to.

She said, "I'm going to watch *Homeland* and turn in for the night, Riley. I hope this helps but please, don't tell her or anyone for that matter how you found her."

With that, she was gone. I again had failed to tell her about Charlene. Any satisfaction I felt about finding Ted's ex within hours of setting out to do so was tempered by the emptiness in the pit of my stomach.

My conversation with Jaime gave me no insight into where we were headed. I'd taken the coward's way out again.

TWENTY THREE

"**H**ow can you even suggest that, Riley? I *am* a woman, or hadn't you noticed?"

"And a fiery one at that. I like a woman with spirit." I did my best Gable.

"Is that a line from one of your old TV westerns?"

Charlene was getting wise to my eccentricities but I still haven't been able to coax her into watching *Cheyenne* with me on the Western Channel. She always seemed to have something more urgent to do, like bleaching her teeth or defragging her laptop.

"Charl, just calm down a minute, okay? I don't think the idea is that outrageous."

"King, you can't have it both ways. Yes, I want to get away with you for a few days. Somewhere romantic. But to use that as a pretext to harass this poor women, that *is* outrageous."

"Do me a favor, just visit the website. The Dewdrop Inn is the perfect getaway. Nestled deep in the Shenandoah Valley with the picturesque Blue Ridge Mountains, standing proudly...."

She said, "Cut the sappy commercial. I'm sure the place is lovely. You know what my problem is."

We'd been over this already and she wasn't budging. She objected to me working for Ted McCarver and had only backed off badgering me because she was on tour and not around to give me grief. But now she was home and boiling over.

"Charlene, just hear me out. The first woman he had me find was a victim of sexual abuse by her father *way* before Ted entered the picture. Ted is not the kind of man who would rape a young girl. He's truly sorry they even had sex. You've never met him. He's a gentle soul."

"He's admitted to you that he's different when it comes to women. He goes to hookers. He pays for his nooky. How is that okay?"

"What would you have him do? He doesn't feel he's able to have a honest relationship with a woman. He's in therapy. And he wants to make amends for those he hurt before he became so self aware. To me that's honorable."

Charlene had just gotten back from her latest adventure in country music land and she was tired from traveling. Added to that was the stress of performing in front of people who came to see somebody else, and not some relative unknown trying to perfect her craft. Her songs from twenty years ago sounded slightly dated and she was having a difficult time coming up with new ones.

"But King, this just doesn't pass the smell test with me. You're looking to bushwack this woman and hit her up with the fact that you're repping her ex husband. Just ain't right."

"I'm trying to see where she's at now. If she'd be open to talking with him. Maybe taking some money if she needs it."

"Didn't he pay alimony?"

"No, when they divorced she got half his assets, which at the time were a whole lot less than they are now. She was able bodied and working and making money on her own. He didn't really strike gold until later with WJOK; he sold it for over thirty million dollars. What she got was a pittance compared to that."

Charlene walked over to the butlers' pantry where the liquor was stored and extracted my Glenfiddich. She poured us both generous measures and sat beside me on the sofa.

"So you're convinced that she'll come out of this ahead, sugar?"

"I am. Ted has given me a lot of leeway here, to do the right thing. I thought having you with me would help. If we come up as a couple, she'll feel less threatened and maybe if she gets to like us, she'll understand that this is on the up and up."

She sipped her drink, deep in thought. One of the things I love about Charlene is that she appreciates good scotch. I've never met a woman who wasn't repulsed by its strong, smoky burn.

She said, "You're going up there anyway, with or without me, aren't you, babe?"

"It's my job. Charl. This is supposed to be healing, for both sides."

"I still don't see how this is detective work. More like some kind of counseling or social engineering."

"You're not the first to bring that up. That's been one of my qualms all along. I'm trying to help a friend, or actually a friend of Rick's. The man has led a good life; he's universally respected in his field. He's now trying to have a real personal life as well. Most of us are afraid to admit our failings. Here's a man who's not only aware of them, but is trying to change at seventy. Takes guts."

She bobbed her head back and forth. "All right, you've worn me down."

"That's not what I need to hear. I can do this alone. If you're not fully on board, we can go up to Asheville this week or wherever you want. I'll go up to Wintergreen on my own next weekend when you're back on the road."

This time she took a deep pull on the whisky. "I won't be on the road next weekend or any weekend in the near future."

I had been so obsessed with my own interests that I had barely paid attention to her mood when she got home. I had asked how it went in a perfunctory manner, but paid scant attention when she merely said, "Okay."

I said, "Why? I'm sorry, what happened?"

"Darius took me aside after the last show. You know, I really respect the fact that he told me himself rather than just get a flunky to do it. He's a cool guy."

"What did he say?"

"Just that I need some better material. Problem is, that most of the top songwriters would rather give their good stuff to a hot twenty-something with a future than some forty eight year old hag with saggy tits and wrinkles."

"Charlene, you are not a forty eight year old hag with wrinkles. You're easily the most beautiful woman I've ever seen. You've got a great body. My God, don't you notice how men's heads turn when you walk into a room?"

"You're a sweetheart for saying that, Riley, but if I ever do go on the road again, you ought to come with me. Or maybe you shouldn't. Some of these young girls make me look like an old cow."

"Impossible. But you wrote your own songs for your first album. Why not write some new ones?"

She sighed. "About what? Botox. Menopause? Vaginal dryness?"

"That would be a first. Maybe there's a niche market there. "

"Said no one ever."

"Not true. I'm sure there are things you have in common with the audience. You just need to find them and write about them."

She shook her head. "You think it's that easy? I just don't relate to sitting in the back of a pickup truck, drinking beer on a Friday night and swimming nekkid in the river after throwing off my tight blue jeans."

"That kind of defines a lot of those songs, doesn't it? Nice fantasy, though. Did Darius close the door completely?"

"Nope. He just gave me the same pep talk you did. I have to find my voice and write songs that resonate with the listeners."

She gulped down the rest of her scotch. "You know, maybe that trip to Wintergreen isn't such a bad idea after all. I just have to get over the idea that you're using me to soften the woman up. Maybe I can find some inspiration up there in them mountains."

"Let's do it then. Pack up Bosco and head north tomorrow. Go on their website, pick out their most romantic looking room and I'll make the reservation. And I'm not using you to soften her up --- that would strictly be a side benefit. I don't even figure on bringing it up to her until we're ready to leave. Let's not plan past that. Like Rick says, we'll go with the flow."

TWENTY FOUR

Charlene was asleep in the passenger seat and Bosco was dozing intermittently in the back. Sirius/XM's *Classic Vinyl* was playing low over the Audi's eleven speakers, not loud enough to disturb either of my somnolent companions. The journey to Wintergreen wasn't much further than Hilton Head, just due north instead of south.

McCarver's file detailing his marriage laid the blame for its failure squarely at his own feet, but reading through the text, it was clear that he didn't fully believe it. He blamed his own neediness as the fatal flaw that led to the divorce. He cited Gretchen/Rebecca's absences as a factor. As a musical comedy singer, she was on the road for weeks on end, during which time Ted frequently took comfort elsewhere. At first, his cheating was confined to periods when his wife was unavailable, but then extended to times when she was. He rationalized this by claiming that none of his other *conquests* (his word) meant anything to him and would be discarded summarily if his wife were to commit more of her time to him.

All through this, Ted assumed that his wife had been faithful. He believed that her physical needs did not match his and felt safe that she did not share his propensity for straying. He wrote that their lovemaking had always been somewhat mechanical; not unpleasant but not especially invigorating either. It was rote: missionary style, brief in duration, and distant in its aftermath.

He was shocked when he discovered that her extracurricular activities rivaled his.

He was doubly shocked by his inability to let go. As unfulfilling as their union had become, when she declared it over, he clung to it with the desperation of a man deprived of oxygen. He made every concession, tried every means of persuasion and humbled himself in ways he never thought possible, but it was all to no avail.

That's when he crossed the line. In the file, he described his descent into the dark side. I hoped that he had exaggerated some of the extreme things he had done to woo her back, but I feared that he may have understated them.

I related to his difficulties. In the few months that Charlene and I had shared space, she had been on the road over half the time. I *have* missed her but my once roving eye has been satisfied to merely look at the menu, rather than give in to my baser appetites. So far Charlene's forays have been in short spurts --- most of the bands she tours with are on what they call a *James Taylor* schedule. Since most of her fellow musicians are married with children, they confine their big trips to the period between Memorial Day and Labor Day, so they can be home while their kids are in school. The rest of the year, they try to schedule their appearances on weekends and holiday breaks. James Taylor had pioneered this approach --- thus the honorific.

But there was always the chance that she'd catch on with some young buck with no family ties to restrict him. These tours could last for months and the thought of Charlene being away that long was not appealing. If that happened, Ted's confession made me wonder if I wouldn't fall into the same trap he had.

There was one notable difference. I would hardly describe our sex life as mechanical. In most relationships I've been in, the *heyday of the blood* as Shakespeare put it, calms after the first few months. With Charlene it has only intensified. She is more demanding and imaginative than I am. I certainly would rather have it that way than the opposite, but it does cause me to worry what she is doing to satisfy her needs when I'm not available. And since she had tried to seduce me and Derek Davis while she was still married, my reservations are grounded in reality.

As we drove through the Shenandoah valley on I-81, I kept looking across at the beautiful creature beside me. Every so often, I peeked at the contented animal dozing in the back seat. Although there is no legal documentation affirming it, this is my little family right now. I love them both, in different ways. I would be crushed if either of them were no longer in my life.

TWENTY FIVE

The Dewdrop Inn. I would hope that a published author, even one who specializes in books for children, could come up with something more original. But there are probably lots of unschooled guests who think the name is exceedingly clever --- and what's in a name, anyway?

The place itself surpassed my expectations. It was set in the Wintergreen Valley, its forty acres were crisscrossed with tributaries, rocky streams and horse meadows, giving way to forests of pine and running cedar as the gentle foothills rise toward Blue Ridge peaks. The Inn was an old Victorian style manse that dated back to the late eighteen hundreds and had been updated numerous times since. The exterior featured the obligatory curlicues and filigrees of the period, although the dark green and white palette was more restrained than the extravagant "painted ladies" of New England.

The interior fretwork was impressive, certainly not achievable today without a profligate budget. The thick crown moldings were exquisite, framing the twelve foot ceilings in majestic grace. The numerous sconces and chandeliers were true to the period, as if modified from oil and gas lamps. The public areas were furnished with authentic antiques or convincing reproductions. The guest suites were wallpapered with tasteful floral designs, extending across the slanted ceilings. Claw foot tubs and pedestal sinks complemented the marble baths, although the ornate brass and silver fixtures represented a slight nod to more modern sensibilities. The larger rooms had fireplaces and bay windows. Since we were visiting midweek, we were the only guests and had our choice of rooms. It was all one could expect for a romantic getaway in the country.

Rebecca Hunter, as she now called herself, was not quite what I expected. It was hard to imagine her married to the trim and debonair Ted McCarver. The headshot I'd found online was at least thirty years old, and time had not been kind to her figure. She had put on considerable weight, and her once pale blonde hair was too brassy to be natural. On the plus side, her face still bore vestiges of its former beauty --- her blue eyes were clear and twinkly. The genuine smile she gave made us feel welcome as guests in her home.

As we exited the Audi, she was there to greet us on the front porch. She smiled in welcome as she said, "Rebecca Hunter. I'm so pleased to meet you. You must be the Kings."

"Riley King. And this is Charlene Jones."

She stared at Charlene in admiration. "I wasn't aware that a celebrity was a guest. Forgive me for not recognizing you right off. I'm a big admirer."

Charlene is not one to accept praise effortlessly. She generally turns it aside with humor, and this time it was particularly awkward for her, given our mission. Her modesty was not an affectation; she is hyper aware of her minor flaws --- blemishes that escape others' scrutiny. When she was twenty, she was runner-up to Miss North Carolina, and I believe that experience causes her to be overly critical of her own appearance. At forty eight, she still puts most younger women to shame. She doesn't see it that way. I do, but I'm not exactly objective.

Charlene muttered her thanks and averted her eyes, which was my cue to pick up the conversation.

"This is a lovely setting Ms. Hunter. Especially this time of year. Do you take care of all of this on your own?"

"Oh no, it's much too large for one person to handle. My husband does the bookkeeping and some of the work around the house and I have a couple of hired hands who maintain the property. They stay out in the bunkhouse when we need them, near the corral and stables. They care for the horses, too, when we get too busy. If you want to ride, I can call down and they'll arrange a time. Wow, I can't believe that Charlene Jones is staying with us, unannounced. I used to sing myself some. Played piano too."

Charlene smiled. "Maybe we can sing together later. You mightn't know any of my songs, but I'm sure we can find some common ground. I did bring my guitar. Riley even knows a few chords."

I halfway expected her to reply, "Oh, pshaw". It was pretty clear that my girl and Ted's ex-wife were hitting it off. I wasn't sure if this was good or bad. If they really were bonding, it might make it more difficult to announce the fact that we'd come with an agenda.

Oh, by the way, I just happen to know your ex husband and he once confided in me that he regretted his behavior with his wife and wanted to make amends. Can I help?

Uh-uh. I'd have to find exactly the right moment to drop the bombshell. Maybe in the middle of one of Charlene's sad songs, while they were singing a duet lamenting a love grown cold.

Nah!

Hunter was excited. "That would be wonderful. I mostly did Broadway, you know, show tunes, but since we moved to Virginia I've become a fan of country. And quite honestly, your first album got me though a tough time some years ago. I still remember some of the lyrics."

I did some quick subtraction in my head and figured that Charlene's only album had come out years *after* McCarver and Rebecca had split. That *would* be a coincidence.

Charlene blushed. "That's one of the nicest things an artist can hear, Mrs. Hunter. Thank you for that."

"Please, call me Rebecca. Now, normally we only serve breakfast here and I recommend one of the fine restaurants in the valley to our guests for supper, but my husband is leaving on business later this afternoon and I hate to eat alone. Would you two like to join me for a home cooked meal?"

This woman was like a kindly old grandma, although the difference in our ages was not enough for her to be my mother. I felt bad that we had come here under false pretenses, but I convinced myself that my mission could only do this woman good. If nothing else, to put some unpleasant memories to bed.

I said, "We'd be delighted if it's not too much trouble."

"Not at all. Is pork roast all right? Neither of you keep Kosher, do you?"

"I'm sure you didn't learn that down here, Rebecca," Charlene said.

She winked. "No. I grew up in New York. I'm not Jewish, but a lot of my friends were. Dinner is served at six. I imagine you'll want to see your rooms and maybe change clothes. We're very casual around here. This isn't Downton Abbey so you don't need to wear a tux to dinner, Mr. King."

We all laughed at that.

She went on. "My husband, Doug, is packing for his trip. I'm sure he'll want to meet you before he leaves. I still can't believe it. Charlene Jones, staying with us."

She led us upstairs and showed us the five guest rooms, each with singular charm. We picked one with a luxurious bath and a marble mantled fireplace. The logs were pyramided neatly over kindling and crumpled paper so that the merest flick of a match would ignite the blaze.

"Again, a lovely place, Mrs. Hunter. We're very pleased," Charlene said. "I'd love to sing with you tonight if you have no other plans. And we'd dearly love to meet your husband before he leaves."

"He'll be thrilled. Why don't you unpack and meet us downstairs when you're done. I haven't really done any singing professionally for some years now, so I hope you'll forgive me a few sour notes. Take your time, Doug's not leaving for another hour or so, in case you want to rest up after your trip."

She nodded toward the elaborately made up four poster bed, a sly look indicating she understood we might have other ideas for its use. Or at least, that's what crossed my mind.

TWENTY SIX

Douglas Hunter's appearance was about as far removed from Rebecca's first husband as Steve Buscemi is from Brad Pitt. He was tall, bald and had the teeth of a ferret. It was hard to assess his build given his loose attire, but his arms looked strong in a sinewy way. He had a jagged scar along his left cheek which gave him a sinister look, even when he smiled. Although you wouldn't expect someone embarking on a two hour car trip to dress formally, his stained UVA sweatshirt and baggy workout trousers were not the ensemble a grown businessman should be sporting to win friends and influence people.

He seemed to be a rather nice fellow in the two minutes it took for Rebecca to introduce us and whisk him away to his beat up ten year old Ford Explorer. All the way out the door, she hounded him with questions and reminders of everything he needed for his journey, making sure he had bottled water, granola bars and that he had packed all his medications.

Once they were outside, I teased Charlene.

"That was for our benefit."

"What do you mean, Riley?"

"There's more to Dougie-boy than meets the eye. Did you notice his shoes?"

"This is going to sound shallow, darlin', but I tried not to look at him more than I needed to. We had a fellow like that in high school. We called him mole boy. To his face. Of course, nowadays, we'd get our young asses kicked out of school for bullying if we did that."

"On his feet were two hundred dollar ECCO BIOMs running shoes."

"So?"

"Okay, I'm bullshitting you with my deductive skills. During your little post-coital nap, I made a quick call to my buddy Dan Logan."

"I thought you weren't going to burn a favor."

"Didn't exactly do that. This was a friendly call. You know how Dan loves Broadway. I just told him we were staying with a real legit singer who did national road shows and played big female roles in some of his favorite musicals. You know before Dan transferred to New York, he saw a lot of shows with the touring companies and I casually asked if he'd seen Rebecca."

"And he'd actually remember if he had? All those years ago?"

"Maybe not unaided, but you know the bureau. They have resources. I heard him pecking away on his little keyboard and next thing I know, he's telling me to be careful. Wouldn't say specifically, but hinted that Doug was a dangerous man."

"That milquetoast? You've got two or three inches on him."

I said, "He's going to Washington for a couple of days, right? So he works for the government maybe? Pentagon? Or Langley? Not saying that he's covert or anything but this guy was underdressed to the nines, or should I say minus nines?"

"And his wife was bossing him around big time. So you think that was all for show? Why?"

"Don't know. I wonder if he typically interacts with guests. But this would be an ideal cover. Mild mannered B and B owner. I just think that Rebecca going from the elegant McCarver to a loser does not compute."

"Maybe he's a tiger in the sack, sugar."

"One way to find out, Mata Hari."

"Hey!!! I agreed to this little adventure under protest to begin with. Don't make me grab Bosco and drive back in the middle of the night while you're sleeping."

Rebecca came back in through the front door. She sniffled as if holding back a tear, sad that her hubby was abandoning her.

She said, "I wish Douglas didn't have to leave. But duty calls."

"What does he do exactly?" Charlene asked, feigning innocence.

"He's a forensic accountant. Audits books. Boring work but it pays well."

The IRS? Dangerous man? Someone who just by coincidence could pull your tax forms and make life hard on you if you bother his wife? Logan usually reserved that term for those who do physical harm for a living. The only forensics involved would be after the wet work was accomplished.

Twenty seven

Dinner was simple, well prepared country fare --- Barbeque glazed pork roast, garlic smashed potatoes, cranberry-orange chutney, apple pie for dessert. The conversation mostly centered on innocent gossip about the celebs that Charlene was touring with. She always told strangers heartwarming human interest stories about the stars, hospital visits to sick children and the like. She never mentioned out of control egos or diva-imagined slights --- no lurid groupie tales or refusals to go on if there were brown M and Ms in the dressing room.

I tried to look like I care about how Dierks loves animals; even Bosco yawned when the subject came up. My presence was mostly nodding in agreement or commenting on how delicious each course of the meal was.

After we ate, Charlene brought down her Martin acoustic guitar. Rebecca found an old Epiphone that she suggested I strum with my thick fingers as she sat down at the piano. The two women proceeded to trade songs --- Charlene sang some of her own and some country classics. Rebecca mostly from Broadway. Both were talented enough to pick up the chords by ear. I was forced to lip read Charlene's cues --- C, A minor, G, E minor. Even though I could see that her fingering was much more complicated than that, she spared me from Adim7ths and the like.

We had killed two bottles of cabernet at dinner. I wouldn't rate their warbling harmonies with the Eagles, but the girls sounded pretty damned good to me. They encouraged me to sing along but I demurred, not wanted to spoil their fun. They took a short break for some brandy midway through their little hootenanny, and as a way of exiting gracefully, I told them that Bosco needed to take care of some business. After we got back, I pled fatigue from the long drive and coaxed the dog up to bed with me. Charlene and Rebecca seemed to care not a whit, and continued singing into the night.

Unlike McCarver's well insulated house on the water, this ancient place amplified the sounds coming from downstairs, so I wasn't able to sleep even had I wanted to. Every so often, a high note would strike Bosco's fancy and he'd howl along. I hoped that Charlene wouldn't think it was *me* mocking their singing. I'd pay dearly if she did.

I revisited an old *Spenser* book I hadn't read in years. Sometime after midnight, the vocalizing stopped and I heard Charlene mount the creaky stairs. The room was dark other than the pale light of my tablet, so she quietly tiptoed in and headed straight for the bath. I heard the shower go on. I closed my book and lay there in the dark, imagining her naked and soapy. It was a nice image.

But when she emerged a lifetime later, she was wearing an unsexy flannel nightie shirt and rather than shoo Bosco off the bed, she merely moved him over so that he lay between us. This was a pretty clear signal that our afternoon encounter wouldn't be enjoying an encore.

"Everything okay?" I asked in a small voice.

"Fine. 'Night."

"Uh, I waited up for you," I lied. I really had no choice, given the volume of the music wafting from downstairs.

"Sorry, darlin'."

"Was it my guitar work? I haven't played in months, you know."

"Do you really want to get into this tonight?"

Since she wasn't referring to her mons Venus, I wasn't sure what I else wanted to get into. Clearly something was bothering her. I had tried to be polite at dinner and not roll my eyes when the gossip got too silly. I thought I did a pretty good job hiding my ennui.

"Well, yeah. If something's on your mind, I want to hear it. Remember, no secrets?"

"Okay, you asked for it. I like this woman. She and I could be friends. But when she finds out why you're really here, I doubt she'll ever want to speak to me again. I'm sorry, I hate fibbing and that's what we're doing."

I hadn't anticipated Charlene and Rebecca hitting it off so well as to become bosom buds the first night. I'd failed to consider the bonds that musicians develop. I hoped their instant friendship would make the transition to McCarver's emissary easier. But the more I thought about it now, the more awkward it seemed.

I said, "I know how you feel. I like her too."

"In fact, playing with her tonight gave me an idea for an album. All those great Broadway songs, countrified. I don't think anybody has done that before and I bet the fans kinda have a vague notion about those tunes, but haven't heard them dressed up in blue jeans and cowboy hats."

"You really think that would work?"

"FYI, smarty-pants, did you know that the Beatles did songs like *A Taste of Honey* and *Till There Was You* on their first record? Where do you think they came from?"

"You have a point."

"Damn straight, I do. But that's just it. I can't go on pretending that we're here to jam with this lady when you have a whole nother agenda."

"I could tell her that you had no idea about Ted and that you just thought we were here for a romantic getaway. Make me the bad guy, which I guess I am."

She huffed. "Another lie. Just dig the hole deeper and deeper. But I guess that's what you do for a living, isn't it?"

We had now crossed from a mild disagreement on tactics into an existential question about our relationship. A few hours ago, I was thinking of how content I was with our little family, and now I was justifying my profession's warts.

"Charlene, that's really unfair. Is your stage persona who you really are, or just the side you want your fans to see? I came here to offer this woman a heartfelt apology and maybe a million bucks, but I had to get in the door first. You and I met under a little deception, but that's worked out, hasn't it?"

"But Riley, when we met, within ten minutes I told you I was married and I told you about my misspent youth, trying to get a record deal. I was honest with you, upfront. I was honest with Johnny, too. He knew I cheated on him. That was the deal we made. You, on the other hand, played dumb until I called you out on it. It's your nature."

She was calling me a back door man. A cheat. In my line of work, you can't always be open and upfront. This wasn't the time to get into a lengthy justification of what I do. But that time would need to come soon if we had any hope of staying together.

I said, "Okay. I shouldn't have involved you in this. I see now that I didn't think this through entirely. I was trying to get work done and spend some quality time with you at the same time. I told you we could go to Asheville this week and that I'd come up here later. You agreed to come along."

"I did. But remember that old proverb, serving two masters at once serves neither, sugar. I just don't want to be there when you tell Becky the real reason you came."

"Becky, now? You two *have* gotten tight. Tomorrow morning, you go riding and I'll tell her the truth. Or if you like, we can spend a nice day here, weather's supposed to be really great. I'll tell her day after tomorrow before we leave. If that doesn't work for you, you can fly back to Charlotte whenever you want and I'll deal with it when the time is right."

She rubbed Bosco's ears and thought for a moment. "Let's get it over as soon as we can. Do it in the morning. I need to look her in the eye afterwards. If she spits in my face, well, I deserve it. But let's not string her along, making out like we're something we're not."

"That's up to you. Like I said, if I do this delicately, she may not hate us. Maybe she'll accept Ted's apology and money and actually be grateful."

"Keep dreaming, babe. Go to sleep. You'll need your rest for the shitstorm you're driving into."

TWENTY EIGHT

"I'd like you to leave right now." Rebecca was definitive.

I'd gotten up before Charlene and come down to take Bosco out. Rebecca was sitting in the kitchen, smoking a cigarette and looking pissed.

"I'm afraid I don't understand. We booked two nights. Is there a problem?" Could my primitive guitar work be that bad?

"Just be thankful I didn't kick you out last night. He sent you, didn't he?"

"Who? What are you talking about?" *HE* could only be Ted, but how could she possibly know?

"My bastard of an ex husband. Don't play dumb and say you have no idea who that is."

I said, "I don't know what you think is going on, but if you'll let me explain, I think you'll understand this is for the better."

"The better for who? I understand that my ex hired you to find me. That you're a sleazeball with no ethics. Is that what I'll understand?"

"Rebecca, just give me five minutes and if you don't like what you hear, we'll clear out as soon as we can pack. Okay?"

She took a short drag and blew the smoke in my face.

I said, "I knew Ted from Toms River. You know he bought a radio station after your divorce. Well, he sold it and he's a very wealthy man. He feels awful about how he treated you. Simply put, he wanted to apologize, in person if you'll have him or through me if you won't. He also wanted to offer you some money if you need it and if you'll accept it from him. That's it."

"And you expect me to believe that? Do you believe it yourself? I had you marked for a bright guy, Guess I was wrong about y'all." She cackled at my perceived foolhardiness "Really let down more by Charlene than you."

"Listen, Rebecca, Charlene only agreed to come because I told her that you could only benefit from what Ted was offering."

She used her dying cigarette it to light another. "And you'll just tell him where I live and maybe the bastard will come here himself. If he decides to do that, tell him I own a shotgun and I'll be waiting."

She was as bitter as buttermilk.

I said, "Look, I haven't told Ted where you live and I won't if that's your preference."

She raised her eyebrows in skepticism. "And what will *that* cost me?"

"Nothing. I get it that you hate the guy. Sounds like you had some pretty ugly times. But he's not that way now. He's in therapy, has been for years. He knows that he's been a failure at relationships with women his whole life and he wants to make amends to those he hurt."

"You don't know him like I do. He's a master manipulator. When we were with other people, he was the perfect husband. Nobody could believe it when I filed for divorce. But only my closest friends know the half of the hell he put me through."

"Is there anything he can do to show you that he's changed? He doesn't want to re-kindle anything with you. I believe he is sincerely sorry for what he did and he's asking for your forgiveness. I think that if you gave him that, even if it's in a letter, he'll never bother you again."

She stubbed out her cigarette. "I don't even smoke any more. Haven't in years. Just the thought of him has gotten me started. Why don't you just write a letter and tell him it's from me?"

"Despite what you think, I consider myself an honest man. I can't do that. But Ted did give me a lot of latitude on this. I understand your trepidation but you should also know that you're not the only woman he's had me reach out to."

"My God. He's tortured others, too? There's no limit to this man's depravity. And he's using you as an instrument. You can't see that?"

"From the start, he told me that he's the guilty party. It hasn't been easy for him to admit how badly he behaved."

She arose from the table and poured herself a cup of coffee without asking me if I'd like one. I took that as a sign that her innkeeper duties took a distant second to her disdain for me. I have to say that Ted is a better host, and he isn't even running a bed and breakfast.

She said, "Bad behavior? Burping in front of guests. Telling dirty jokes in mixed company. That's bad behavior. What he did to me was so much worse. I don't know why I'm bothering to tell you this. Maybe you've been taken in by Ted like I was. I certainly fell for his charm, his looks, his sophistication. But if you really knew him half as well as I do, you'd put him in your rear view mirror before he fucks you over. And sure as I'm sitting here, I can tell you that if Ted and I ever meet again, one of us ain't walking out upright."

"Rebecca, the reason I came here was so I could see if you needed anything and if you were in a state of mind to deal with your ex. Obviously, you aren't. He told me about the restraining order, but he said he never laid a hand on you. Did he hit you? Is that what this is about?"

She shook her head. "No, he never physically hurt me. He terrorized me. He broke into the house I was renting after we split and left little notes. Threatening ones. He went through my things --- clothes, papers, letters. Smeared blood on a letter from a man I was seeing. Went to his house with a gun and threatened to kill him if he ever saw me again. For months, I didn't feel safe, like he was following me everywhere I went. He ruined an audition, making a crazy scene with the casting people while I was singing. Bad mouthed me to directors. He flew that damn plane of his to a regional theatre I was appearing at and disrupted the cast party. Had someone like you follow me when he couldn't do it himself. He ignored the restraining order but I could never prove to the police that he was orchestrating the whole thing. I even hired a body guard for a while. Finally, I had to move away, change my name and disappear. I couldn't stay in show business, I was too exposed. I thought I'd finally gotten him to give up and now all these years later, he sends you."

She was absolutely justified in her fears. McCarver had traumatized her to the extent that she had given up her identity and career. Ted seemed incapable of such things now, but he did admit he had done dreadful things, although not in quite the graphic terms she described.

"Rebecca, all I can say is that he convinced me that he's truly sorry and wants to make it up to you. He's authorized me to write a blank check."

"I don't want a dime of his money. All I want is that he leave me alone. Oh, and one more thing. When I told him that I had met somebody while I was touring, someone I really cared for, he began listing the dozens of times he cheated on me, starting a month after we were married. Chapter and verse, lurid descriptions. I tried to leave the room rather than listen to that poison and he wouldn't let me. He followed me through the whole house and even shouted through the door when I locked myself in the bathroom."

One last try. "All right, consider this. Tell him that you know that people change and that you're willing to accept his apology but seeing him again would only cause you more pain. Could you write a letter like that? Because if you could, I think that would be enough for both of you to get on with your lives. And I promise not to tell him where you live."

She bowed her head and buried her face in her hands. When she finally looked up, it was with a look of cold determination. "Listen, Douglas is a good man. We're happy here. And I meant what I said before. If Ted McCarver ever shows up at my door, we'll shoot his sorry ass. But I'll write that note. I hate giving him the satisfaction but if you think it will get him off my back, I'll do it."

"That's all I can ask. Charlene and I will leave as soon as I can get her up. She told me how much she enjoyed singing with you. She said that under different circumstances you could have been great friends, but she'll understand why you'd never let that happen now."

"I'm sorry for that, too. We had a fun evening last night, but she's right. Your girl has loose lips when she drinks."

"Wait a minute. Did Charlene tell you I was here for Ted?"

She started a smile, then quickly suppressed it. "Not in so many words. But she mentioned a name in passing, telling me a story about your best friend. Man named Rick Stone. A name I vaguely remember from the past. And lo and behold, Rick Stone, radio star, has a public Facebook page. On it, there's a picture of him, you and Ted on Hilton Head Island, all smiling and laughing. Didn't take much of a detective to figure that one out."

TWENTY NINE

Charlene didn't bother to shower and apply makeup. She had thrown on the same clothes she was wearing the night before and carelessly tossed the rest of her gear into her suitcase.

I was feeling pretty low.

This whole debacle had morphed into the very definition of *mission creep*. I was trying to serve many masters and wound up serving none. My intentions were honorable: I wanted to help my client live out his days without guilt and recrimination. I wanted to give his ex-wife a heartfelt apology and a nice check. I wanted to give Charlene a respite from her career crossroads and some time to decompress. I thought a nice little ride up the Shenandoah Valley would accomplish all three of those objectives and make me a hero.

Instead, I now had two women seriously upset with me. One I figured never to see again. The other --- I had succeeded in undermining her trust.

On top of that, I still had to finesse how to present what I had learned to Ted, without telling him where I had found Rebecca/Gretchen. I had to tell Stone to leave me out of his Facebook posts.

For a Georgetown educated man who had spent ten years with America's most esteemed crime fighting institution, I had made a mess of things lately. Two of my female clients had been killed in the last five years, when a little more foresight by me might have saved them. I'd screwed things up with Jaime --- first, by moving away and then by not telling her about Charlene before there was very much to tell.

Even the last case I dealt with that had turned out relatively well had its share of major missteps. My ham fisted inquiries had gotten a man killed. He was a bad man, but I don't know that he deserved to die the way he did.

My instincts told me to walk away from the whole McCarver mess and spend every minute I could on lavishing attention on Charlene Jones in hopes that she'd forgive my misguided attempts at chivalry.

What would happen with McCarver then?

I came up with two possibilities immediately. Ted would hire someone else to finish the job, someone who might not share my honor code of not revealing Rebecca's whereabouts. Someone who might handle the third mystery woman clumsily and create even more trouble for both her and Ted.

The other possibility is that Ted would sink into despair, believing that no one could help him resolve the issues with the women he had wronged. He'd continue to use the services of prostitutes. Maybe one day he'd pick the wrong one and her pimp would roll him or worse. That didn't seem like a very satisfactory outcome, no matter how badly he treated his women in the past.

I had to see this through. Maybe it's vanity, but I still believe that I'm the person who could best handle this dicey mission. Maybe there will be salvation with this third woman. It could hardly be worse than the first two: One was dead and the other hated his guts.

On the bright side, old Teddy boy wasn't out two million bucks.

I didn't have to make a decision right away. We had a five hour drive ahead of us. I generally think I'm a guy who has a positive attitude. Now I was dwelling on my failures and thinking negatively. After all, I had a nice house, a business that allowed me to work as hard and frequently as I want. I am healthy as a horse. I have no money concerns. I am living with a beautiful, talented and intelligent woman.

I'd find a way out of this morass. It just couldn't come soon enough.

THIRTY

My newly rediscovered optimism had what seemed to be an immediate payoff. When Charlene and I came downstairs, bags packed, buttoned up and ready to head home, Rebecca stopped me in the foyer. She shot Charl a regretful look, then averted her eyes and nodded toward the kitchen. I followed her as Charlene took the hint and herded Bosco out to the car.

Rebecca Hunter spoke slowly and deliberately. “While I don’t have any sympathy for my ex and his quest for love at seventy, I want to put an end to this, once and for all. If saying that I’ve put it behind me helps, I’ll tell him that lie. I wrote this note while you were upstairs packing. Short and sweet. It’s not sealed and you’re welcome to read it if you want to.”

She handed me an envelope, the front devoid of his name, as if she couldn’t bring herself to write it down.

“I’ll see that he gets it. And I do promise not to tell him where you are.”

“I hope you mean that. Now, some business between you and me. I realize that you booked two nights in advance. I don’t want your money, or Ted’s money if he’s paying. I don’t want anything from him but to be left alone.”

"I get that. I won't submit anything to him as an expense so he can't trace you that way. The charge is on my card. There's no need to refund the money."

"It's already done. While you were getting ready, I did call the Wintergreen resort, friend of mine up there. If you want to spend the next day or two in the area, they have condos for rent on the mountain. Tell them I sent you and they'll give you a rate. Up to you, but the views high up are spectacular with the leaves and all."

"That was very thoughtful, thanks." I hadn't expected this kindness and felt ashamed accepting the favor. I hoped I could convince her one last time that I wasn't the enemy.

"Look, whether you believe me or not, my intentions were good. And please don't think less of Charlene. Whatever you may think of me, she really wanted to help and she insisted I tell you the truth after she got to know you."

"King, you still don't understand. This is a man that told me more than once, 'if I can't have you, no one will.' A direct threat on my life. You seem to think the years are enough to let bygones be bygones. This man terrorized me. You say he's in therapy. I spent years in counseling trying to get over what he did and I still have nightmares that he's hiding in the closet with a knife. I won't recite chapter and verse of all the things I did to compensate, but I gave up what was a pretty good career doing what I love to be safe from him. You just picked open that scab."

That seemed to define my vocation these days, *professional scab picker*. "That was never the intent. I'm sorry."

She said, "And that's best done by leaving me alone. I don't even want to be in the same time zone. And trust me, I meant what I said before. We keep guns in the house. We won't hesitate to use them if he comes anywhere near me."

"I do believe if I tell him to stay away, he will. But if I'm wrong, just be careful you don't allow him to destroy what you've built here."

There was nothing left for me to say. Charlene had finished loading the car, and was sitting in the passenger seat, thumbing her tablet while Bosco roamed the back seat, nervously awaiting me. As I got in, I saw Rebecca staring at us through a side window.

In silence, we rode down the long gravel driveway to the front gate. I stopped the Audi there and turned to my distant companion.

"She said she hooked us up at Wintergreen, luxury condos on the mountain. Great views, nice restaurants. No need to hurry back. We could stay a couple more nights."

"I think I'd rather go back to Charlotte. This trip is going to have nothing but bad memories."

We'd argued about things in the past. She'd been mad at me before. But normally, after a few minutes of pouting, we cleared the air and went on as if nothing had happened. This was different.

"Charlene, I was trying to help. I was trying to help Ted get on with his life and maybe find some happiness in whatever time he has left. And I hoped that Rebecca would see this as his attempt to make up for what he did to her. I didn't appreciate how those wounds never fully healed. I'll do everything I can to make Ted understand that she's doing okay now, with her husband and career and that he should leave her alone."

"Right." She wasn't giving an inch.

"I'm not sure what to do going forward. I just don't want to make anything worse."

Her tone was arctic. "You should have thought of that before, shouldn't you?"

THIRTY ONE

Rebecca's note was concise, one paragraph: she accepted Ted's apology and hoped that he was truly a changed man, but had no desire to see him or accept any money from him. She signed it Gretchen, no last name.

Ted again insisted on flying up to Charlotte when I informed him that I had located his ex-wife. As soon as the doorbell rang, Charlene ran to the bedroom, as if Ted had a communicable disease and her immune system was compromised.

We sat in my living room. I offered him a drink, but he was eager to hear what I had unearthed and declined. I'd never seen him quite this antsy, as if his whole world depended on what I was about to tell him. I guess in a way it did.

I said, "She's fine. She has a business that has done well. She doesn't need or want any money from you."

"And?"

"That's it. She doesn't want an apology in person."

"Where is she now? And how does she look?"

The dance begins. "She has put on quite a bit of weight since the time you were married, but I could see how she was once very pretty. She seems happy where she is."

"And where is that?"

"She's married to a very nice man. She doesn't want any complications in her life. She wrote you this note."

I handed it over and he read it slowly, as if he was looking for something in code or invisible ink that I hadn't seen. After a minute, he waved the letter in his right hand, dismissively.

"Why doesn't she want to see me? It's been almost thirty years."

"Ted, you see, that was my reservation from the very start. You approached this as a chance at redemption. You hoped that these women would forgive and forget and that the money would pave over any wrongs you had done. I was afraid that we'd be reopening some chapters in your life, things you'd be better off forgetting."

"What else did she say? And how do I know she actually wrote this? It's been done on a computer and the signature could be forged."

All his words about how he trusted me to do the right thing rang hollow now as he accused me of fabricating the letter. I was not in a great mood to begin with, since my efforts for him had endangered my relationship with Charlene. Now he was reproachful that I hadn't created an outcome to his liking.

"If that's the way you feel, let's call it quits right now. You don't owe me anything. Just leave."

"I'm sorry, King, I don't mean to impugn your integrity. But it's obvious that you're holding something back. I trusted you to be honest with me and let the chips fall where they may. I don't know who you think you're protecting, but I think I'm entitled to the truth."

I had made a vow never to use Jack Nicholson's *you can't handle the truth* line since Stone had worn me out with it in the months after *A Few Good Men* had captured the whole of his psyche.

"If that's what you want, here it is: Gretchen changed her name and her career to get away from you. You scared the hell out of her. She feared for her life. It's taken years for her to finally sleep at night and she doesn't want to revisit this. She said that if you try to contact her in person, she'll kill you."

Ted was stunned speechless for a moment, but his preternatural calm remained.

"King, I know I made some pretty terrible threats back then. But I never would have acted on them. I never would have harmed her. I was just desperate. I was trying to make her see how much I needed her and show her I'd go to any lengths to keep her. But in the end, they were hollow. I wouldn't have done anything."

"She says you did. That you broke into her house. You confronted her lover. You stalked her. You're denying that?"

"No. I did those things." The legendary Ted cool was breaking, and his voice rose. "I couldn't accept losing her."

"Ted, you told me that you never really loved her all that much. That you married her for companionship.

The sex was mechanical. You cheated on her. What was there to lose really?"

We were headed into Dr. Mills' territory again.

"I was afraid of being alone. Gretchen and I were never passionate in the conventional sense. We were friends who shared common interests, who always got along. She was my safe harbor, someone I could count on to just be there for me. Even when she was on the road at first, I could always call her and she'd be there. But that changed. I'd call and get voicemail and she wouldn't call back. I was adrift. Then it happened. She confessed that she had taken a lover. That was the ultimate betrayal."

Tears were not welling up in his eyes, but his face betrayed as much emotion as he'd ever let on. "I settled for her. I opted for a comfortable existence, without the highs and lows. I thought that's what she wanted too. I never thought she was good enough to be a star, but she could play competently in minor productions. She was never good enough to make a living at it without me subsidizing her, which I was happy to do. All she had to do was be there for me when I needed her."

"But what about the other women?"

"Sex. That was all it was. I could let out my inner animal like I couldn't with Gretchen. I never took any of them seriously. I guess I needed to prove to myself that I could be attractive to other women, not just a wife who did things by rote. Gretchen approached the marital bed like it was a duty. She wanted it over as soon as possible. That's why when I broke into her house I read her boyfriend's love letters to her, I was stunned. He described things they had done with each other, things I knew she hadn't wanted with me. It was worse than catching them in the act."

"So after all that, why did you still hold on?"

"I committed everything to this woman, accepted the ennui of our life together. I wanted stability. I thought I had found the mirror image of myself. Under control at all times. And despite all I had given her, all the compromises I made with myself, she walked away with some worthless third rate actor."

His was a classic case of the exterior not matching the interior. Ted seemed to be the guy who had everything. A man others would envy. And yet underneath it all, he was a scared little boy, afraid to be alone. And these insecurities caused him to act out. He knew that he could never actually harm Rebecca/Gretchen physically, but she didn't.

"So what's next, Ted? Maybe it's time to give up this fight."

"That's what Jackie Mills has been advising of late. But I need to see this through. I haven't told you about the third woman. If this works with her, it will all be worth it. And finding her won't be hard."

"I have to be honest. I'm not sure I want to keep doing this. I think we both need to take a breath and re-think what you're trying to do. "

"I can't quit now. I'm moving forward. With or without you."

THIRTY TWO

Charlene emerged from the bedroom as Ted was leaving. She strode toward the kitchen, casting a rueful glance our way, but making no attempt to acknowledge our visitor.

It wouldn't be wise to call her out for her rudeness, since she was already at wit's end with me. I hustled Ted out and walked into the breakfast area, where she sat perusing the *Sunday Observer,* sipping reheated coffee.

"Not interested in meeting McCarver?" I said, meekly.

"Not in the least. He's actually better looking than I imagined, I'll give him that," she said, turning back to the paper.

"Your timing was exquisite. You must have heard some of what we were saying since you conveniently came out just as he was leaving."

"Maybe. I heard a lot of *ifs and buts and re-thinks*. Nothing final, or did I miss that part? You told me you were reconsidering the whole thing. Are you in or are you out?"

"I'm not sure. He gave me more food for thought just now. I need time to digest it."

Her sour mood had now lasted two days longer than usual --- this wasn't a passing storm. She wasn't ready to talk it out yet so I retreated to my office and sat down at the computer, checking some cyber-jobs that had emerged while we were in Virginia.

I'd barely started working when the phone rang. Stone managed to be upbeat and reproachful at the same time.

He said, "So you're thinking of quitting, huh? Not like the Riley King I grew up idolizing."

"News travels fast." I told him more about the ex-wife and her fears and how Ted's motives had come in question. If that wasn't enough, there was the fact that Charlene was into a nuclear freeze phase with me over the matter.

"So what are you saying, mate," he said. "you think Ted is some kind of psychopath who wants revenge against these women?"

"You know how you hate when some old girlfriend tries to friend you on Facebook now that you're a star? Imagine if after you ignore the request, she sends a detective out to hunt you down to try to arrange a meeting? Even if she did you wrong and wants to make amends, do you really want to hear from her again?"

"Well, if she's still hot and looking for a quick boff, why not?"

I said, "As hard as it may be, Neanderthal, try to think like a woman. One who's been terrorized and threatened by someone bigger and more powerful. That's how his ex-wife feels. Maybe it got even worse with the next one after her. I don't know much about this third woman."

"Neither do I. But I told him if you quit, I might be able to help."

"Okay, hold on cowboy. You're a public figure. You have a successful radio career to worry about. If this turns bad, your rep could go with it."

He acted hurt. "Don't think I'm up to the job?"

"Not the point. There's been something a little off about this all along. If Ted acted in any way toward this last woman like he did with his ex, she might do something irrational. His ex-wife said if he approached her, she'd shoot first and ask questions later. No offense, but I think I might be in a better position to handle that than you are."

I heard him take a couple of deep breaths. As an ex-Marine, he was no stranger to danger, but these days, his work was mostly sedentary and driven by his glib wit. He'd recovered from his death waltz with Lisa Tillman, and I didn't fancy him throwing his newfound stability to the wind in service of an old friend with questionable motives. He'd already almost lost his life protecting me.

We left it there. Back to reality in Charlotte. I'd told Charlene I was thinking of bowing out of the McCarver case. If I get pulled back in, how will she react? Maybe this is a stress test, like the government does with the banks every so often. If our relationship could withstand this, it would only grow stronger.

If it couldn't, we were wasting each other's time.

THIRTY THREE

The Airbus was airborne less than 75 minutes, gliding from Charlotte/Douglas to Newark/Liberty. I hoped to make this a surgical strike --- do the job and head home within forty eight hours.

Charlene Jones had been truthful with me about her past, painfully so. Within ten minutes of meeting her, she revealed that she had lost her virginity in New York City attempting to score a recording contract. That furtive coupling was followed by many others --- with promoters, A & R men and producers --- with equally unsuccessful results.

She told me about her adventures in the drug culture while trying to make the grade as a singer. I already knew she was married to a dangerous felon, but she asserted that it was a platonic business arrangement and that she had no knowledge of his criminal activity. She said that she had been accorded license to cheat during her marriage, and had exercised that option whenever the mood struck her.

But I asked her to move in with me anyway.

On the other hand, I had met her under false pretenses, pretending to be a star struck fan when in reality, I was trying to get the goods on her husband. It didn't take long for her to see through that ruse. I told her that Jaime Johansen existed but didn't explain how she was still in my life and potentially a threat to our happiness. Another deception on my part.

I never told her that Bosco was once owned by another woman I had fallen for, and that the lovable dog's presence was a constant reminder that my incompetence was responsible for that lady's demise.

Given her history, she swore at the outset of our relationship that there would be no lies or secrets between us. I had no reason to believe that she hadn't honored that vow. She told me of recent advances made by music business sharks, who were aware of her reputation. She rejected them now. Drugs were backstage as well, and although she admitted being tempted on occasion, she had resisted.

Even though Charlene was holding up her end of the bargain, I was failing. I was on my way up north to finish the job I had started for McCarver, a job Charlene clearly did not approve of.

McCarver had manipulated me again. He knew that by enlisting Stone to complete the task, I'd have little choice but to intercede again. But when I told Charlene I needed to fly up to Jersey to help Rick, I didn't explain that it was to protect him from blowback if he accepted the McCarver mission. A lie of omission, but a lie nonetheless.

And why did I lie? Was it that I don't trust her professed love for me, based on her past meanderings? Or am I so racked with doubts over my own history that I didn't think any woman worth having would accept me as I am?

How did this make me any different than Ted McCarver? He has avoided commitment in the autumn of his life, fearing repetition of his lifelong behaviors. At least now he was confessing his sins and trying to make amends, yet I continue to obfuscate mine to the person living with me.

It fits a pattern I am not proud of.

Especially with Jaime. I hadn't told her I was harboring Charlene in my home, even before anything sexual had happened between us. I had plenty of opportunities, but chose the coward's path. When Jaime found out on her own, she was deeply hurt by my lack of candor. She had asked for time to reflect. The clock might still be ticking on that.

The cynicism of my profession has seeped into my personal life. I frequently need to deceive to accomplish my mission. My job has corrupted me.

Or is it the other way around, that I am by nature a liar? Have I subconsciously chosen a profession that perfectly fits my unreliable character? Will I ever be able to fully reveal myself to Charlene, or do I think so little of the real me that I'll never summon up the courage?

The wheels mercifully bumped down on the cold New Jersey tarmac, and my thoughts turned toward the task at hand, relegating my self-doubts to be dealt with later.

THIRTY FOUR

"How you feel about driving a pickup truck, Goober?" Stone asked me.

"Least I'd have some cred driving it. Not like you, Urban Cowboy."

We were speeding down the Garden State Parkway, doing over 80 on a 60 mile per hour freeway.

"Aren't you afraid of getting stopped, Ricky?" I asked, begging him to slow down. The parkway isn't engineered for such high speeds, and the curves and sudden traffic stoppages make 80 feel like 120.

"Just showing you what my new baby can do, brother," was his flippant answer. "Besides I got so many PBA badges after that little tiff a couple years back that no self respecting cop in the state will ticket me."

Funny, how his near fatal wounds now were *that little tiff.* I was glad that he'd been able to put aside his physical wounds so quickly; it had taken him substantially longer to heal from what Lisa Tillman had done to him.

"Mid life crisis, eh? A shiny new Mustang convertible with a 5.0 L V8. Sad." I was trying to shame him into reducing the speed, but it wasn't working. His other vehicle was a seven year old Ford F-150 pickup, which he only used when he needed to haul heavy loads or when his main ride was in the shop. That's the slick motor I'd be tooling around in while sleuthing in Jersey.

"When did you turn into a little girl? I'm trying to break my world record. 66 miles home. Best I've done is 56 minutes. I bet I can beat that today, do it in 53. By the way, does Charlene know what a wimp you are?"

"Charlene hasn't said much to me at all lately."

"So I've heard. She was *Cold as Ice, Willing to sacrifice* to Ted when he was down there, didn't even say hello. Oh yeah, he noticed. But he has a great plan to warm her up to him. And you sir, will reap the benefits."

"Whoa there, partner. This whole thing started because Ted has problems dealing with women and now he has a little scheme to help me with mine? No thank you."

Stone laughed at my naïveté. "Wait 'til you hear what he has cooked up for her. Charlene knows enough about computers to stream audio, no?"

"About twice as much as you and me put together. Why?" Charlene had set up a mini recording studio in the extra bedroom that Stone used to do his radio show when he visited me in Charlotte. She could record multiple tracks into her laptop, and was toying with the idea of cutting her own album and selling it on the internet. A couple of positive "likes" from Darius, Keith and company might make it profitable, eliminating the middlemen.

Stone said, "Tell her to stream Country 94 in New York at around three this afternoon."

"She doesn't exactly have fond memories of New York. Besides why listen to some faux country station when we have the genuine article down in Charlotte?"

"Are they playing her record?"

"What record? The one she did twenty years ago?"

"That's the one. You see bucco, when Ted sold WJOK, it was to a huge radio group. Cirrus. Part of the payment was in company stock. So he persuaded the group programmer to play one of her songs on their New York station today. Who knows, if it gets enough positive reaction, it may force the label to re-release it. Could be a big boon to her career."

Another example of Ted trying to buy his way into a woman's heart, not with a million bucks this time, but with airplay. Like his previous forays, I believe he meant well, but I wasn't sure how Charlene would take it. Timing is everything in her line of work. She might not want her old material out there as representative of her current sensibilities. She would welcome radio exposure, but only when she had new material to promote. Either way, it was doubtful Ted's gift would be accepted gracefully, especially since she didn't like him to begin with. And one spin, even in New York would hardly be noticed.

I said, "You know, Ricky, you could do me a favor and deliver the news yourself. She's mad at me and she might see this as my attempt to weasel my way into her good graces again."

"Riles, this ain't weaseling. I know you're not in the business, but formats are so tight today, there's no way an unknown artist gets played on a New York station without buying a big package. A few spins could cost a half million bucks to a new artist."

"I spent some time investigating payola with the FBI. Now they've essentially legalized it."

Stone agreed. "Radio found a way around those old rules a while back. They sell an artist or record company a package. The package includes commercials, promotional appearances, maybe a free concert and, oh by the way, airplay. They will actively promote your music if you pay them. The FCC is pretty toothless now and even if they weren't, it's all perfectly legal."

"Back then, we were investigating individual deejays."

"The big radio groups didn't want their low level employees profiting when they could rake in the big bucks. The deejays were doing nickel and dime stuff under the table, and that was undercutting the big earnings the corporate owners could make. Deejays don't spend millions lobbying in DC."

"Another reason I'm not working in Washington anymore. Den of thieves. Still, why don't you call Charlene and give her the news?"

"Why me? Don't you want to be the hero?"

"I'm afraid this might backfire if she thinks I put Ted up to it. It might be the straw that breaks the camel's back."

"Things are that fragile? I thought you guys were tight. No offense to your priors, but she's the hottest number I've ever seen you with. *She is terminally pretty in the heart of the cold, cold city*. Maybe not the sweetest girl around, she does have her moods, but hey, that's *life in the fast lane*."

One more song quote and I'd jump out of the car, even at eighty. "This McCarver deal has driven a wedge between us. She sees the guy as a rapist who got away with it. I didn't tell Charlene I'm here for Ted. I told her that I'm helping you with something, which is technically true, but she won't see the distinction."

Stone chewed on that for a minute. "Now I feel bad. You came here to protect me in case this blows up, even knowing that it could ruin you with Charlene? And this is all because I jumped in front of a loaded gun for you, once upon a time?"

"Payback's a bitch sometimes, man."

THIRTY FIVE

The woman looked tough. I couldn't imagine her taking shit from anybody. Her voice was husky from years of cigarettes and the acrid smell of smoke radiated from her pores. But there was something striking about her, a fierce beauty that emanated from someplace deep within. Maybe it was her eyes, the kind you see in animal shelters, resigned to their fate but pleading to be loved.

I could envision her in a mixed martial arts competition, lean yet strong at five seven, one-ten. Long elegant fingers, short clipped, unvarnished nails. Her sharp features were heavily made up, dark mascara highlighting expressive green eyes.

She had full mouth of nearly perfect whitened teeth, stained ever so slightly at their base from the nicotine. Her attire was simple: tight jeans and a pale yellow cotton sweater fraying at the collar. Practical flat shoes.

I knew from Ted's notes that she was pushing fifty. Tiny wrinkles around her eyes and mouth surfaced when she smiled. There was a thin white scar underneath her chin that stood out proud against her deep tan. A hardboiled detective from a bygone era might have called her a hellcat.

We were sitting in the Starlight diner, the one Stone and I used to frequent when I lived in Bayville. In the shank of the evening, the few remaining patrons were nocturnal workers who came for breakfast and yesterday's paper before their shifts. Cops, always cops. I suppose there is something reassuring in that.

I said, "Thanks for agreeing to listen to me, Stephanie. I wasn't sure you'd be receptive."

"Call me Stevie. And dispense with the Journey jokes. I've heard 'em all."

Her last name was Perry, we were in a diner in New Jersey. This could be the final scene of *The Sopranos*, if *Don't Stop Believing* was playing on the tiny jukeboxes that they still keep on the edge of each table in authentic Garden State haunts.

"Hadn't crossed my mind until you mentioned it," I lied. "I get that stuff too, sometimes. Riley King is B.B. King's birth name."

"I didn't know that." Her menthol cigarette pack was on the Formica table in front of her and I could tell she wanted one, chafing at the state's no smoking ordinances. "So ... how did you find me?"

"Facebook. You said on your page that you were headed out to see John Cafferty play tonight at the Rocking Horse. So I just hung out by the door and waited."

"So, what the hell does Ted McCarver want from my life these days? And why did he hire you, when he could have found me himself. I'm not exactly in hiding."

"Well, for starters, he said that you were the woman in his life that he loved the best. Better than all the rest."

"He had a strange way of showing it. We fought all the time. Then he slugs me to put a cap on it. I'd hate to be his enemy, if that's the way he treats the girl he says he loved best."

"Yeah, well. Ted's retired now. He's been reflecting on his life, and you happen to be his biggest regret."

She sipped her coffee, her eyes boring right through me. "Well, he was mine, that's for damn sure. In one sense, I'm sorry I ever met the bastard. In another, he was the most important man in my life. I loved him a lot. Don't know why. Just chemistry, I guess."

"Let me cut to the chase here, Stevie. I won't waste your time. Ted wants to apologize to you. And help you in any way he can. If it's money, a job, a new condo. Whatever he can do, he wants to make up for what he did."

She laughed softly. Shaking her head rapidly, back and forth as if to dislodge something foreign stuck in her brain.

"So if I said I wanted a million bucks, he'd do that? Bull----shit!"

"He's authorized me to do that, if that's what you want."

"This from the man who demanded I return everything he ever bought me after we split. You're shitting me."

"I'm not. I told you, he's very regretful these days. A million dollars isn't a big deal to him. If it buys him peace of mind, he thinks it's worth it."

"And this is for real?"

"Stevie, my job was to find you, express his apology and extend his offer. He'd like to see you and hand you a check in person. But if you can't abide that, he'll wire the money to your account."

I had done my homework on Stevie Perry, not just on Facebook. She had worked for the same small building supply company since getting out of high school thirty years ago. Her salary was just over forty thousand a year. Her checking account contained no more than two thousand bucks at its peak. She had a couple of short term CDs at a miniscule rate of interest. She lived in a small condo that she still owed a hundred grand on.

"What's your deal in all of this, King?"

"Ted is a friend of my best friend. This is not normally something I'd do. But Ted personally asked that I handle this for him and I promised I'd see it through."

"This is fucking unbelievable. A man I haven't seen in twenty years wants to give me money because once upon a time, he hit me when we both were drunk. Did he mention that I came at him with a baseball bat?"

"He said that there was only one incident involving physical violence and that he would never do it again. Honestly, it's hard for me to think of him that way. He's one of the gentlest souls I've ever met."

She stared out the window at the passing cars on Route Nine, the maze of colored lights mesmerizing as they reflected off the wet macadam. Even now, in the harsh florescent illumination, Stevie Perry was stunning --- twenty years ago, she must have been outright irresistible.

She had never married, which I wondered about, since I couldn't see the cheap Jersey shore Lotharios giving her a moment's peace.

She was about the same age as Charlene, but Charlene had womanly curves and this chick was all chrome and hard edges. Angular cheekbones, no chest to speak of. Auburn hair clipped in a style that went out in the nineties.

She interrupted the reverie. "Okay, Mr. Riley King, if this isn't some sick prank, what's the next step?"

"That's up to you. If you'll agree to meet Ted, name the time and place. Specify how you want the money. I can put you directly in touch with him and bow out now. It's your call."

"Let me think about it. Where is Ted now?"

"At the moment? I imagine he's home. He lives on Hilton Head Island full time, but he's got a condo up here. I'm sure if you're amenable to meeting him, you choose when and where."

There was still doubt in her eyes. "You know, I haven't really seen him since that night he hit me. I changed my phone number. He pounded on my door a number of times and I never answered. I hid out at my folks' house. He even showed up at my work once. I swore I'd fucking call the police and press charges if he didn't leave me alone. It took a few weeks, but he finally gave up. Although I guess he never gave up if he hired you."

I was relieved that my role in this mini-soap opera was nearing the end. The best outcome would be for her and Ted to work out the details, have one final meeting and be done with it.

I said, "Do you even remember what brought on that fight?"

"Something about where we'd spend our honeymoon started it, I think. We were going to be married, you know. But once we got going, every little thing I had done that Ted didn't like got thrown out at me. Small stuff, like he didn't like my fucking language in mixed company. And I gave him shit right back. Made fun of his penis that didn't work after a couple of pops. I think that put him over the edge."

That would do it. This was way over the *too much information* line for me. I looked around for the waitress. She was tied up flirting with a couple of Ocean County cops at the end of the counter and managed to ignored my gestures.

"Well, now there's Cialis and Viagra so I don't think that's a problem," she said. "You know, Ted was everything I grew up thinking the perfect husband would be. Smart, rich, good looking. And he was actually not bad in the sack. He made up for his weenie in other ways, silver tongued devil."

This was more stuff I didn't need to hear. "I've got to get back. Why don't I give you my cell number and you call me and let me know how you want to proceed. Am I okay in telling Ted that you accept his apology and you'll contact him about meeting or transferring the money?"

"I'm still not a hundred per cent buying this. I've had a lot of time to think about what happened with us. I was immature, in my twenties. I could have handled things a lot different. I suppose he did feel threatened by that baseball bat, even though I never would have used it."

"You both were drinking, things got out of hand. But don't blame yourself. Ted doesn't assign any of this to you, at least that's what says. He never should have laid a hand on you, no matter what you said to him or how you came at him with a bat. He says he could have taken it away and left after that. Here's my card with my number. Call me when you've decided."

I left a twenty on the table and gave her the card. God willing, she'd call soon and relieve me of this burden. Then I could go home and deal with the other difficult female in my life.

THIRTY SIX

I have a plan Meet at La Cantina Bay Head noon Stevie.

I didn't read the text message until I was back at Rick's Mantoloking digs. My friend was MIA when I got in. He had a promotional appearance for the station that evening, hosting a party at a local chain restaurant celebrating the World Series.

It was too late to call Charlene, and I couldn't very well share my discovery with her anyway. And as far as I knew, she hadn't responded to Stone when he left her a voicemail about her New York airplay. Although there might be a perfectly reasonable explanation for her radio silence, it was troubling nonetheless.

I started watching the game but fell asleep in the bottom of the seventh. The participants held no rooting interest for me, but baseball is still my favorite sport, probably because my dad took me to so many games. When I woke up during the endless postgame analysis, Stone still hadn't gotten in. No point in waiting up any longer --- I trudged upstairs to the comfort of his guest room, leaving a note that we'd talk in the morning.

Despite my physical fatigue, I didn't sleep well. On one hand, I was optimistic that whatever Stevie's plan was, it would mark the end of my excursion through shrink-land with Ted. Hopefully, it would also mark the beginning of rehabilitating my relationship with Charlene, which was on uncertain turf recently.

Around six, I finally gave up trying to go back to sleep. The smell of fresh coffee was wafting up from downstairs. As I fetched the *Asbury Park Press* from his front porch, I noticed there was another car in the driveway, parked next to the pickup. It was a sleek looking but older Mazda MX-5, the kind of spare vehicle someone like Ted might keep at a second home, just in case.

When I got back to the kitchen, the occupant was not Ted McCarver, but someone far more captivating at this early hour. She was wearing tight orange satin shorts, and a tank top bearing the unmistakable *Hooters* logo. Rick, you naughty boy!

I said, “Hi, I’m Riley King. Friend of Rick’s. Hope he told you I was here.”

“Of course he did. I’m Cindy. Uh, I’m uh, a friend of Rick’s, too.”

“Nice to meet you.” At the risk of sounding like the sexist pig I can sometimes devolve into, this girl was *Hooters* personified. Blonde, blue eyes, large boobs, a great ass, and a perky disposition. Not that there’s anything wrong with that.

“Rick awake yet, Cindy?” I asked, feeling just a bit awkward.

“He was stirring when I left. I’d love to talk with you, but I have an early class and traffic sucks on the causeway to the mainland, even this early.”

"Well, don't let me keep you. Where are you studying?"

"Ocean County Community. Second year. I want to study law. Springsteen did a semester there, you know."

"I did know. But he wasn't studying law. Well, it was an unexpected pleasure meeting you."

"Me too. Rick should be down soon. Bye."

She moved that great butt out the front door un-self-consciously, as only a nineteen year old can do. Rick is handsome, a radio star, but at least thirty years her senior. After two cups of coffee and finding the three stories in the local paper that might sustain even the slightest interest to me, Stone wandered in from the main floor master. He was freshly showered and dressed for work, which in radio these days means jeans, cross trainers and a polo shirt.

Saving the lecture about young Cindy for a more appropriate time, I filled him in on the previous evening's developments. His face grew dark halfway through the story. Clearly, he suspected that something was amiss, perhaps a detail I'd overlooked in my haste to be done with this.

"So hopefully, her terms will be reasonable and Ted can do his thing and move on," I said in conclusion. "But you look troubled, man. Am I reading this lady wrong?"

He ran his fingers through his dark blonde hair. "Yeah. I'm afraid there's another complication."

This was the last thing I needed. I was hoping for a clean getaway today, maybe even a flight back to Charlotte and Charlene tonight. I waited for his explanation.

He said, "You and Ted never told me her name until now. Stevie Perry, you say? Slender. Tough looking but still attractive in a Joan Jett Jersey girl kind of way. Forty five to fifty?"

"Closer to fifty, yeah. Why?"

"I fucked her."

THIRTY SEVEN

"**P**lease tell me you're kidding."

He wasn't kidding. Rather than answer directly, a simple what-the-hell shrug of the shoulders told me all I needed to know.

"Why?" I asked.

"Like Mount Everest, because it was there." He was taking this a lot less seriously than I was. "There was a Beatlefest in Red Bank. *I saw her standing there*. We were interested in the same memorabilia, started talking, one thing led to another and before we knew it, I was on top of her."

"At least you remembered her name. Do you even know Cindy's last name?"

"Cindy who? Oh, her. Ah, it's Hudson, Houston, something like that. She's on my speed dial under CIN-SIN so last names don't matter that much. Stevie Perry struck a chord because of the guy in Journey."

Rick had been so badly burned by Lisa Tillman that he decided to take it out on the entire gender. My experience with Ted led me to speculate that twenty years from now, Stone might well be hiring someone to undo the devastation left in his wake.

I shifted to damage control. "Does Ted have any idea about this? Did you know he considers Stevie the love of his life? More so than his ex-wife even."

"I did not know that," Stone said, channeling his best Johnny Carson.

I'd had enough. "Okay, Rick, I know you don't take this seriously, but how do you think Ted will take this if he finds out? I take it his name never came up when you were on top of her, as you so delicately put it."

"Nope, both of us were preoccupied then. Although you got me thinking, this might have been a vengeance fuck on her part. Using me to get back at Ted. *She's the kind of girl you want so much it makes you sorry.* And I thought she just had the hots for a fellow Beatlemaniac."

"Maybe you can put the post-coital bliss with Cindy aside and think about what you did. You claim this man is your friend and mentor. And you screw the woman he almost married."

"Years later. So shoot me."

"Don't give me ideas. You've put me in a bad spot, by the way. Ted wants to talk with her and she seems open to it. I must say after meeting her just this once, she and Ted make an odd couple. She's all street, he's luxury high rise. I don't think I've ever heard him curse and she swears like a longshoreman. Ted is circumspect: he speaks everything very carefully, like a lawyer almost. She has a certain earthy charm and she just says whatever's on her mind. Now she might have something she can throw in his face if their meeting doesn't go well."

"He's a big boy. He'll roll with it."

"Don't be so sure. This could result in losing him as a friend --- at the very least. And since you've become so self centered, how about losing your gig as another consequence? He still has a share of WJOK and if he becomes an enemy instead of a benefactor ..."

My friend was turning into an asshole before my very eyes but the thought of losing his job sobered him up. "You really think Ted would do that?"

"I don't know, but he has a long memory. Think about it. At seventy, he's trying to make amends to the women he wronged over a forty year period. You don't think it could work the other way, too?"

"Bummer."

"And now that I've got your attention, did you ever consider that this Cindy may not be as old as she says he is? You know that Mary Chesterton, the first woman I investigated for Ted, was fifteen and claimed to be eighteen."

"Cindy's 21. She told me the first night we shagged, brother. Besides, there's no way she cries rape. You saw her this morning. Didn't she look like one satisfied customer?"

This man had saved my life. There was no one I could depend on more. But right now, I had all I could do to keep from slapping some sense into him. So I just threw up my hands and left. I had business to take care of.

It was still too early to meet Stevie. I had my tablet with me so I found a Starbucks that was not crowded and hunkered down with an almond scone. Not exactly a healthy breakfast but I was feeling none too healthy at the moment and maybe the sugar rush would lift my spirits. I Skyped Charlene. She answered, video off.

I tried to sound cheerful. "Morning, sweetheart. I'm not calling too early? Your camera isn't on."

She was drowsy. Charlene, like most musicians, is not a morning person.

"I look a wreck. Up late working on some songs." I couldn't read anything into her tone. At least it wasn't overtly hostile.

"That's good. You happy with the way it's turning out?"

"Yeah, kind of. I'm re-doing that song *Cockeyed Optimist* from *South Pacific*. You know," she sang, with a twang "*When the sky is a bright canary yellow...*"

"That could work. I like it. Dan Logan will have a conniption maybe but who cares. Hey, did you get Rick's message about your old CD getting a spin on that New York country station?"

"I did, but I was out and didn't hear it."

I was a little surprised that she showed absolutely no enthusiasm. I would have thought it a big deal to get New York radio exposure.

"There's an MP3 of it in my inbox this morning. Should I forward it to you?"

She didn't answer right away.

"Riley, did you put McCarver up to it? He's the only one I can think of that has the juice to do this."

"I had nothing to do with it. Ted's idea totally."

"Like I figured. Don't you see it? He's trying to buy you off. He knows the money ain't a big deal to you. So he's trying to lure you back into his clutches by doing something nice for me. On one hand, sugar, it's lovely that he's thinking that you care for me that much, but it's pretty blatant."

Men are from Mars. My woman questions Ted's motives and takes his every good deed as a cynical effort to attain nefarious goals. He has a lot of resources in his repertoire -- charm, intelligence, integrity and yes, money. One uses the tools one has. Maybe I should have heeded my initial misgivings about Dracula.

I could wimp out and try to hide the truth from her, hoping she would never find out on her own that I was up here for Ted. That tactic hadn't worked out so well with Jaime when I neglected to tell her that Charlene was temporarily under my roof.

Or I could confess and risk it being a deal breaker.

I decided that I had to man up and tell her the truth. I'd meet Stevie Perry, work out a solution and tell Charlene about it --- face to face --- when I got back to Charlotte. And play out however the Fates decide.

THIRTY EIGHT

La Cantina was a dive. I'd driven past it before but never ventured in. Not only did it look like it might harbor rats, but that they might be featured prominently in the cuisine. I'm sure there is a Spanish word for it. La vermina? For a classy berg like Bay Head, the joint stood out like a turd in the punchbowl.

It made me wonder about Stevie Perry. Most women, who assume that their companion is springing for the vittles, would pick a nice place. And there were certainly a host of trendy bistros in Bay Head, overlooking the bay or the ocean. My guess was that she opted for this sinkhole because it was A) close to her job and/or B) nobody she knew would be caught dead in there.

I arrived a few minutes before twelve and ordered a diet coke. They served it out of a can and handed me a Styrofoam cup, so I felt fairly safe from dysentery. The place was empty, which didn't bode well for business unless the midday crowd arrived fashionably late. Not exactly the type of café for ladies who lunch, unless they were ladies of the night.

Stevie arrived at noon. She was wearing yellow paisley corduroy jeans, topped by a shiny light blue blouse. In the sunlight, she looked her age, but despite the hard edge, she radiated a cool sexiness.

"I see you got my text. Not hungry?" she said, eyeing my soda.

"I'm keeping Kosher. One day only."

"Open mic night at the Stone Pony is Tuesday. But we're not here to eat, are we?"

"Thank God for that. How close is the nearest ER?"

"I hope you're a better PI than a comedian. Well, at the risk of enduring any more of your fucking one liners, let's get down to business."

I could see why Ted had such a hard time forgetting this woman. She was unconventional in every way --- her hair, her attire, her voice. Nothing matched yet all these incongruous parts meshed into a very alluring sum. Or was I just missing Charlene?

"Let's," I said, awaiting her opening gambit.

"I'm curious to see Ted again. I told you, I had a part in what happened at the end of our relationship. I'm not worried that it would happen again. I'm not exactly afraid of a seventy year old man."

"You said you had a plan?"

"Oh, now it's Mr. Let's-Get-Down-to-Business."

I was here strictly to listen. Ted's instructions all along were not to negotiate but to accede to any demands these women might have, within reason. Reason to a multi-millionaire.

"I just thought you probably need to get back to work, so I was being considerate." She'd quickly pick up on the bullshit that line encompassed.

"Okay," she said, ignoring my sarcasm. "Here's the deal. You said Ted lives on Hilton Head. I was there once and I loved it, always wanted to go back. So, if Ted wants to see me, I want first class tickets out of Newark, roundtrip, leaving tomorrow morning and returning Monday night. Four star hotel, two nights. The Sonesta on the ocean looks nice. And ten grand in my checking account before close of business today."

"Okay."

"Okay? Just like that? You know what they say, if the other side agrees too quickly, you should have asked for more. I'll talk to Ted on the phone but if he wants to fucking meet in person, he'll need to up the ante."

What puzzled me was how a woman as sharp as this could hold the same menial job for twenty plus years. Maybe her generous use of certain adjectives? Of course, this whole affair amounted to blackmail, but my client had approached her, not the other way around. And if he was willing to pay that kind of price for an audience with his old lover, well, it beat paying for hookers.

"All right, Ms. Perry, this is how this will work. I'll contact Ted with your terms. I'm sure he'll agree, but my only concern is that the money can be transferred that quickly. Not that he doesn't have it, but in my experience, wire transfers sometime take a bit longer to clear."

"You claim Ted has beaucoup bucks. Let's see if he has the clout to make this happen. If not, then he can't afford me."

Ironic. We were sitting in a shabby taco joint that was just now starting to fill up with Central American laborers, most of whom were here illegally. Her condo was one step above government subsidized housing; her car a five year old Honda; her clothing a pastiche of leftovers from T.J. Maxx, however imaginatively they had been assembled. Her price on a Saturday night might be a few drinks and a ride in a fast car. But this afternoon, it was ten grand and a first class vacation. Instant inflation.

"I'll call him as soon as we're through. If it *can* be done, Ted will do it. That kind of dough is beyond my pay grade, but he probably pays that much for his suits."

She gave me a wistful smile. "He always was a great dresser. Just one of the things I loved about him. You know, after he hit me, I was bombarded with all kinds of feminist crap from my friends about how if he does it once, he'll do it over and over. I just cut him off cold, threatened to press charges if he ever came near me again. But after a while, I realized that I had said some fucking hateful things, threatened him with a baseball bat, and we'd both been boozing. He had never raised a hand to me before in the two years we were together. I don't think he ever would again, to be honest with you."

"I shouldn't say this, because I'm representing a client: it's not feminist crap. In my line of work, I've seen a lot of domestic abuse. I'd agree that Ted doesn't seem the type to be a serial offender, but you can't always tell. Better to be safe than sorry."

"And that's what I did. It wasn't easy and he was persistent with his apologies. But understand, Ted was the love of my life. We were two strong willed people. Neither one of us knew how to back down or compromise. We fought all the time, but the makeup sex was always great. Maybe that's mellowed in us both over the years."

In twenty years, maybe the blood had calmed to the point where a lasting truce was possible. That wasn't my affair, I'd fulfilled my role. "I hope so. Then you both can move on, without regrets. But there is one other item we need to address."

"And that is?"

"Rick Stone."

"Well done, detective. How did you come by that little tidbit?"

"Not important. All I can say is that if Ted finds out that you slept with Stone, all bets are off. He doesn't know about it. Stone will never tell him. There's no way anyone else can spill the beans, especially Riley King. But believe me, if Ted finds out, I can't say how he'll deal with it."

I'd caught her unprepared. I could see her mind, calculating the probabilities, the risk versus reward. It was almost like those little spinning circles your computer spits out at you when it's buffering or doing something else in the background.

Finally, she reached a conclusion and rationalized. "It was a Saturday night and I was lonely. He was a great looking guy. We both were into the Beatles. It wasn't like I was trying to pay Ted back by sleeping with his friend. He was a lousy lay anyway."

That little morsel was too luscious not to use on Stone, although given his current state, not any time soon. I'd file it away for an appropriate time.

I told Stevie that I'd speak to Ted and call her cell when the arrangements were made. Given what Ted had expressed, there was no doubt in my mind that he'd enthusiastically agree to her terms and the money would be in her account within the hour.

I left to get some real lunch.

THIRTY NINE

How did I end up on a plane, sitting next to Stevie Perry?

The invisible hand of Ted McCarver was guiding my life these days, almost as if he was a god who had predetermined my course and I was powerless to change direction. Ted had agreed to Stevie's terms, as expected. The money transfer posed no problem. The tickets were waiting at the American Airlines check-in at Newark/Liberty. When I mentioned that I considered my role in his affairs complete and that I wanted to return home as soon as possible, he suggested that I ride to the airport with Stevie in the car he ordered. He'd be happy to book my flight at the same time as hers.

Although I had hoped to be back in Charlotte, I stayed at Stone's place Friday night. He was out on another promotional night for WJOK. He invited me to join him but since the limo was due at five a.m., I passed. I watched some baseball, falling asleep again in the seventh inning. Sometime around midnight, I heard rustling by front door and some girlish giggling, either Cindy or a new conquest. I didn't fancy initiating battles with Stone and Charlene at the same time, so I deferred my man-to-boy lecture with Stone for another time.

There are no direct flights from Newark to Hilton Head, which I knew but hadn't thought of. They all required a short stopover in --- Charlotte! Ted had booked two first class seats next to each other. I'd disembark in North Carolina and Stevie would move to a smaller plane capable of landing on the island's shorter runway.

I didn't mind the company. After an espresso at the airport, she opened up and chatted away about any subject that caught her fancy. Nervous flyer or just more trusting?

"You must think I'm frigging crazy or greedy or both, don't you, King?" she said, shortly after the wheels went up.

"I don't know you well enough to say one way or the other. I don't imagine I'll ever be in your situation and I don't know what I'd do if I was."

"Aren't you in my situation right now? I mean, I'm sure Ted is paying you well. He gave us both top shelf travel arrangements. I don't think you ever came close to marrying him, but you must have a pretty high opinion of him to do what you're doing or you're more of a sleazeball than I take you for."

"I barely knew Ted when I took this job. It was a favor for a friend at first." I wasn't sure if she knew that Rick Stone was that friend.

"What I don't quite get is why he's reaching out to me now, after all this time. Is he like, terminally ill or something?"

I didn't think it was my place to tell her that I'd found two other women from Ted's life before her --- one was dead and the other, terrified of him.

I said, "I asked him that right after he approached me. He says no. He said that he has few regrets in his life but that you were the main one. The one that got away. He felt bad about how it ended and wants to make amends. Apologies and whatever else it took. Money, if you needed it."

"Just so you know, I don't want his money. I plan to return the ten grand. Asking for it was my way of seeing if this whole thing was legit. If you were some crazy asshole who somehow hacked into my life. I figured ten thousand would blow that out of the water."

"And what if I was some kind of eccentric wealthy kook with money who just happened to know your history with Ted?"

"I did some homework on the internet. Former FBI, eh? And I know a couple of local cops down here who come in for building supplies occasionally. One of them knew a lot about you. Spoke highly, as a matter of fact. Was kind of surprised you'd take on something this trivial."

"Name wouldn't be McCullough, would it?"

"Bingo! Our man Flint we call him. Said you two had quite an adventure a few years back.

That we had. McCullough was a straight shooter who had helped me out on a case when I lived in Bayville. I was trying to track down a missing author, but wound up uncovering a plot with much bigger ramifications. We weren't exactly pen pals since I moved south, but I always figured if I needed something in my old stomping grounds, he'd be there for me.

I figured now was a good time to ask the big question. "So, it's really none of my business, but if you don't want any money from Ted, why are you on this plane? You said yesterday that the ten thousand was merely a down payment."

"Maybe it was, in a way. You see, I never fully got over Ted. Sure, I've had lovers since, but well, even though we were constantly at each others' throats, Ted and I had this fucking thing for each other that's hard to find. No one else since has come close. He even loved all the Jersey shore bands I idolized. Bruce. Bon Jovi. Beaver Brown. Southside Johnny. He wasn't intimidated by me and my mouth like so many other men are. I met my match. I like to think I'm a pretty sharp cookie, but he's sharper."

"Now that you bring it up, how is it, with all your smarts, that you're still working at the same place since high school and at the same job."

"I like it there."

Just then, the flight attendant came by and asked if we'd like anything to drink. Stevie ordered a Bloody Mary. At eight in the morning, that might be a clue as to why she hadn't climbed a corporate ladder somewhere. Or maybe she felt she was going on a vacation and could indulge at will. I let it go.

"So Stevie, why see Ted again? What's the best outcome for you? Are you just curious how he's aged? I can tell you, he still looks great."

"I'd expect nothing less. Cary Grant, that's how I saw him. That slightly stilted way of speaking, like he comes from New York money. His style. Like John Slattery in *Mad Men*. You know, I don't even remember exactly what part of the honeymoon arrangements we were arguing about the night we came to blows. It was no worse than any of the other fights we had."

"You pushed a button you didn't know was there. Maybe he didn't know it, either. But aren't you a little afraid that you'll accidentally push it again?"

I don't know why I said that. Maybe I liked this woman and was feeling protective. Although we were more age appropriate than her and Ted, she wasn't physically my type --- too thin, too hard looking. But beneath the tough exterior, there was a little girl, still seeking Prince Charming.

"I'm staying at a nice hotel on the beach. Ted will call the room in the late afternoon when I'm settled. Said he had an earlier commitment he couldn't get out of on short notice. We'll meet in the hotel bar. Lots of people around. Maybe go out to dinner. Give me a chance to see where he's at. We'll see how it goes."

"Then what?"

"Then --- we'll see how it goes. I might remember a lot of things that I've romanticized away, things I didn't like about him. Or I might invite him up to my room to fuck my brains out. I don't know."

"Oh." I tried to hide my prudish reaction to her colorful language.

"Shocked, are we, Mr. King? Ain't like I get credit for saving it up. It could be just for old times with him, or maybe we both will realize that we blew it way back when and are now smart enough not to screw it up this time. I'm coming at this with an open mind."

She took a sip of the Bloody Mary and smacked her lips. "You know, I'm not really what you'd call a feminist. Or maybe I am more feminist than these snooty women who think they are. Think about it. We claim we're equal to men in every way. But if a man hits us, it's somehow worse than if he hits another man?"

"It's the strong brutalizing the weak," I said.

"The weak? Like women are the weaker sex? So we can insult a man, threaten him, or like I did, come at him with a bat and he can't strike back? How is that equality? I think if you give somebody shit, you better be ready to take whatever they give you back in return. Like if you poke a bear and he mauls you, it's his fault? No, it's *your* frigging problem. He's just doing what he's biologically programmed to do."

"Ohh--kay,"

I wasn't going to debate this with her now. I doubted anything I could say would change her mind. She'd lived almost a half a century and her values were locked in, so I changed the subject.

I said, "By the way, I think you'll like Hilton Head. People who live there call it paradise and it won't take you long to see why."

The rest of the flight was engaged in small talk about the island --- the beaches, wildlife, places to eat. She had a gleam in her eye that I hadn't seen when we first met, a gleam of anticipation. The more she spoke the more I realized that she still held Ted in the same high regard he held for her, despite what had happened. Like she had acknowledged, perhaps she was romanticizing. She seemed to have hopes for their future together but she swore she was going into this with no expectations.

After we landed, I walked her to the gate of her connecting flight and waited with her until boarding. She gave me a quick kiss on the cheek and thanked me for taking good care of her. As she entered the tunnel, she looked back at me and winked.

It was the last time I ever saw her.

FORTY

It was Tuesday morning and I'd been home for three days. Three days since I had resolved to lay it all out for Charlene; how my trip up north was not just to help Rick out of a jam but to finalize my dealings with Ted. I was waiting for the perfect moment, knowing that there was no perfect moment to deliver the news.

She'd been rather cool since I'd been back. No physical intimacy or even mention of it. She now was reading the paper during breakfast, looking up only to refill her coffee. Most of her days were spent in the makeshift studio, working on her music. I'd seen this kind of preoccupation before when she was preparing to go out on the road. Her intensity reminded me of the cases I've handled for professional athletes over the years. Their whole being was focused on the next game. They allowed no distractions, even though more important personal matters were at hand. That's why they were so good at what they did.

I gently knocked on Charlene's studio door, where she was hunched over her laptop.

"There's something we need to talk about."

She sighed as if I'd interrupted her from doing her nails. "I guess I have a few minutes. But I do need to lay down some tracks today and it might be better if you found somewhere else to be. Why not hit the driving range?

You've been complaining your game is rusty and Stone kicked your butt."

I got the message: Get lost, kid and don't bother me. I've got more important things to do.

"I may do that. But I need to tell you something first."

"Shoot."

"When I went to New Jersey last week to help Rick, there was more to it than that."

"My mama didn't raise no fools, Riley. It had to do with Ted, didn't it?"

She had been doing a slow burn since I returned, waiting for me to come clean. And now it was Judgment Day. The chance to plead my case and clear my name in the court of Charlene.

"Ted wanted Rick to contact the last woman on his list. I couldn't let that happen. Rick's got a lot on his plate now and besides, he's not a pro. I was afraid he'd mess up and get in trouble. Being a public figure and all."

"Bull-shit. Rick's a big boy. An ex-Marine. You don't think he could handle one of Ted's victims and make whatever bogus offer Ted had in mind?"

"It wasn't that simple. Look, I never shared all the details with you on this one, but the relationship ended because Ted hit her after she came after him with a bat."

"Oh, great. So I was right all along. The man's a serial abuser. And you were working for him. In my book, that makes you an accomplice."

"I was trying to calm the waters, not aid a criminal," I said, bristling at the suggestion. "We can do this two ways, babe. I can lay out the whole story for you, or you can just connect the dots however you choose and come to whatever shitty conclusions about me you want. You've had it in for Ted right from the start. Never gave the man a chance."

"Damn straight."

"That's not how I read it and this is what I do for a living. Ted came off as sincerely sorry for what he did twenty years ago. He wanted to try to make up for it. And whether you choose to believe it or not, he succeeded."

"How do you figure that, King? His ex-wife said she'd shoot him if he came near her. The one he raped is dead, maybe because of what he did to her. So what did this girl do, take the money and run? And what does that make her? Lower than a snake's belly and no better than any of them whores he's been with."

"Charl, you're passing judgment on people you never met, probably never will. You're going off half assed on Ted and Stevie without knowing the whole story."

"So, it's Stevie now? First name basis. Sounds like you got a little closer to this chippie than just this envoy business."

Trying to stay calm, I said, "You're acting like a jealous teen age girl. It's beneath you. Yes, I got to know her a little bit. It took me all of ten minutes to find her. She was open to meeting with Ted. She even took some responsibility for what happened."

"So now we're blaming the victim. Poor girl has such low self esteem she thinks she asked for it. Really, King, I thought you were more enlightened than that. Guess I was wrong."

This was spiraling out of control. All the pent up anger she had repressed for the last couple of days came spewing out. Jealousy, rage, rash conclusions --- ugly stuff. She seemed on the verge of throwing something at me.

"This isn't about me. Bottom line is, she went down to Hilton Head to meet with him this weekend. Apparently things went very well. Ted emailed me that they're getting back together."

"What?"

"Charlene, they both told me that they were the love of each others' life. They were sorry they broke up the way they did. They're twenty years older now and they realized that through all those years, they never had it so good. So they had a great weekend in Hilton Head, and they're considering moving in together."

Charlene turned her back and stomped away. "Un-fucking-believable."

"They're two grown-ups and if they think it's true love, who are we to question it?"

"Don't you get it? This man has a history of abuse toward women. Rebecca Hunter was no nut case. She's a smart woman. Yet she lives in deadly fear of this man."

"For something he did thirty years ago. He convinced me that he's changed. And obviously convinced

Stevie, too. If I had a hand in helping two damaged souls find happiness, I'm good with that."

"Oh my Lord, you sound like Doctor Phil. He hit her once, he'll do it again."

"Now who's playing shrink, Charlene? How do you know that?"

"Because I lived it."

Now it came out. She had sworn to me that as loveless and sterile her marriage to Johnny Serpente was, he'd never struck her. His only abuse was verbal, in the form of sarcastic and demeaning comments which both sides can be prone to. Charlene could certainly dish that out and take it in return without flinching.

"Johnny hit you?"

"No, not Johnny." She sniffled but composed herself quickly, continuing in a soft voice. "I told you about my time in New York. The few A and R men who I slept with, stupidly thinking it would help get me on a label. Well, one of them seemed different than the others. He was very handsome. Didn't fancy himself an artist, just a businessman --- didn't dress down like the rest. Always was elegant, polished. Didn't talk down to be a good old boy around the artists. I thought for a while that we had something."

She was re-living a part of her life that she'd long since buried. From her description of this man, I could see the similarities to Ted. No wonder she had taken an instant dislike to him.

"One night after clubbing, we had an argument. I was getting the idea he was stringing me along with his promises of a record deal. He accused me of being a little tramp who was using him. He slapped me hard, almost knocked me unconscious. But he broke down soon as it happened, said how sorry he was, didn't know what came over him. We'd both done some blow that night. I had said some nasty things to him. So I forgave him and we stayed together."

It didn't take a detective to figure out the next part.

I said, "But he did it again."

"Yeah. This time, he broke my nose. Oh, he paid me off not to press charges. Paid for a plastic surgeon to fix me up. That was it. I left New York, moved back to Charlotte and got a job at the Capital Grille. That's where I met Johnny. He was kind and gentle, almost to a fault. Nothing like that bastard from New York."

"And Johnny kept you safe. You told me there was nothing sexual with him, but you could live with that, as long as he looked the other way when the need arose. But I must say, you did overlook some heavy shit with him."

"I guess I went from one extreme to the other."

"I get it now." I really did. She had told me a lot of terrible stories about her time as a struggling singer in New York, but not this one.

She said, "Do you? A big strong guy like you. Ever know what's it's like to fear someone you love? That they might just explode one night and kill you? Do you understand that?"

"Of course not. I don't have the numbers, but there have been studies on people who do something bad once and never do it again. If I really thought for an instant that Ted hadn't changed, I'd never have taken this one. I talked to his shrink. I did my homework, trust me. And besides, this woman Stevie Perry, is a tough cookie and if Ted still has violence in him, she'll know it and get out in a hurry."

Charlene giggled through her tears. "Stevie Perry. The dude from Journey?"

"Her parents had a sense of humor."

"Or maybe they wanted to toughen her up. Like *A Boy Named Sue*."

More laughter.

"Your country roots are showing, babe." She had that look in her eye, like everything was going to be all right with us.

But hey, looks can be deceiving.

FORTY ONE

Ted deposited money in my account by wire, way over what I had earned. I emailed him back a note and snail mailed a check for the excess, enclosed with a detailed expense report and a summary of the hours spent on the case. I didn't charge him for our contemplative dog walks along the water, billable hours which I'd justify as *consultation time* to a less favored client. When my check came back shredded after three days, I was mildly surprised but I wasn't going to continue to fight him over it. I had saved him three million bucks and re-united him with his one true love. Not a bad couple weeks' work.

Things were just okay with Charlene after our difficult talk. She seemed distant but understandably so, given the surge her career was taking. A prominent agent had contacted her about representation, and wanted to hear some tracks from her new project. She was now spending twelve hours a day polishing the simple arrangements, fully aware that most labels would demand more sophisticated production values.

I did some light computer work for a few continuing clients, and hit the range to work on my game. I hadn't spoken to Stone since we had seen each other in New Jersey, and as the days went by, I became less inclined to lecture him about his juvenile promiscuity. I doubted my words would have any effect, and all it would do is discourage him from driving down to Charlotte Thanksgiving week, as we had planned months before. I just hoped Cindy wouldn't be making the trip, or Charlene would be even more impossible to live with.

Ted called two weeks later.

"Hey, Riley, how goes it?" he began, innocuously.

"Life's good, Ted. Yourself?"

"Never been better, thanks to you. I know you feel that I overpaid you for all you did, but frankly all the money I have couldn't begin to be enough for the happiness it's brought."

"That's me, Bringer of Jollity."

"Thank you, Gustav Holst. Classier than those rock songs Rick's always quoting. But seriously, these last weeks have been wonderful. Stevie and I are like newlyweds. I spent the last couple of weeks up in my condo in Toms River with her."

I'd never heard Ted so upbeat, even at the height of WJOK's popularity when the ratings actually eclipsed several New York City stations. I was glad to have played a part in it, but equally cautious that such innocent joy rarely lasts. Sometimes things that start so promisingly have a nasty habit of backfiring when you least expect it. But why rain on his parade?

I said, "That's great. Glad it's working out. So are you leaving Hilton Head?"

"No. Stevie feels she can't leave her bosses in the lurch after all these years, so she's going to give them notice and stay on to train her replacement for as long as it takes. She'll sell her condo and that might take a while. So I'll fly up and stay with her as often as I can, then when she leaves her job, she'll move in with me down here. After we get married."

"Married. Wow. That strikes me as kind of sudden, but you know what you're doing."

He cleared his throat. "I think so. You see, I've learned that most of the disputes people who care for each other have aren't worth fighting over. I've learned to compromise, which in most cases, means just going along with what Stevie wants. So if she wants seafood and I prefer a steakhouse, we're eating fish. It's like Phil Jackson's philosophy of winning basketball. Implicit trust in your teammates, in this case, your lady."

I wondered if I'd ever reach that level of accommodation with Charlene, then quickly banished the thought. I still needed things to go my way a decent amount of the time, but if it makes Ted happy not to sweat the small stuff, who am I to question it? Maybe at seventy, I'll feel the same way.

"Sounds like you've come a long way, Ted. She's good with moving South?"

"She loves the island. It *is* paradise, you know. I'd love it if you and your charming lady would come visit us down here once we're settled. You have an open invitation."

As much as the idea might appeal to me, liking Ted and Stevie as I did, I couldn't push that on Charlene, not after she told me about the dread memories the sight of Ted evoked.

"That's very nice of you. Hey Ted, I'm glad it's going so well. You deserve it, man. You had regrets about the way you conducted yourself in the past and you did something about it. Not many can do that."

I was sounding like Tony F. Robbins with my self-realization bullshit. As sudden as it seemed, they had been in love years ago, and both regretted their role in its downfall. It was like Indian Summer in a way --- the fierce heat of summer subsides, an early frost, then the remaining days turn warm and agreeable before winter closes in.

"There's one more thing I need to tell you Riley, and I hope you'll be all right with it."

Uh-oh.

He continued when I didn't reply. "I've taken an interest in your --- how do you want to put it --- girlfriend? I think she's really talented and just hasn't met the right people. So I made a few calls, agents, PR folks, radio programmers, and spread the word. I don't know if any of them have been in touch yet, but I think some of them will be. I don't know how you feel about her career and her being out on the road a lot. I told you I had a hard time with that with my ex-wife. But if you don't mind, I'll stay on these people. I think she has the goods to do very well. What say you?"

That explained why that agent had called Charlene. But if she didn't have talent, I doubt Ted's influence alone could get her a deal. "I'm not sure what to say. I want her to be happy and if that means the life of a wandering minstrel, then that's what it will be."

"Well said and exactly how I thought you'd take it. We'll see if any of the seeds I've sown bear fruit. By the way, have you heard from Rick lately? I've rung him a couple of times to share the good news and he hasn't responded. Calls went right to voicemail."

"Haven't spoken to him recently myself. I'm sure the World Series kept him busy. The station was doing a lot of promotional nights with it. He told me you were right that radio is really struggling now and they're constantly trying to find new revenue streams. People they'd never get in bed with in the past, they're soliciting now."

"Seems I got out at the right time. If I hear one more commercial about a *Gentlemen's' Club* or *male enhancement* product, I'll toss my radio into the Atlantic. Or how you can make millions flipping houses, like anybody can do it. I'm afraid integrity is a thing of the past in my old business."

"Okay Ted, I've got to run. And my best to Stevie. I really like her."

"So do I. And thank you, Riley. Let's get together soon, with the ladies or not."

FORTY TWO

I used to hate loose ends, unresolved storylines, especially on significant cases where I'm tasked to find the absolute truth. I grew up watching Perry Mason; my dad was a big Raymond Burr fan. Perry, Della Street and Paul Drake would sit in their favorite watering hole with the client after he was exonerated and Perry would explain how he unmasked the killer. It was mostly owing to a seemingly insignificant clue that had escaped the others' notice. Sherlock Holmes had no edge on the world's best criminal defense attorney and his merry band of operatives.

Lately, I've come to accept the fact that life is full of questions that have no discernible answers.

My last two important investigations ended with no Masonic (Perry) denouement. I tracked down a missing author. Turns out he was a bad guy. Stone shot him dead. Case closed. But two principal actors in that little drama remain unaccounted for. They are either dead or in witness protection. I'd really like to know which.

The other case started as a simple undertaking, namely, to find out who beat up Derek Davis, a builder friend of mine in Charlotte. The most likely culprit turned out to be Charlene's husband, who had deeper blemishes in his past than either of us had imagined. He also was shot dead, but by whom? The local authorities were willing to chalk it off to the Russian mafiya, who owed him a bullet for absconding with some of their ill gotten plunder. But my friend on the force, Pete Shabielski, caused me to doubt their conclusion. He implied that the Char/Meck coppers were too eager to close the books on this as *BAD GUY DEAD*, next case please, that they failed to follow up other promising leads.

Charlene didn't seem obsessed with finding the truth, either. I agreed that digging into the Brighton Beach mob to avenge the death of one of their own was a no-win proposition and let it go. She was glad to be free of him and I was glad to have her, so the sleeping dogs were left to lie.

Speaking of sleeping dogs, Bosco lay slumbering at my feet as I worked on the computer, tired from our morning three mile jog. I labored at putting a nice shiny ribbon on the McCarver case. Rebecca Hunter had indeed refunded the lodging charges back to my card, and all my other incidental receipts were in order. I catalogued the records for tax purposes. My financial arrangements with Ted were over.

Finally, I had a case with a Disney ending. It would have been nice if Mary Chesterton was alive and forgiving, but I had to be satisfied that whatever Ted had done forty years ago had little to do with her suicide. Although Rebecca Hunter was not really on board with letting bygones be bygones, she had communicated to Ted that all was water under the proverbial bridge and she didn't need his money. She was doing very well on her own, thank you. He seemed to accept it without the need of further contact.

Then there was Stevie. Ted's ideal goal in all of this was to find true love, and tenderness on the block.

(Thanks for that phrase to the late, great Warren Zevon. I wonder what he meant by that. Another unanswerable question, since Zevon isn't going to be around to explain.)

Pardon the digression, but I was in a digressing mood. Business had slowed as the holidays approached. The weather had turned chilly. Charlene was in Nashville, talking to one of the agents Ted had sent her way. I was reading a lot of history, bored ever so slightly, but content that the year was ending on a positive note.

I was daydreaming that someday, I might want to seek resolution to some of these unresolved issues. Maybe the trails had to get really cold before they were safe enough to explore. I wouldn't want to wait until my eighth decade like Ted had, although I'm not nearly as financially independent as he and therefore less able to indulge my curiosity. Maybe if Charlene hits it big, I'll have some money to play with.

Although I resisted at first, I came around to admiring Ted for identifying the mental roadblocks to his peace of mind and proactively setting out to resolve them.

Stone called. I still hadn't talked to him about what I saw as a lifestyle that would be fraught with regrets, but I wasn't in the mood to do that today.

He said, "Hey Riles, you've been kind of incommunicado lately. Everything okay?"

"Yeah, never better actually. Just been busy, cleaning up some stuff," I lied.

"Me too. Well, have you heard the news? It's on WJOK's website."

"Don't tell me. You're pregnant. Congratulations."

"Close." He put on his best radio voice. "Mr. Theodore Chesterfield McCarver, former owner of WJOK and current shareholder, proudly announces his engagement to Stephanie Elizabeth Perry. No date for the wedding has been finalized, but the happy couple hopes to tie the knot by year's end. No gifts, please, as they plan to celebrate privately with a bottle of their favorite wine, Silver Oak 1991."

"You could have saved the dramatic reading, you ham, and just linked me to the site. I'm there now. Nice picture of the two of them. Ted actually told me about the wedding himself, said he was trying to reach you and you hadn't returned his calls."

"Thought I'd talk to you first. I'm a little bummed by this."

"What do you mean?"

"Are you forgetting, I shagged the bride to be? Unless they elope, I'm sure Ted will invite us to the wedding. Awkward! How do I face the two of them, knowing what I know?"

When did I become Dear Abby?

I said, "Ricky, grow up. These things happen. You're not going to say anything to Ted, are you?"

"That's just it, I think maybe I should. Riles, not bragging or nothing, but it wasn't like I had to try real hard to get her legs in the air. More like she wanted it worse and more often than me, and that's saying something. Then, the way she blew me off. Not like I didn't win an Olympic gold medal for my performances, and I do mean multiple, that night."

I was tempted to share Stevie's less than favorable review of his prowess but restrained myself. "What do you hope to accomplish, other than piss Ted off and maybe mess up their plans?"

"All I'm saying is, she's twenty some years younger than him. No offense to Ted but if she's got needs like that, an old man can't possibly satisfy them. All the Viagra in the world wouldn't get him up to my level."

"Again, not to brag."

"It ain't bragging if you can back it up, partner. This Stevie Perry might be a gold digger. Boink him for a few months then take half his dough. Been known to happen. I might be saving Ted a world of hurt if I hip him to that."

Since I've known him, Rick had a pretty high opinion of his swordsmanship with the ladies. "Stone, let's do the math with you and Cindy. Closer to thirty years difference and you keep telling me how satisfied she is. And by the way, have you ever considered that Ted and Stevie may be in love?"

"Who's the hardboiled detective here? Think about it, they haven't seen each other in years then all of a sudden, they're getting married? That pass the smell test with you, Pancho?"

"Remember that Red Sox pitcher, Bill Monbouquette?"

"Why are you changing the subject?"

"Not. He died not too long ago. I read the obit and it said that he ran into a girl at his fortieth high school reunion who had turned him down for a date when they were kids. They hadn't seen each other in four decades. They got married a few weeks later. It happens."

"Touching. But Monbo probably still had his fastball. Okay, you've convinced me to hold my fire for now, but I'm going to stay on top of this. And if I see the slightest crack in this arrangement, I may go public with Ted."

"Talk to me first. Don't be a jerk."

"Have you ever known me to be a jerk, bro?"

I didn't answer that. Some questions are best left unanswered, after all.

FORTY THREE

Charlene and I were walking Bosco along the lake. She had just returned from Nashville and I could see she was bursting with news of her journey but for some reason, she held back. As soon as she walked through the door, she made a big fuss over the dog and practically ignored me, save for a desultory peck on the cheek. She then insisted we take him for a long walk while the weather was still mild.

The autumn colors had descended on Charlotte and they were spectacular. The maples and oaks that line the lake were ablaze with yellow and crimson. Some of the poplars had already shed most of their leaves, glittering our trail with a rustic carpet.

Once Bosco was harnessed up and on his way out to taste the crisp fall air, I said, "So tell me what happened. I can tell you can barely contain yourself, babe. Good news?"

She gave me her full wattage smile. "Yes. And no. I have a decision to make and I need your input."

Dear Abby again. Maybe I should start a blog. Was I starting to look like Yoda or what?

"I'm at your service."

"All right, here's the short version of what went down. Radio stations across the country do Holiday concerts, starting in a few weeks. They usually don't pay much, if anything. They just cover expenses. Most of them donate the profits to charity"

"Even WJOK does some of those. They figure sports fans like music, classic rock in particular. Plus, they can usually get a few ballplayers who live in the area to act as emcees."

"Right. So anyway, there's kind of a circuit for these now and since so many of the stations are owned by the same corporate group, they've made it into a package."

Bosco was heeling extremely well. Maybe he thought that Charlene had gone away to punish him and was afraid she would leave again if he misbehaved. Or maybe he was just getting older and was too tired to tug at the leash and go running off after whatever temptation he saw off the trail.

"So if you do this, how long would you be away?"

"I'd do wherever it takes me. Probably be gone from Thanksgiving to New Years. This is for exposure and airplay." She frowned and bit her lip, as if the next part was going to be distasteful. "This agent, his name is Harrison Mitchell, also wants me to cut a Christmas single, or I should say download. He's got hold of the Band's *Christmas Must be Tonight*. The backing track is already done with guide vocals, waiting for someone with pipes to cut the final version. And he thought that we might be able to convince Darius to duet on it, which would make it even more saleable."

"Isn't kind of late to cut and release a new record? So how does that work? Would it be Darius' record or yours?"

"Not with the technology today. It could be recorded and released within a week. I'd get top billing. Sort of like Carly Simon's *You're So Vain* with Jagger. It was her record but the fact that he was on it got the attention at first."

I said, "Sounds like a no brainer."

"It can put me on the map. I'd do radio and newspaper interviews, tell my story about how I had a record out twenty years ago and am on the comeback trail. He heard some of my Broadway stuff and thinks it could work, once it gets produced a little heavier than I can do at home. I'd need to get that out early next year to take advantage of the momentum the Holiday tour creates."

There was an old green wrought iron and wood slatted park bench facing the water and we stopped to sit on it. Bosco jumped between us and laid his head on Charlene's lap, purring like a kitten as she stroked his muzzle.

I said, "So what's for me to say?"

"You wouldn't mind me being away all that time? I'd probably have to record in Nashville, so I might be gone pretty much through next January. Then if the CD takes off, I'd be on tour spring through Labor Day."

"How do *you* feel about all the traveling? I thought you weren't crazy about waking up in a different bed in a different city every night."

"The reality is that artists don't make much money recording these days. Remember U2 gave away their last album on iTunes. Touring is how you make money. That and merchandizing. Tee shirts, memorabilia. Last year, there was only one million selling record. Kids expect their music for free these days and even when they do pay for it, they share it with their friends and the artist gets zero."

"So I've heard. In answer to your question, yes, I'll miss the hell out of you," I said.

"You could come along with me."

"And be Mister Charlene Jones? I like to think I don't have a big ego but that's where I'd draw the line."

I stood up and walked toward the water. I was thinking about Rebecca Hunter and how her traveling undermined her marriage to Ted. The idea of me hanging around backstage at Charlene's gigs was a nonstarter. Ted had eventually cheated --- would the temptation get to me, as well?

The fact that Charlene's earning potential could dwarf mine didn't bother me in the least. Her name recognition could easily surpass my little brushes with fame. Not a problem.

Absence makes the heart grow fonder is a crock as far as I'm concerned. I need someone to be there for me. It's not like we need a lot of money. My youthful frugality and some luck with real estate investments had blossomed into enough of a nest egg to live comfortably, if not extravagantly. Hell, even the government owed me a pension in a few years.

This was about Charlene finding herself. She had subjugated her talent and taken the safe way out for a long time. Even though I was a much better bet than the late gangster Johnny Serpente, she couldn't and shouldn't bury her ambition forever, lest she wind up a bitter old crone wondering *what might have been.*

I suppose I should have been thrilled about her exciting opportunities but in truth, I wasn't. It meant I had long, lonely winter nights to look forward to instead of cuddling up with the most beautiful woman I'd ever known.

Maybe Dear Abby had the answer. I sure didn't.

FORTY FOUR

"You have any plans for lunch?"

McCarver's hearty baritone crackled over my landline. Charlene was out shopping with girlfriends for the day and I was left to my own devices.

"What do you have in mind, Ted?"

"I'm flying up to Jersey to stay with Stevie for a while, and I thought I might stopover in Charlotte. A friend of mine is soft-opening a restaurant in Davidson and I told him I'd come by for lunch. Interested?"

There weren't that many places to eat in Davidson, and the town could use another, given the affluent residents that the sleepy college town was now attracting. My dance card was fairly empty today, so I accepted the offer.

"Sure, when and where?"

Ted rattled off an address on Main Street near the school, and said that one was a good time. I killed some time organizing some old paperwork, although using the computer, no trees were harmed. Thanksgiving was just around the corner, and Stone was planning to come down for the holiday. With Charlene likely on the road, I welcomed the company.

I lit out for Davidson at 12:30, leaving a note for Charlene in case she came back early. I somehow forgot to mention that Ted was my lunch date.

The restaurant was pretty cool. Ted's friends had done a nice job, freshening up an old storefront just south of the college. They retained the old beams and aged timbers in a style that might be considered industrial with all the ductwork exposed, but industrial harkening back to the eighteen hundreds. The walls featured a lot of worn red brick and the floors were wide plank pine, lightly polished to a rich patina. The place would accommodate fewer than a hundred diners, with leather upholstered booths on one side and black four top tables across the main area. The ambience was nice and if the food is any good, the place should prosper.

Ted was resplendent in a russet cashmere sweater and designer blue jeans over soft suede boots. It was as casual as I'd ever seen him dressed and he seemed far more relaxed and informal. Stevie's influence?

"Riley, thanks for joining me," he said after a jovial handshake. "Jose, come over and meet a friend of mine. Jose is the main force behind this project, which I have a small interest in. This is Riley King, Jose Montero."

A tall, handsome Latin man came over to our booth and smiled warmly during the introductions. After the obligatory small talk, he hustled off to supervise the kitchen staff.

"So when did you become a restaurateur, Ted?" I asked.

"I've always appreciated the fine dining experience. Since I've had some money to play with, it's kind of a hobby. I have a stake in a few spots, like the place we dined on the island when I first approached you. I've known Jose for years and his track record is excellent."

There was an awkward pause as I wondered where to go next. Fine dining for me could be a well cooked burger or Staten Island pizza. I'm not a foodie and details as to its preparation hold little interest.

"So," I said. "Getting married. Set a date yet?"

"Actually, that's one of the reasons I wanted to talk with you. We're aiming toward New Year's Eve on the Island. Sea Pines has a beautiful Inn, hard by the ocean. We were thinking of a sunset ceremony, outdoors, weather permitting, and a small reception for friends and family only. I don't want this to be a business deal where I invite all the radio execs I've worked with over the years. Just small and tasteful. Stevie's folks are gone as are mine and I'm an only child, so there won't be a whole lot of family. I'd love you and Rick to be there, obviously."

"Well, you didn't need to buy me lunch for that. Even an email invite would have been okay,"

"Oh, I know. But I also wanted to discuss your fee. You claimed that my retainer was excessive."

"That was very generous of you Ted, but to be honest, I felt a little guilty taking anything from you, other than expenses. It really wasn't all that taxing."

"Perhaps, but you handled it deftly. Another investigator might not have accomplished what you did. Ah, the wine. I insisted they stock Silver Oak '91. My sole contribution to the menu."

I wasn't sure that wine and aviation fuel mixed, but I wasn't about to censure Ted. He seemed to be a meticulously prepared pilot and I was sure that he wouldn't dream of flying under the influence. FUI? There must be laws, no?

"But Riley, I do have a favor to ask. I'd like Charlene to perform at the reception."

I took a small sip of the Silver Oak. "Ah, I can't commit for her, Ted. She's headed out on a tour soon and I'd imagine New Year's Eve might be a pretty important date."

"I'll make it worth her while. Name a figure."

I had no idea what Charlene would want for a private party and if she'd even consider the gig. Her dislike for Ted was palpable and I wasn't even sure if she'd be open to attending the wedding as my guest.

"Ted, you should probably look for someone else. I don't know that her style would lend itself to a wedding reception."

A waiter materialized. Ted whispered something to him that I couldn't make out, and the man vanished as suddenly as he had appeared.

"I took the liberty of ordering for both of us. Basically, tapas plates of the top items on the luncheon menu. We can sample whatever we choose. I'm sure you'll find most of it to your liking. If not, we can get you something else."

"Fine." It really wasn't, but I wasn't about to protest. I felt like a girl on a first date with a domineering suitor, who insisted on ordering what he thought she'd like without consulting her. I couldn't imagine the willful Stevie Perry putting up with that for long.

"So, back to the wedding, Riley. Look, country isn't my bag especially. Tom Petty said that today's country is bad rock and roll with fiddles. But I mentioned to Stevie that Charlene was your girl and she took a liking to her old CD. Said that she'd love for her to play at the reception. I think part of it is an excuse to see you again, not that I'm jealous. I told her you'd be there anyway, but she really seems to like Charlene's music. Weird for a Jersey shore girl, but there it is."

I'd have to try another tack. If I told him the truth, that Charlene didn't like him, he might pull the plug on his attempts to aid her career. Either that, or try to charm her into accepting his entreaties. I know that when her mind is set, she is immune to persuasion, no matter how enticing the carrot might be. Only bad things would ensue.

"Ted, what I'm saying is that I can't interfere in her career and ask her for favors --- that would make things pretty awkward. I just don't want to tie you up thinking Charlene might perform when I don't think it's in the cards. I'd even be willing to explain it to Stevie if you'd like."

"Look, I told you, the thing that led to our unpleasantness years ago was an argument over honeymoon and wedding arrangements. Stevie is pretty strong willed as you undoubtedly observed and I'm afraid she's turned into Bridezilla. She wants what she wants and if I have the means to accommodate her, I will do everything in my power to do so."

I tried to get him to drop it, but Ted didn't get to where he is by giving up easily. He spent the remainder of the lunch trying to convince me that I should work things out so that Charlene could perform. I grew weary of trying to come up with fresh excuses, but thankfully by the time an excellent flan arrived, he stopped insisting.

The rest of the meal was consumed by an awkward silence. He fended off my attempts to talk sports or music with monosyllabic grunts. It seemed out of character for him to behave so petulantly and it was not a flattering portrait. He was frustrated that for once, he couldn't have his way.

We parted on Main Street with brusque goodbyes. After one last attempt to change my mind failed, he suddenly exploded and cursed me

"I can't believe that after all I've given you and all the help that I've provided for your semi-talented girlfriend that you can't do this for me. You're a fucking ingrate and you know what? Forget coming to the wedding. You won't be welcome."

He turned on his heel and stomped off.

I'd finally seen his dark side, the one that had caused Rebecca and Stevie to quake at his wrath. A temper that arose violently with no warning --- up until the last moment he had been as tranquil as a calm sea. Then a burst of violent anger, a murderous look in his eye. I'd seen it before with the feds --- natural born serial killers who strike when it is least expected. But it was shocking to see from the gentlemanly Ted McCarver.

After this last unpleasantness, I wasn't sure that I hadn't steered Stevie Perry into a hornet's nest. She knew

Ted better than I did, but my eyes aren't clouded by love. Could I come up with a way to warn her or would that only make things worse?

FORTY FIVE

I tried to reflect on anything I could to take my mind off Ted McCarver.

I was stewing over Ted's last comments, doing a slow burn as the Audi headed across the lower edge of Lake Norman. The ungrateful bastard. Within a fortnight, I had located two women from his distant past without having the benefit of their names, and then reunited him with a woman he planned to marry. He figured that a generous paycheck would be enough to show his gratitude.

He didn't know how Charlene had fought me from the very beginning about taking on his case, and came close to leaving me when she saw the consequences of his actions firsthand with Rebecca. I hoped that by politely declining his invitation for her to play the wedding reception, he'd let it go and use his juice in the industry to book someone else. Instead, he kept pushing.

Although he'd been honest in his writings how his explosiveness had gotten him into trouble with his women, seeing firsthand how quickly and intensely it flared was a revelation. I wanted to believe that time and therapy had becalmed this madness, but the pilot light still burned within him, prepared to ignite at a moment's notice.

When I got home, a quick text from him awaited on my tablet. He apologized for his language; said that he was just trying to give Stevie the perfect wedding she deserved, and how he wasn't looking forward to telling her he'd failed. Well, I'd like Bruce Springsteen to play at my wedding *if and when*, but I don't think it would be a deal breaker if he declines.

Regardless, the books were now officially closed with Ted. I'd find an excuse not to attend the wedding and I'd leave his text unanswered. I'd done my good deed for a friend. I told myself that Stevie Perry was a grown-up and that if she was convinced that Ted had changed enough to accept his proposal, then who was I to interfere?

The good news was, I came home to my own private fashion show, which further put Ted on the back burner. Charlene had been shopping for outfits to wear on tour, and each one was hotter than the last. Seeking my expert opinion, all I could do was nod in appreciation and confirm that none of them made her butt look too big.

"So all the paperwork is set and you're definitely on board with this tour?" I said.

"Not yet, but everything seems in order. I'm just waiting for the final contract. You think this one shows too much cleavage?" she asked, modeling an outfit that displayed her bosom to great advantage.

"Is there such a thing?"

"Come on, I'm pushing fifty, babe. I can't get away with dressing like a teenager."

"That Catholic schoolgirl look on you still works. Might take the focus off your music, but I don't see it drawing any complaints."

"Oink oink. Since we're talking about my breasts, that Mitchell guy did have some suggestions."

"No, not that again. Tell him you have a big bad boyfriend who'll kick the crap out of him if he tries to put the moves on you."

She said, "No worries there, sweetie. I'm pretty sure he's gay. But he did say that I could use a little boost in the tittie department. And that one of those lifestyle lifts to get rid of my turkey neck would be a good thing."

"Turkey neck? Please. Your neck is fine. You don't look a day over forty. And breast implants? No way I'm living with Dolly Parton."

"That's kind of what I told him. I'm a thirty six C. With the right bra, I can push that up to look like a D."

"Really? I think I need to see proof before I accept that."

She proceeded to phase two of my private showing, modeling her latest trove of lacy unmentionables. They all passed muster, and to show my approval and appreciation, I helped her remove them and vigorously attended to what next arose.

We took a late afternoon nap afterwards and got dressed for dinner. We'd made plans to see my old friend Derek Davis, the builder who had accepted a project in San Miguel when the housing market slowed in the States. The mountainous Mexican climate suited him and his wife and they had made friends with numerous American ex-pats who had retired there. But he longed to build in Charlotte again, and the market was heating up enough to make it feasible.

We ate and drank into the night, reminiscing about how Derek had restored my humble abode in Denver to its current state. The only part of the evening that was a bit disquieting was when Derek told me how the CEO of his venture in San Miguel often asked about me, in a polite but overly inquisitive manner. I had some suspicion that our paths had once crossed, but this was another story I'd relegated to the cold case file.

We got home around ten. The battery on my phone had run down, so I plugged it into the charger on my nightstand. It immediately flashed that I had one missed message.

Rick, sounding urgent.

I called him back. "What's up, pal? I was out to dinner with Derek. Sends his regards."

"Great. Riles, there's no way to sugarcoat this, so I'll tell you straight out. Your worst fears came true. Stevie's been murdered. They've arrested Ted."

FORTY SIX

Charlene and I had split a bottle of cabernet at dinner. I was feeling good, but far from buzzed. Stone's call made me want to open another bottle.

"What happened? Have they actually arrested him, or just brought him in for questioning? Have you talked to Ted?" Jumbled questions mixed with guilt raced through my mind.

"Ted was out, came back to the condo and found Stevie lying on the sofa. He thought she was asleep but then he saw blood. He called 911. Cops came. While they were questioning him, a neighbor came forward and said that he'd heard them arguing earlier. No sign of forced entry, no signs of a struggle. They surmised it was someone she knew and that plus the argument --- well, they hauled him in."

I was in the bedroom, still dressed. Charlene was in the bathroom, getting ready for bed. I didn't want her to overhear the unfiltered news so I took the phone into my office and closed the door. With any luck, she'd be primping for a while and I could break it to her gently.

"You say you spoke to him. Before they brought him in?"

"Yes. Right after he called 911, he called me. He was pretty shaken up. Look, from the way he sounded, he wasn't worried that he'd be blamed. He sounded more in shock that the woman he loved had been murdered."

I'd seen this play out from both angles. Murderers who pretend to discover the body and fabricate elaborate ruses to cement their claims of innocence. If guilty, a man of Ted's means and access to a private aircraft could have done the deed and disappeared. By the time the body was found, he could be somewhere beyond United States' extradition agreements. It would be tantamount to an admission of guilt, but depending on how quickly he could lay his hands on his money, he might live out his days comfortably somewhere in Africa or the Middle East.

Knowing Ted, I'd bet on the former approach. That 3-D chess master mind of his could concoct a scenario to sell a jury on his innocence, aided of course, by the best legal counsel money could buy. Perhaps he'd already begun the process with an attorney.

"Does he have a lawyer? Do you know what he's already told the police?"

"I don't know what he said to the cops. After he called me, he said his next call was to John League, that hot shot shyster who defended Tony Gazza back in the day."

"But he called you first. Why, do you think?"

"Said he needed a friend with a cool head. Said he would have called you but that you were pissed at him."

"Yeah, I was. I mean, I am. God, I don't know what to think. I found Stevie for him, got her to agree to meet him. Now this. The whole damn thing is my fault."

"Hey, come on. Look, I know you didn't hear his voice, but he didn't sound like someone who just killed his fiancée. I worked with this guy practically every day for over twenty years. I'd never believe he could do this. And don't forget, I knew Stevie too."

"And don't think that little factoid won't come up at a trial if it gets that far. League is a great defense attorney. He'll do whatever it takes to win. Even if it means suggesting that you killed her."

He obviously hadn't considered that possibility but it didn't seem to bother him. "You think you and me would be asked to testify against him?"

"For sure. Maybe as hostile witnesses, you being his friend and all. Honestly, Ricky, if he did this, I want the bastard to fry."

"I thought you were against the death penalty."

"I'd make an exception."

"Well, in that case, I feel weird telling you this, bro, but Ted says he wants to talk to you. ASAP. Damn the expense, just get here."

I wasn't sure that any contact with Ted was a good idea, for either of us. I could claim confidentiality until the cows come home, but there wasn't anything I could say that would help his case. And if he did do it, I wouldn't shade the truth to make him look good.

Stone must have read my thoughts. “He didn’t do it. I can feel it in my gut, man. He loved her.”

“Yes, well, he loved her twenty years ago and nearly knocked her unconscious. Do you know who caught the case? Was it McCullough? My old friend?”

“Don’t know. I can find out.”

“Do that. Keep me posted. I’ve got some serious thinking to do on how to handle this. I may have aided and abetted a killer. I’ll have a hard time sleeping, I guarantee you that.”

“Don’t beat yourself up. You did this for me. And I’m convinced he’s innocent.”

“Even if that’s the case, she’d be alive today if I hadn’t hooked her up with Ted. Unless this is a totally random act and a complete coincidence, and I find that hard to believe. Stay in touch. I’m going to have to tell Charlene now. That’ll be fun.”

FORTY SEVEN

It wasn't exactly fun but the next few minutes were damned revealing. I expected a ration of shit and *I told you so* from her, and I deserved it. There was an obvious opening for her to second guess my every move, and she drove right through it.

She was wearing man-tailored black silk pajamas. She smelled great. Normally after a night out with friends, a nightcap and a long, slow session of lovemaking would be in order, but it was the furthest thing from our minds just then.

She said, "Riles, face it. You were played. I told you all along. Is there any way they can come after you on charges?"

"You've probably heard the expression that a grand jury can indict a ham sandwich, so anything's possible. But I can't see how they could make anything stick. That doesn't make me feel any better about my role in this."

"But what about the negative publicity you're sure to get? If I was looking for a PI, I certainly wouldn't hire one who was involved with a murderer like Ted McCarver."

"Charlene, this isn't about me right now. Poor Stevie is dead."

"Could they put you in jail for refusing to cooperate like they do reporters who won't give up their sources?"

"I don't think they'd try that on a former FBI agent. They can't think I'd be that naive. No, they'd probably try to smear me, like you suggested. Try to damage my rep."

"Would that be enough to get your license pulled down here?"

"Depends on their connections."

"Admit it. You're thinking Ted didn't do this and you want to vindicate him."

"I want whoever did this to pay, whether it's Ted or not."

"So how do you go about doing that? I suppose you could let the police handle it and cooperate as much as you can within the rules of your profession. That's the smart move."

She winced and shook her head. "That's not you, is it? You're going to work this on your own, aren't you?"

I said, "You know me pretty well."

"I don't like the way you always approach things from the side door. In the end, it's coming back to bite you in the ass. Why didn't you listen to me?"

I tried to kiss the top of her head, but she pulled away.

I said, "Okay, maybe you were right and I was wrong. Is that what you need to hear? Sometimes the direct approach doesn't work. I've got thirty years experience doing this and I've been right far more than I've been wrong. Like with that Rebecca Hunter woman. If I had just shown up at her door saying that Ted sent me, she would have slammed it in my face."

"And now you have three dead women and my husband to show for it."

"That's a low blow Charlene." She knew my vulnerabilities and hit me hard with them. Jaime never blamed me for the death of her mother and she very well could have. And this was the first time Charlene had laid her husband's death at my doorstep. I could retaliate in kind, but I was afraid that in our present state of alcohol fueled anger, I'd say things that couldn't be unheard. Things that would send her packing.

Sitting cross-legged on the bed, she had no such trepidations about recounting past grievances. "Like when we first met. You side-doored me too, Riles. You were digging dirt on Johnny and you pretended to be a fan of my music."

"I *am* a fan of your music. You forget, at the time, Derek thought that maybe you had arranged his beating because you were pissed that he spurned your advances. I had to find out for myself if you were that kind of woman. I found out otherwise or we wouldn't be here tonight."

Charlene was still sensitive about her marriage and my disapproval of the whole arrangement which allowed her to cheat at will. She had attempted to seduce Davis while he was working on her bathroom, but his moral code didn't allow for sleeping with married women. That stopped her in her tracks for a minute.

How did it come to this? We start talking about the tragic events in Jersey, and now I'm being put to the test about my whole career.

She said, "I gather you're headed back to Toms River, first thing tomorrow, aren't you?"

"Like I said, you know me well."

She turned her back to me and shut off the lamp on her side of the bed. She exhaled in frustration and said, "And what's your plan when you get there?"

"I've got a nine hour car ride ahead to figure that out."

FORTY EIGHT

"So where is Ted now?" I asked Stone. I was tired from the drive, and the nice cabernet that he had poured upon my arrival was having a soporific effect.

"Hotel TR. His condo is a crime scene."

"So they haven't arrested him yet?"

"Nope. They asked for his passport and alerted the Monmouth Jet Center about keeping his plane grounded. All voluntary but he didn't fight it. They gave him the typical 'don't leave the area' rap."

The sunset from Rick's Mantoloking house was stunning. Between the effects of the wine and pastel panorama over the bay and ocean, I could almost forget why I'd come. "I would guess that *anything* the cops asked Ted would be referred to League. The guy is shameless but he gets results."

"When do you want to see Ted?"

"Tomorrow morning. After a good night's rest, unless you're planning on bringing one of your noisy young harlots around."

"Can't help it if they shriek in ecstasy, my friend, it's what I do. But no, I figured I'd stay in tonight, maybe watch some NBA with you. Show you what you missed for lack of talent."

Another dig on my college career at Georgetown. He couldn't help it. "At least I was varsity hoops for a D-1, not baseball for a D-3," was my weak rejoinder, putting down his resume as a mediocre college pitcher at a small school.

The next morning, Stone was off to the station early and there was no Cindy or any other member of his chippie brigade to greet me. After breakfast and the newspapers online, I drove to the Hotel TR on Route 37. It was a converted Holiday Inn, which I thought was named after Teddy Roosevelt until it hit me that TR stood for Toms River. *A pleasant place for the entire family, not far from the water.* Not as upscale as McCarver's usual haunts, but I expect that was part of the strategy. League had probably instructed him to lay low and avoid the press, and this place was not where reporters would suspect a multi-millionaire to be hiding.

Ted looked awful. His normally crisp attire looked like he'd slept in it, as I later discovered he had. His hair was all over the place, his face was a riot of two day stubble, and his eyes appeared rheumy.

He skipped his normal handshake and hearty greeting and motioned me to sit at a small table near the courtesy bar. I cleared off the fast food wrappings, planted myself down, looked him in the eye, and waited for him to begin.

"Thanks for coming, King. I wasn't sure you would after the way we parted the other day. God, that seems so long ago, when was it?"

"Day before yesterday. Look Ted, let's get something straight right from the outset. I'm not here to defend you. You have a high priced lawyer for that and I'm sure he has his own investigators."

"Four figures per billable hour. Even for the likes of me, that qualifies as high priced. But worth it if he keeps the police at bay."

"So why me? I'm not sure I can help your case, only hurt it."

"I want you to find out who killed Stevie. John League sees his job as creating reasonable doubt. If that leads to identify who is responsible, all the better but that isn't his primary goal. I won't rest until I know that whoever did this is brought to justice."

His breath smelled of hard liquor, a beverage he had given up years ago in favor of fine wine. I didn't know if that meant he was a self medicated alcoholic, or simply if his drink of preference had changed.

The transformation of his visage was startling. For the first time, I noticed age spots on his face, leading me to wonder if he'd disguised them with makeup. He was even paler than normal. Broken veins mapped across his nose, dark circles under bloodshot eyes.

"Ted, here's the deal and there's no negotiating. I'm not going to work for you. Not now, not ever again. I'm here for me. Our goal is the same. I want whoever did this to get the max. If it happens to be you, so be it."

He nodded his head slowly several times, taking it in, before calmly replying. "You really think I could have done this? We were getting married in six weeks."

"It's been known to happen the night before the wedding so that doesn't mean anything. And I know the mood you were in when you left me in Davidson. I saw that famous temper of yours first hand. So let's cut the prelims and get down to it. Tell me what happened that day after you flew up here."

"There's not much to tell. Stevie was supposed to work until six, I landed at the Monmouth Jet Center around four thirty. I went to the Ocean County Mall, looking for a little gift for her. I found a nice pearl necklace I thought she'd like. I got to the condo just after six. She had gotten off early, and was already into a bottle of Silver Oak."

"When you say into, what does that mean? Was she drunk?"

"No, there was plenty left in the bottle, I couldn't imagine she had more than one glass. I didn't have any, I wanted to wait until dinner. I thought it was kind of strange, because she thanked me for the wine. I guess I had left some after my last visit, I don't remember. Anyway, we talked a bit and then I broke the news that Charlene wouldn't play at the reception. She became incensed, way overreacting. I said we'd find someone even better maybe even Bon Jovi, but she started in on how I promised that Charlene would sing and she had already told some of her friends."

"Had you promised?"

He balled his hands together in a cleansing motion. "I said it shouldn't be a problem. Is that a promise? I wanted to give her what she wanted, what she deserved --- as I told you."

"So you fought."

"We fought. This was the first big blowup since we got back together. I really believed those days of screaming matches were over. And I have to say, the anger was way out of character for her. She had really polished off her rough edges. Even cut down on the swearing. I think I kept my cool pretty admirably, given some of the nasty things she was saying. I chalked it up to Stevie having a bad day at work and I just left before it went any further. Went for a walk along the water."

"How long were you gone?"

"An hour and a half maybe. It was around eight when I got back. I figured that would be enough time for her to cool off and maybe mellow out with more wine. When I got back, that's when I found her."

He stopped, swallowed hard, trying to keep his composure. "She was lying on the sofa. I thought she had finished the bottle and dozed off. Then I saw the blood. Not a lot of it. Just a small spot on her chest."

"I know you're not a forensics expert, but it looked like a gunshot wound?"

Again he hesitated. "I thought so, but I couldn't be sure if it wasn't a stab wound. Like an ice pick or something."

His efforts to stay in the moment failed. He began to tear up and then wept openly, reaching for a soiled tissue in his pants pocket. If he was putting on an act for my benefit, it was a pretty convincing one. A display raw emotion from a man used to bottling it up.

I gave him a minute, then asked, "You called Stone first. Why?"

"I called 911, then Rick. I told him to get a hold of you and see if you'd advise me on what to do, being former FBI and all. Then I called John League's office, but it was obviously too late for anyone live to answer. Luckily, he had an emergency number and he sent a man out."

"He didn't come personally?"

"No. But his associate got there pretty soon after the police and gave me instructions to say no more."

I'd been there dozens of times. Attorneys always instruct their clients to clam up until they hear the story first, and then usually spirit them away before they can say something either incriminating or contradictory to what the evidence would later show. As a fed, it was damned frustrating when I had a person of interest cornered, but in civilian life, my attitude was more sympathetic. Sometimes things can get misconstrued and used against an innocent party later.

I said, "So I take it they ran you in for questioning and you said nothing on the advice of counsel."

"Pretty much. They claimed they had a witness who had heard screaming coming from the condo. The lawyer said not to confirm that because this witness may not exist. That's about when League himself showed up and told them either to arrest me or let me leave."

"And the name of the homicide detective who caught the case?"

"I'll never forget it. A name from my youth watching Wagon Train on TV. Flint McCullough."

My old pal. McCullough was a straight arrow, but an honest cop who didn't take shortcuts. We had history together. This was about to get even more convoluted than it already was.

FORTY NINE

Flint McCullough is a creature of habit. One of his daily rituals is lunch. He eats at the same diner every day at noon precisely, unless work intervenes. He eats the identical meal --- an egg white omelet, with spinach and broccoli, doused with ketchup, hold the home fries. It is washed down with two cups of hi-test coffee, and sixteen ounces of Toms River tap water. He allows himself fifty minutes, no more --- occasionally less if working a particularly urgent case.

It had been several years since I had last seen him, but I was pretty sure that time had not eroded his commitment to his noon repast. He had two grown kids and was still on his first wife, who he had met in high school. I would wager that she was the only encounter he'd ever experienced with living female flesh. It wasn't that he couldn't have strayed had he wanted. There are plenty of cop groupies in the area who would gladly spend a night with a rugged man in uniform, no questions asked.

Flint's uniform these days consisted of a five day rotation of off-the-rack conservative suits, altered smartly to accentuate his chiseled physique. Although I'd never seen him sans shirt, I guessed that his six foot, hundred and sixty five pound frame was as tight and ripped as his facial features. I had told him more than once that he reminded me of the actor Scott Glenn, but his response was always the same. He said he didn't know who that was, but when I reminded him that he played Alan Shepard in *The Right*

Stuff, he always let out a long slow "aaahhh' --- no other reaction.

Sure enough, when I strode into the Starlight Diner at 12:05 p.m., he was seated at his customary small booth in the back, newspapers spread out, nicked white china coffee cup in hand. I wouldn't be surprised if the place held that cup aside for him. He looked up from the paper briefly upon my arrival and then went back to his reading as if I were a fly that he had brushed aside, rather than an old colleague that he hadn't seen in years.

"Well, well, well," he said, still not looking up. "You saved me and the department several hundred bucks. I was ready to book a flight to Charlotte and now it seems I won't have to."

"And it's great to see you too, Flint. You haven't changed a bit."

Indeed he hadn't. Other than a smattering more gray in his close clipped hair, he looked remarkably the same.

"You seem a little trimmer than when last we met," he said. Amazing how such a quick glance from him could observe that I had lost twenty pounds over the last couple of years.

"Clean living. So you were ready to visit God's Country, eh? Maybe I should just vanish now and you should book that flight. You're looking a little pale and a couple of days in the Southern sun might do you some good."

He snorted. McCullough was anything but pale, always sporting a coat of tan on his weather beaten countenance. His face was all sharp angles, from the slits of his eyes to his thin lips.

"So Mr. Riley King, you decided to head me off at the pass and cooperate fully this time. Maybe the South has changed your rascally ways. I can only hope."

The last time our interests had intersected was a case I was given by Jaime Johansen's mother, Paige White, a literary agent in search of an author who had submitted a hot manuscript and then gone AWOL. McCullough liked me for Paige's murder. Luckily, he wasn't a lazy cop who fixates on one suspect to the exclusion of all others, and he gradually came around to helping me find the real killer. That's what I would be asking him to do now.

"Not that I'm keeping count or anything, but you have quite a track record with dead ladies. Let's see King, first there was Elizabeth Huntington, then Paige White and now Stephanie Perry. I knew her, you know. Bought lumber and fixtures at her place when I finished our basement. Fine lady."

"Yes, she was. Before you waste time trying to tie me to this, I was six hundred miles away. I have probably a dozen people who will back that up."

"I know. I already checked. Just routine, you understand, gets the boss off my back." He gave me a tight-lipped little leer that passed for a smile.

"I'd expect nothing less. So how did you come to the conclusion that somehow I was linked to this case?"

He took a sip of coffee and contemplated whether he should share any information. "Computers. We have the decedent's laptop and McCarver's. There are numerous email and doc files pointing in your direction. Anything you want to tell me?"

"Much as I love you Flint, we both have rules we have to follow. I can tell you some things that my client has given me permission to, but I do have to honor confidentiality."

Before leaving Ted, I had asked for and received written permission from him to share everything I knew with the authorities. I was sure that John League would never have allowed it had he been present and no doubt he would challenge it in court if it got that far. It wouldn't. Even though my former client had agreed, I wasn't about to give the cops anything of value. My ask was a test, and he passed.

"I'm waiting, Riley. Let's hear it."

My game was to reveal as little as possible but in return, receive something useful. Tricking a hard bitten cop like McCullough into divulging anything worthwhile off the record would be tough, but I had to try. "Can't be one sided, Flint. Anything you have will come up in discovery anyway if this goes to trial. And I can save you a lot of time chasing down dead ends."

"And of course, you would never tell me that something is a dead end that might actually incriminate your pal. There's trust and then there's trust, King. I'm with the great Ronald Reagan on this one---*trust but verify*."

"Equating me to Gorbachev? I'm flattered. Let me explain one thing from the outset. Ted McCarver is no longer a client. I've told him and I'll tell you --- my reason for being here is to find whoever killed Stevie Perry. And if that someone is McCarver, I'll let the chips fall where they may."

"Again, I can't just take your word. I wouldn't be much of a detective if I did."

"Understood. Same goes for me. Let's just agree not to lie to each other. If there are things you can't tell me, don't. But don't make shit up, okay?"

"Deal."

I proceeded to tell him about my role, how Ted had hired me to locate three women in his life that he had wronged and offer restitution. I wasn't sure how much they had gotten from Ted's computer, since he may have sent me info from his desktop in Hilton Head, so I was careful not to confirm anything they merely suspected. When it came to Stevie, I said she had decided to meet with Ted and agreed to marry him of her own free will, as far as I knew.

"And were you aware that he had struck her previously?"

This was my first test. If I said *no,* all bets would be off since Flint likely had already discovered references to the incident in McCarver's file.

"I was."

He said, "And it didn't cross your mind that since he'd already abused this woman, that he might try it again?"

"Of course it did. But call me stupid, I think that people can change and that a seventy year old man who examines his life and wants to rectify his mistakes deserves a second chance. That is, if the woman in question is willing to give it to him. But if he pulled the wool over my eyes and he's responsible for killing her, I hope he fries."

He said, "You know King, I'm not the hard ass you might think I am. I want to see justice served and I'll do everything I can within the rules to accomplish that. The difference between us as I see it is that you'll push the envelope and color outside the lines when you think it's justified, and I won't."

"Well, that does make you a hard ass in my book." I winked and he looked back with a blank expression. "I've heard Ted's story about what happened. Tell me what you have."

"Victim was found condition D as a result of a single small caliber bullet, fired at close range that penetrated her heart. Death was almost instantaneous. Her body bore no signs of a struggle. Toxicology showed a high dosage of gamma hydroxybutyrate, commonly referred to as a date rape drug. Overdoses can lead to deep sleep, even death. Upon searching the condominium, a bottle of wine was discovered, heavily laced with this substance. Next to the bottle was a gift card, with the inscription, 'I'll be in this evening. Be ready for a special night. Don't wait for me to enjoy the wine. Ted'."

"Sounds like your incident report, verbatim. Good memory." Ted's story was already at odds with McCullough's findings. He had claimed that he didn't know where the wine had come from --- that he might have left it there from a previous visit.

"I try to be clear, concise and correct."

"Does that sharp memory of yours include the name of the wine?"

"I'm not wine expert, more of a scotch drinker myself. Let me check my notes." He produced a large smart phone that doubled as a tablet. "Here it is, if it means anything to you. It's called Silver Oak, 1991."

FIFTY

"**W**hy would he need to give her a Spanish Fly to get her in the mood?" Stone asked.

"You're showing your age, Ricky. Haven't heard that term since high school. But in a way, I'm glad you're not familiar on a first name basis with this stuff."

"Never needed anything but my dashing good looks and quick wit to score with the ladies. *I'm a hard headed man who is brutally handsome*."

Stone and I were eating pizza and drinking beer. It had turned chilly on the Jersey shore and he had fired up the gas logs. The sconces in the gathering room were on a low setting, so the blue and orange flames illuminated the room with their rugged glow. The sun had already set, nature's cold memo that daylight hours were dwindling and winter was closing in.

My latest tack was to ignore his music references in hopes that they'd go away. "Whatever. The issue here is Ted. You do understand that anything I tell you about this can go no further. I mean, to Ted or anybody else. Especially one of your young bimbos."

"You think anything I say to any of them holds any truth at all?"

"I'm not playing with you. You've always been a great sounding board and you've given me perspective on a number of cases before. But this is different. We're dealing with murder and so far, all the signs point to Ted."

"Based on a bottle of wine? Really?"

"Think about it objectively, forget you know him. He hit her once before in anger. He admits to me and his shrink that he has a problem with women. He sweet talks Stevie into getting back together. She's making only a modest living, and she sees him as a ticket out of her lackluster life. Way back when, they argued all the time. Now they have another knock-down, drag-out. There's a gun handy in the condo. In a fit of anger, he shoots her. Then goes out and tosses the gun in Barnegat Bay."

"But why spike the wine? I told you, she wasn't all that hard to get in the sack."

"And as long as you stick to that lie, you'll do nothing but hurt your friend's case."

"I don't follow."

This was going to be tough but it needed airing. "Stevie and I spent five hours together the morning she flew down to meet Ted. We talked a lot. That's how I got to know her a little and came to like her. She told me about her time with Ted, first time around. She said that he took her to a lot of station functions, described meeting famous sports and music people. You really expect me to believe when you ran into her at that Beatlefest that it was the first time you'd laid eyes on each other?"

Stone leaned back in his chair. He looked about the room nervously and took a healthy swig from the long neck. "I didn't think it was all that important. I did run into her at the Beatlefest like I told you. First time in years. But

I had the hots for her even when she was with Ted. I never let on until that day. After a few drinks I told her that and she said she'd been attracted to me too. We had a fling, didn't last long. She broke it off, said she felt like she was betraying Ted, even though they'd split years earlier."

"Why did you lie about it to me? You didn't think I'd find out?"

"Really pal, I didn't think it mattered much. And then I started feeling guilty about it when I heard they were going to tie the knot. That's why I called you and said that Ted should know about what happened."

"You didn't tell him, did you?"

"I sent him an email, explaining what happened and apologizing for it. I did it out of respect --- because he needed to hear it from me first. Not from her or through the grapevine. I felt I owed him that, even if it jeopardized our friendship."

"God damn it Rick, I told you to talk to me first. When did you send it?"

"The night she died. Around six o'clock or so."

Another brick in the wall. Stone didn't have to say it -- I thought of that one all by myself.

FIFTY ONE

The text from McCullough requesting a meet was unexpected. The succinctly worded message said that McCarver had been arrested and that at nine p.m., Flint would be in his usual place.

I arrived a few minutes early, but the fastidious detective was already waiting in his favorite booth at the Starlight. No newspapers this time, merely coffee and his tablet/phone. I wonder how long ago it had replaced the little notebook he used to carry and whether he'd been meticulous enough to digitize annotations on his past cases. Given his experiences, there could be a major publishing deal in his future, but I doubted McCullough would ever take advantage of it.

"How can you drink that sludge this late at night?" was my greeting. "How can you get to sleep?"

"Don't sleep much anyway," was his reply. "Four hours a night usually."

I wasn't about to say how unhealthy that was --- he was chained to the behavior and nothing short of a heart attack would change it.

"So, you arrested Ted."

"Arraignment and bail hearing within forty eight hours. You know the drill."

"Don't imagine a judge will allow bail. Flight risk and all. Second degree?"

"Yeah. Not pre-meditated, at least until we get more. Either way, he's looking at hard time."

So far, Flint was telling me nothing I couldn't read in tomorrow's Asbury Park Press. He didn't call me out on a chilly night to preview the next day's headlines.

"So, you're convinced he did it."

Careful not to say anything that might be used in court if I decided to violate our trust, he said, "My boss is. And his is the vote that counts."

I knew better than to press him too hard right now about his own misgivings, which might be the reason he wanted to talk. "What tipped the scale?"

"Couple things. The computer guys dug a little deeper. Seems your friend Stone wrote an email confessing that he slept with Stevie. Don't imagine that went over too well with McCarver. I'd guess that could start a little tiff, finding out your intended had slept with a friend."

"You're sure he saw the email? You're positive he opened it?" Stone had checked his sent file and confirmed that the message had been sent at 6:03 p.m.. Ted had told me he got to the condo at around six oh five. I had my doubts that the first thing he'd do after not seeing his lady for a few days was to excuse himself and check his email. Never worked that way with Charlene.

"Not on his laptop. But it could have been opened on a smart phone. We didn't get his phone and now it seems to be missing. We're looking to subpoena the service provider to check that."

"Seems like a pretty big loophole if you can't prove that he saw the message."

"That's not all there was."

"Do tell."

McCullough looked uncomfortable, which was unusual for a man used to seeing the dregs of humanity in their worst possible light. "McCarver kept doc files on the laptop. Notes of his conversations with his shrink. Emails back and forth to her. I don't know if she billed him for these little exchanges, but bottom line, we know some stuff we might not otherwise know."

This was a prelude to something bigger, but I'd have to draw it out of him.

"And that was enough to arrest him?"

"I'm sure League will try to get it disallowed, being that it is doctor-patient privileged. But we didn't get it from the shrink, so who knows how a judge will see it. Did you know that McCarver's father killed his mother?"

It was hard to conceal my surprise. Ted had mentioned his mother in passing and Dr. Mills had told me he had 'mommy issues'. His dad killing his mom? That qualifies.

"Ted said they died in a plane crash. That's not so?"

"Oh, that much is true. But apparently, his father crashed the plane deliberately. He'd said as much to the tower before he rammed it into the side of a mountain. He couldn't take the humiliation anymore."

"Wouldn't this have been in the news?"

McCullough said, "Sure, today it would. The air controller would have tweeted it to the universe. But back then, social media didn't exist like now. Ted's father had a politician friend who wanted to protect the man's reputation. So he somehow got it suppressed. Hard to believe that the FAA didn't investigate it further, but apparently the friend was a U.S. Senator. In fact, Ted didn't even find out until years later. I expect that's what led him to psychotherapy. The dates match."

"And this could be used in court?"

"Establishes a pattern of behavior based on his past. I'm sure that League would try to suppress that, too. Depends on the judge. You know that."

In all the time we'd been talking, no waitress had even ventured near our table. They knew McCullough so well that they understood when police business was being transacted and when they needed to give a wide berth.

"Flint, I appreciate the heads-up. You've got quite a circumstantial case here. Murder weapon?"

"We've got divers going down first thing along the water where he could have walked that night. 'Course it's possible he threw it down a storm sewer and it's washed out to sea by now, or tossed it into a dumpster close by. We have a couple of uniforms checking that out."

"So it's Ted or bust?"

"That's why I wanted to talk to you. I don't know what it's like in Charlotte, but up here, the county, the towns, even the state are cutting budgets. Manpower is tight. We can't go chasing every lead, so we concentrate on the more obvious ones. What I'm proposing is this --- even though you told me that you're not looking to clear the guy, that's the direction you should go in. We're compiling every bit of data we have to build a case against him and we have access to a lot of material, mainly because of his laptop."

"Even stuff that his doctor and I would normally have to keep confidential."

"Look King, I can't keep feeding you intel, because if it got out that I was helping the defense, they'd have my badge. We can't even be seen together after tonight. I've only given you what I have so far because it'll come out in discovery anyway."

He looked over his shoulder, his quick grey eyes scanning for eavesdroppers. "So just saying, if I were you, I'd chase down every possible suspect other than McCarver. We have his ass covered. And I *will* promise you this: if we have an airtight case against him, like if we find the gun and it's clearly his, I'll tell you to stop spinning your wheels. You said if he's guilty, you want him to hang. So do we. But I do want to be sure and I don't know if we'll be able to chase down every flimsy lead when we have such an obvious perp."

It seemed he might already have someone in mind. "You have any gut feeling, if it isn't Ted, who it could be? Anybody who might have a grudge against Stevie from down here? Some contractor who hit on her at work that she rejected?"

"There's only one other possibility that makes any sense at all as far as motive."

"Save me the riddle. I'm tired."

"Rick Stone. Now before you cut me off, if you read the email he sent to McCarver, he says she was the one who broke off their little fling."

"Flint, that's ridiculous. He's been banging every twenty something waitress in the county lately. Not like he's missing her. Come on, you need to do better than that."

"I'm just saying, think about it. Lotharios like that are okay dumping expendable women after one nighters without a second thought. But if they are the ones getting dumped? Need I remind you of how badly he took getting pissed on by that female sportscaster, what was her name, Lisa Tillman? So despondent that he walked into a bullet for you because he had nothing to live for."

He was twisting the most brave act I'd ever witnessed into a motive for murder. My best friend *was* acting like a total dickhead lately, screwing everything in sight. Was it because he'd fallen for Stevie and was trying to dull the pain? And what if his insistence on sending Ted that email, despite my objections, was intended to break them up so that he could swoop in on her? Or to punish her for rejecting him?

If I didn't know Rick like a brother, that might be plausible. But unlike me, he shared everything about his exploits in the sack, including the few that didn't go so well. He categorized them as "their loss", but quickly made up for that with a few easy victories. He would have written Stevie off without a second thought.

"Tell me one thing more, McCullough. Is Rick a serious person of interest here?"

"Manpower, my friend. We don't have enough to go digging much in that direction, just enough so that League at trail can't insinuate that we stopped looking after McCarver. But you asked, I answered. It's just something you may want to look into."

FIFTY TWO

Stone was already asleep by the time I got back to the house and as far as I could determine, he was alone. No strange cars in the driveway. I envisioned a scene where I awake him roughly, shine a bright incandescent bulb in his face and grill him about killing Stevie. The idea was as absurd as the notion that he had anything to do with it.

McCullough was a smart man who tried to hide it sometimes behind a Columbo-like veil of middle class sensibility. It was possible that he didn't want me developing any realistic alternatives to McCarver's guilt, so he sent me on a wild goose chase involving Stone. To believe that, I'd have to buy that Flint had been magically transformed from a relentless seeker of justice into a bureaucratic toady, desperately trying to please his superiors in order to protect his pension.

No way.

Nonetheless, he had planted a seed that I needed to quash, lest I allow the nagging doubt that Stone might be responsible to fester within me. It was just past midnight. I logged onto my laptop to check email and see how the newspapers were dealing with Ted's arrest. My mailbox contained nothing but junk come-ons for obsolete products that nobody wanted but I could obtain for pennies on the dollar.

I noticed on my AIM window that Charlene's computer was active. We hadn't spoken all day, so I Skyped her and she answered immediately.

Her tone wasn't as antagonistic as it had been before I left, but it wasn't exactly her normal seductive purr either.

"What are you doing awake, Riley? You normally are tits up by ten."

"You have such a charming Southern way of putting things, Charl." I gave her an edited rundown of my day. "Have you got your tour dates yet?"

"No. Harrison Mitchell hasn't returned my calls. His secretary says he's been sent my messages, but no, nothing new. I'm getting a little worried. We were supposed to cut that side early next week."

"Probably got his hands full with the tour and hasn't had time."

"Yeah, I guess."

I said, "Hey, is the McCarver thing getting any attention down there? I'm just wondering if the national media has picked up on this yet."

"Saw a small blurb in the Observer, one of those bullet point things."

"Let me know if you see anything more. Local papers have played it up but so far, nothing much in New York. Doesn't help my job if the city tabloids start sensationalizing it."

"And what is your job exactly? From what you've told me, they seem to have Teddy-boy dead to rights."

I hadn't told her about Rick and even though we were in full disclosure mode, old habits were dying hard. I didn't want to poison her mind against Stone when I had nothing more than a cop's flight of the imagination to go on.

"I met with the lead detective. An old friend. He said they were compiling a strong case against Ted and that I should concentrate on alternative scenarios. Makes sense, but I don't know."

She leaned in toward the camera. The lighting wasn't flattering but I could see through that and appreciate how beautiful she was. "You're wastin' your time, sugar, but you just do what you gotta do without minding about little old me."

"I always think about you, Charl. I hope you believe me that if Ted is guilty, I'm not going to pull any tricks to get him off. I just need to be sure as I can be so I'll chase down every lead that the cops won't."

"Like what?"

"I'll start at the lumber company in the morning. See if any of her co-workers know anything. If she had any jilted lovers, stuff like that. She has a sister up in Bergen County so I may take a run up there."

She was dismissive now, annoyed further that I was still trying to find alternatives to the killer that she had already convicted and executed in her mind. She said, "Try to get some sleep. You look tired."

"Kiss Bosco on the snout for me."

"I will. He's lying next to me right now on your pillow. 'Bye."

It made me sad to think that Charlene and I weren't going to be spending much time together in the near future. At least this last conversation was civil, but we had a lot of work to do if we were going to make a go of it. Even if, out of the blue, I discover a smoking gun tomorrow, she would be headed for Nashville to record that Christmas song and then to parts unknown to tour. The thought didn't help me sleep, but the melatonin did.

I awoke at just after eight to the smell of breakfast downstairs. Stone had been up early, visiting a nearby Dunkin Donuts, returning with some flatbread sandwiches. I pulled on a pair of jeans and joined him at the table. He looked fresh and rested, ready to take on three hours of hot sports talk, killing the Jets for a recent trade that amounted to no more than a salary dump in the wasteland of their latest season.

He seemed invigorated. "Sleep well, Riles? What time did you get in?"

"Late. Hey, something I need to ask you. Did you send a return receipt with that email to Ted?"

"Not sure what you mean."

"It's just that the cops can't determine yet if he read it before Stevie was killed and if so, it was motive."

"Jeez, I don't know. I never thought about it. You mean, I can see if somebody reads my email?"

Stone was more of a computer Neanderthal than most. The station employed ghost writers to put together his daily blog, which Rick quickly scanned to make sure he wasn't misrepresented. If anything didn't work properly on his tablet, he passed it to the IT guy and boom! it was fixed. He looked at it as appreciating the specs of his sports car but not being a mechanic. That was somebody else's job.

"Mind if I check it out? You may have a default setting for receipts, but they might be hidden files. Likely it wouldn't register unless you looked. So after you sent it, what did you do? I'm sure you must have had an idea that Ted would either want to talk or want to kill you after he read it."

"Me, maybe, but no way will I ever believe he'd kill Stevie over it. No, I stayed home that night. I did kind of think I'd hear from him. And of course I did, after he found her."

"And you were alone? No Cindys?"

"Yeah. She actually was going to pop in for a quickie after work, but given what happened, I told her not to."

"Damned considerate of you. Think hard Rick, did Ted say anything when he called you after finding the body that indicated he'd read the email?"

"No. Now that I'm thinking about it, if he was pissed at me after reading the email, why would I be the first call he made after the 911?"

"To cover his tracks. That would take a lot of clear thinking under stress, but if anyone is capable of that, it would be Ted."

"I mean, he's smart but come on. You're saying they fought over me and Stevie bumping nasties, he kills her, and then tries to cover it up by calling me and saying he found her like that. That would be pretty cold."

"Yeah, just spit-balling here. And that would mean he'd need to get rid of the gun someplace the police wouldn't find it."

I told him about Ted's parents.

Stone was surprised. "My god, that happened while I was working with him in Woodstock. I went to the funeral. Ted was strong, didn't shed a tear but you could tell he was devastated by what happened."

"Well, apparently he didn't know it was murder/suicide until years later."

"Wow. Poor guy. But what's a DA going to imply, that killing your loved ones is genetic?"

"They may try. Don't you have to get to work?"

He checked his watch and started to take up the dishes but I assured him I'd clean up and told him to be on his way. He went into the bedroom to gather his gear and the lit out for the Mustang.

So, he was alone in his house during the time Stevie was murdered. He didn't give it a second thought when I asked if he was alone. He didn't think of coming up with an alibi because he knew he didn't need one.

Rick didn't do it. Period. I needed to exorcize the thought and move forward.

I re-read his email to Ted, checked the time stamp and indeed, there was no request for a return receipt. No proof on this end that Ted had seen the message prior to Stevie's death.

So if that proved out, why would he kill her? Over Charlene not playing the reception? He sure seemed crazed with me over that, but really? Motive for murder?

FIFTY THREE

Boulos Building Supply amounted to a colossal waste of time, as Charlene predicted. I had no trouble speaking to the owner, an old Greek named Bart Boulos. He had nothing but wonderful things to say about Stevie, whom he considered to be another daughter, to go along with the two who bore his name. The only piece of information I was able to glean was why she had stayed in such a menial job for so many years. Boulos whispered that although Stevie was a whiz at math, she had a reading disability that kept her from advancing her career. He also opined that she felt safe and comfortable cocooned in a small family business, far away from corporate politics and backbiting. All his employees, from those in the office to the outdoor workers operating forklifts moving plywood, wore black armbands in Stevie's memory.

Bart had a PA system the covered the acre or so that comprised his supply yard on the barrier island. Without asking me, he announced to his charges that there was a detective present in the office who was investigating the murder and if any of them had relevant information, they should report immediately.

Two things struck me. No one from the police had questioned Boulos or anyone there. Secondly, Stevie had not mentioned my name to anyone, for if she had, I doubt that her friends would be forthcoming to the man who had engineered her return into McCarver's clutches.

It didn't really matter. The four or five coworkers who showed up had nothing to add, other than their undying affection for the victim. They probably welcomed the opportunity to escape the morning's chill for a few minutes to drink coffee and sing the praises of their fallen colleague.

Stevie's thrice married sister was named Janet Gennaro, a housewife, no children, residing in Ridgewood, so I pointed the Audi north, a ninety minute ride on the Garden State Parkway. I'd spent some time in that borough with Jaime, since its compact downtown area boasted restaurants that rivaled those across the Hudson. The thought of those nights in Ridgewood made me yearn to call her, since her agency was barely ten minutes away. Rather than call, I texted and suggested we meet for dinner if she was free since I was in the area. That way, she could easily beg off and I would have done my duty by asking.

Janet Gennaro lived on a quiet street, (is there any other kind in Ridgewood?), not far from the high school which perennially is Top Five in the state. Education comes at a cost, as property taxes are among the highest in the state as well. This leads to a population of young, affluent families who value learning above all else, and an outward migration of older middle class folks unable to afford the taxes.

I got to Gennaro's address around noon. "Mrs. Gennaro. I'm an investigator, looking into your sister's murder. I'm sorry for your loss. Can you spare me some time to ask a few questions?"

She looked me over without requesting further ID or the name of my employer. She nodded slightly and motioned me in. She was a petite woman with fine features, but her face was heavily sun damaged. She was a few years older than Stevie, and there were no other siblings. Her blonde hair was streaked with gray and her eyes were red.

The house was nicely appointed. All the modern must-haves were visible --- crown and dentil moldings, chair rail above wainscoting in the marble entry hall. The furniture was modern and tasteful, subdued Oriental area rugs covered most of the dark stained oak plank flooring. Probably a designer had been engaged some years back to upgrade this older house to the neighborhood's HGTV standards.

She said, "Can I get you anything, Mr. er, I'm sorry, I didn't get your name?"

"Riley King. And no thank you, I won't stay long. Were you and your sister close?"

"Yes, but we live quite a ways away from each other and she was about to move even farther away before..." she broke down.

I gave her time to recover. "Take your time, Mrs. Gennaro. I know this is hard. When did you see her last?"

She pulled herself together enough to speak. "This past weekend. Hall and Oates are back touring and we saw them play a small college down the shore."

"How did she seem to you then?"

"She was happy, the happiest I'd seen her in a long time. She was planning the wedding. Excited about living in Hilton Head. Raving about that bastard who killed her."

"Ted McCarver. Did you know him?"

"I hadn't seen him since they were together the first time, when he hit her. I wasn't really enthused about them getting back together but she believed that he was a changed man. They were getting along great. He mellowed, she said. She trusted him, she said. Yeah, well I trusted my first two husbands and they were assholes in the end."

I let her stew for a bit. "Was there anyone you can think of, other than McCarver who might have had issues with your sister?"

"Why? They arrested the bastard. He did it."

"We want to make absolutely sure that the man is guilty. That there are no other possibilities."

"Wait a minute. I'm in such a frigging fog, I don't even know who you are. You said private investigator. Who's paying you?"

"Nobody's paying me. I'm doing this on my own."

She looked befuddled. "Come on slick, nobody in this world works for nothing. Who's cutting your checks?"

"I'm sorry you don't believe me, but it's true."

"Why would you...." I could see her mind processing all the connections through the confusion of the last few days. "Oh my God. Stevie told me she'd been approached by a sweet talking dick who told her about Ted wanting to see her. That's you, isn't it?"

I couldn't lie, not now. "Yes. Ted originally hired me to find your sister. But I'm not working for him now. I want to be sure that her killer is brought to justice and if that means Ted, I want him to pay."

"Bullshit. He's your friend. You want him to skate and lay this on somebody else. Get out of my frigging house now or I'll call the police."

"Mrs. Gennaro."

"Out, you son of a bitch. You're the reason my sister is dead. Live with that, you bastard."

Defeated, I left.

FIFTY FOUR

So far today, I'd struck out swinging on long shots. I hadn't expected much from any of them and I was beginning to despair that I could turn up a candidate for Stevie's murder other than Ted.

I regretted my decision to text Jaime and regretted it even more when she wrote back that she had a commitment that evening but was available for coffee and could I make it to the Red Oak Diner in Fort Lee by 2 p.m.?

The Red Oak was where she and I first bonded, following the death of her mother. I didn't think the relationship would lead to anything given that she was fifteen years younger and seemingly had no interest in men. I was very wrong about the latter and during the course of our quest to find her mother's killer, we fell for each other. My decision to move to North Carolina put a big crimp on our relationship. I tried to persuade her to join me but her duties running her mother's literary agency precluded that. Or so she said.

I prepared for the worst. When she discovered second hand that Charlene had temporarily moved in with me, she felt betrayed. She would not accept my explanation that I was only offering an endangered woman protection from a vengeful spouse. I like to think that if the situation were reversed, I would trust her enough to accept her justification, but when she saw glamorous pictures of Charlene online, she rejected the notion.

I got to the diner shortly before two and took a booth near the front window. Jaime got there a minute later, wearing a light cashmere car coat, a black skirt with tall boots, and a green cotton sweater that highlighted her opaline eyes. Her auburn hair was now shoulder length: in short, she looked like a million bucks. I couldn't help noticing how innocent her face was compared to Charlene, who was more than a decade older. I wondered if my lack of sleep added years to the way I looked to her since we hadn't seen each other in quite some time.

"You look great, Jaime. I'm glad you were able to break free."

"Slow day in the word factory. I'm yours," she said. Did I detect a flirtatious tone?

"The way the day is going, I might have a lot of free time as well."

"You don't sound happy about that. Tell me."

We were talking as if nothing had happened over the last year to pull us apart. Things were starting out fine but I doubted they would end that way. I continued the charade by detailing the l'affair McCarver for her.

"So you're doing this on your own dime, why? Because you feel responsible for what happened?" she said when I was done.

"Basically, yeah. If I hadn't put the two of them together again, this never would have happened."

"Just like with my mom. Even if we hadn't gotten together, you weren't about to send me a bill me for helping find her killer. It's a wonder you stay in business."

"Long tradition of fictional private investigators. I'm the exception in reality. I've been lucky with real estate and a few big contingency cases. I can afford to do pro bono work when conscience dictates."

"And it does in this case. But I'm sure you realize that even if you didn't facilitate them re-kindling the relationship, this man would have found someone else to do his bidding. You don't sound like you're convinced that this McCarver fellow didn't do it, though."

"The Ocean County cops are working that angle harder than I ever could. Even with their limited manpower, they've got more guys on the case than I do, because you're looking at my team right now."

"You know from what you've told me, I think maybe...oh, never mind. I've just been reading too many of my father's novels."

Her father was Peter Johansen, better known to the reading public as John Peterson, New York Times bestselling author with more books sold than McDonalds' hamburgers. I found his writing simplistic --- wildly unrealistic in the portrayal of his septuagenarian protagonist Elton Spicer, but the loveable old curmudgeon had wormed his way into American reader's hearts. His fans eagerly awaited the bi-annual installments of his latest adventures.

"No, Jaime, tell me what you're thinking. At this point, I'm like what Dylan said: *When you ain't got nothing, you got nothing to lose*."

"Before my time. What's that, *Positively Fourth Street*?"

"*Like a Rolling Stone*, but good guess. There's hope for you young-uns after all. I guess Stone's got me in the habit of turning to song lyrics when I can't think of a better way to put things."

She rolled her eyes. I constantly teased her that she should find a man more her contemporary, but she scoffed at the suggestion. Seeing her across the table now, she seemed like a co-ed compared to my more mature housemate.

"What if --- and feel free to make fun of me --- what if Ted was the target and not this Stevie woman. What if the killer wanted to kill Ted and she just happened to be there?"

I rolled that around for a bit. It wasn't the most ridiculous thing I'd ever heard. If Ted was telling the truth about not sending the wine, someone else had. And if the wine was spiked with enough hydroxybutyrate to knock out a horse, wasn't it logical to think that Ted would have partaken as well? It would have been easy to kill one or both of them if they were lying unconscious. Whereas I hadn't exhausted the possibility that Stevie had deadly enemies, so far, it seemed that no one hated her enough to kill her. Ted might have business rivals or disgruntled employees that he had fired in the past. Anyone who had made the millions that Ted had must have broken a few eggs along the way.

"It's not crazy, Jaime. It's worth investigating. How about you? Busy?"

"Been spending a lot of time on the Coast. We're close to getting Harrison Ford to commit to three Spicer flicks now that Eastwood is out, but he insisted on script approval and he's rejected two of them so far. We're trying to sell the idea that an older man can solve crimes without taking a nap at three every day. We need to find a way to put action into the films without it looking ridiculous. Dad is trying to come up with a different young sidekick for every story, rather than have a son for Spicer or a regular protégé. Doesn't want it to feel like *Ironside*."

It all seemed so trivial given the real life tragedies I was trying to sort out. But I was glad that Jaime didn't have to carry my burdens and could deal with Han Solo instead of whoever was evil enough to have killed Stevie.

"Good luck with it. So...we should talk. It's been almost a year since you told me you needed time away and other than when I called you for some help locating that writer, I've honored your wishes. But some things have changed in my life and I need to tell you about it."

"Charlene?"

"Yes."

She said, "You know, I saw her this summer. She was opening on that shed tour for some hick band down in Holmdel at the Arts Center. Anyway, she sounded great and looked fabulous. I was going to go backstage and try to talk to her but I didn't want to come off like some crazed stalker. And what would I have accomplished, anyway? Tell her to stay clear of my man? So I just left before the headliner."

"I'm sorry. Look, I was being honest with you. When she first stayed with me, it was only so I could protect her from her husband. And after he was killed, she stayed away from me for weeks on the advice of her attorney. But when I couldn't talk to you and she contacted me after the smoke cleared, well, I was lonely and we started hanging out together and, I guess you can fill in the rest."

I expected tears, anger, some kind of reaction. But Jaime seemed unfazed by the news. "So you think that this Charlene is the one?"

Stone couldn't have asked the question more dispassionately. It was asked more out of curiosity than concern.

"I don't know. Things have been pretty rocky with her of late."

"I'll quote you a song. *You don't like weak women, you get bored so quick. And you don't like strong women, because they're hip to your tricks*."

"Joni Mitchell. Very good, kid. Song came out way before you were born."

"Oldies but goodies radio."

"So, are you seeing anyone?" I wasn't sure I wanted to know, to imagine Jaime with another man, but I had no claim on her and I had just told her about another woman in my life.

"No one in particular. I've been dating, but all very casual."

I read between the lines on that one. She was out there and available, but hadn't found anyone yet. With all she had going for her, it was only a matter of time.

"So where do we go from here? I still care about you Jaime, but I'm not leaving Charlotte, and it sounds like you have your hands full here and in Hollywood. So is this it for us?"

No tears still, no anger. "Sounds like that's where we're headed, doesn't it?"

"Was it just bad timing? If I had told you about her situation before Charlene moved in, would it have made a difference?"

She drummed her fingers on the top of her head, intertwined around a lock of her auburn mane. "Back then, maybe. You know, Riley, I've never caught you in an out and out lie. All your deceptions are lies of omissions. Things you don't tell me because you think I won't like them. The thing is though, that if I find them out on my own, I draw my own conclusions. You don't get the benefit of explaining beforehand. And maybe my weakness is that I don't like confrontation. So I simmer inside until I reach hard answers."

"Again, for the record, when Charlene first moved in, it was platonic. Nothing happened."

"Riley King, I don't want to lose touch. I hope that you can call me if you need something, same with me. And whenever you're up here and I'm free, dinner would be nice. And if I ever have business in Charlotte, you'll be the first person I call."

"That sounds awfully final."

"Nothing's final. That's just the way it is now. I can't predict the future."

She looked at me with those green eyes, expecting an answer but I had nothing. She was so much gentler than Charlene, so much easier to talk to. No rough edges, no past life that I needed to overlook.

She said, "I have to get back to work. At this point in my life, the business comes first."

She arose, touched my shoulder gently, and walked away, maybe out of my life.

FIFTY FIVE

I drove south down the Parkway, feeling sad. There hadn't been harsh words, just a solemn realization on both our parts that what might have been might never be. Victims of circumstance, as the Bard put it. Or was it Billy Joel?

I spent most of the ride back to the shore revisiting my time with Jaime, especially since I'd made the journey on this road often during the days we shared. My reverie was interrupted by a call on my cell from an unknown 732 number on the Audi's center display screen.

It was Stone.

"Hey, Riles."

"Where are you calling from, Ricky? I don't recognize the number."

"A friend's place. I turned off my cell. I don't want the cops to be able to track me or listen in."

"And why would they?"

"They were waiting for me when I got off the air today. Two plainclothes guys in the parking lot."

"Was McCullough one of them?"

"No. But he must have sent them if he's lead on this case."

Was this a game-changer or was Flint merely covering his bases? "So what did they want? Did they take you in?"

"Not downtown. They just asked if I'd mind answering a few questions and we sat in their car. Whole thing took ten minutes but they wanted to know where I was the night Stevie was killed."

Ten minutes constitutes a pro-forma interview. If they really considered Rick a person of interest, they would have hauled him in and made him wait an hour before grilling him. I told him as much.

He said, "So Riles, you think they just need to say they followed all their leads, if it comes up at a trial, as opposed to honing in on just Ted. I hope you're right. What should I do? Hire an attorney?"

"That's up to you. Usually the good ones are going to want a substantial retainer. I really don't think the cops are serious about you unless McCullough's feeding me misdirection but that's not his style. If it was me, I'd hold off on a lawyer for now, but again, it's your call. Actually, I was hoping you could do a little legwork. Nothing too demanding, but if you're afraid of the fuzz, I'll do it myself."

"Rick Stone knows no fear, compadre. What do you need?"

"The whole deal on the wine doesn't add up. Ted claims she had already opened the bottle before he arrived. But he says he didn't send her any wine, period. If he did, that would require premeditation and far as we know, he had no motive to kill her at that point. The argument about Charlene was spontaneous. I could picture him getting angry and killing her out of passion after reading your email, but how does drugged wine play into that?"

Stone pondered that for a beat. "Unless he planned this whole thing from the beginning, all the way back to when he asked you to find these women. One was already dead, one you wouldn't divulge her whereabouts, so he settles on killing the only one left. But then why go through the charade of getting back together and planning a wedding? Why not just kill her straightaway after she agreed to meet with him?"

I said, "Stevie wasn't hard to find at all. Why even hire me when he could have just found someone willing to knock her off for ten grand if that was his game all along? Now the police have a whole resume of bad behavior towards women pointing at him. Makes no sense."

"So you don't think he did it?"

"Not saying that. He's still the most logical suspect. I saw some of his temper earlier that day. Maybe he was under a lot of stress with this wedding and all and just cracked when she went into a hissy fit over Charlene not performing at the reception. Or if he had opened your email and confronted her about sleeping with you. But that still leaves the wine."

Stone said, "I should have listened to you and let sleeping dogs lie. My email just makes it look worse. Maybe they were drinking spiked wine all along as an aphrodisiac?"

"From what you say about Stevie, that hardly would be necessary. Look, here's what I'd like you to do. That wine they both liked, the Silver Oak 1991. It can't be inexpensive and I don't imagine too many places stock it.

Draw a ten mile circle around the borough and see how many places have it. Then, if it's as few as I think it might be, hit them up tomorrow and see if we can find out who sent the bottle. If it wasn't Ted, it might be the real killer. I'll be back by dinner time. Got plans?"

"Another club date for the station. New joint opening in Bayville, sports bar. I think the hostess is into me."

"Contain yourself, Ricky boy. Not the best idea with everything that's going on to add to your harem. Just do what you need to and come home early. Alone."

"Yes, mom. See ya later."

McCullough had sent his guys to question Stone, but if he wanted to make a show of it, he could have done it at the station itself. Ten minutes in an unmarked car? He was only demonstrating to a jury that indeed, the prosecution had explored all other avenues. In any case, I'd try to pop by the Starlight Diner at noon tomorrow to see if my instincts were correct.

But tonight? No Stone. No leads to follow. Maybe a little pasta, and a quiet evening at Rick's watching some mindless reality show. But almost as soon as I was easing into those plans, a text on the Audi's display disrupted everything.

It was from attorney John League. Could I be at his house in Rumson at eight tonight to discuss a matter of some urgency? Directions to follow.

How could I refuse?

FIFTY SIX

Rumson, New Jersey isn't a place for the faint of heart or light of wallet. It's a small borough bordering the Raritan River, which empties into the Atlantic Ocean a few miles east. It is Brahmin horse country, rural in nature, yet within commuting distance of Manhattan. It numbered Bruce Springsteen among its affluent and celebrated residents at one time.

I expected John League's mansion to be magnificent and it didn't disappoint. The brick and stone exterior mimicked a medieval castle with parapets and towers, leaded glass windows and massive arched ironclad doors. The two acre property was surrounded by an eight foot wall and the requisite gated entry house contained a 24/7 security guard.

League might have been overdoing his precautionary measures, but it was understandable, given that he was about as popular as Ebola. He was the high priced lawyer to the stars, the stars of tabloid crime that is. He defended high profile socialites, alleged mobsters and corrupt politicians, of which there were many in New Jersey. He always managed to find some seam in the legal statutes that allowed his clients to escape the punishments they richly deserved in the court of public opinion. If Ted had asked me, I would have advised he seek different counsel, someone like Jack Furlong. In the minds of the populace, engaging League is tantamount to an admission of guilt.

On the surface, it seemed like League and McCarver were cut from the same cloth. Both tall and aristocratic, their elegantly attired presentations were superficially similar. League was a former basketball player at Princeton, the small forward successor to former senator Bill Bradley. But whereas Bradley was the champion of the little man, the Average Joe was beneath League's attention. His fees command more in one day than most of them make in a month.

After a brief Q and A at the gate, I was allowed to slowly drive the Audi up the long cobblestone pathway to the main house. League's manservant greeted me at the front door and ushered me into his master's private library, a large paneled room encased by floor to ceiling bookshelves, no doubt filled with rare first editions that League had once read cover to cover.

All this grace and elegance was mine to peruse for ten minutes until League deigned to make his appearance. The appearance he made was not only unexpected but quite at odds with the elegant surroundings. He was sweating profusely, attired only in black nylon running shorts, a tattered and torn Princeton tee shirt, and cross trainers.

He said, "Whew, what a workout. Hello. John League."

He wiped his hand on the towel draped around his neck before offering it to me. Not too many men physically dwarf me, but League had me by four inches and his imposing frame and huge hands would be a match for anyone in a dark alley.

"Riley King." His hand crushed mine. "Although *you* summoned *me* --- so I take it you know who I am."

"Yes I do, I surely do. Too bad I didn't think of it before, but you were quite the shooting guard at Georgetown a while back. I was just scrimmaging with some underclassmen from a local community college in my gym. You look like you might still be able to give them some game. Perhaps another time."

He continued to towel off, rubbing his head vigorously, which sent his three hundred dollar haircut flying askew. He didn't pat it back down; it just seemed to gradually fall into place as if on command.

"You have an indoor basketball court?" I asked.

"Only half court, I'm afraid. Shares space in the same building with the pool. I have plans with the town to expand but they have these silly ordinances regarding lot coverage. I haven't had the time to get personally involved, but if I don't get my variance soon, there will be hell to pay. Can I have Marlowe get you something, King? I've discovered a wonderful IPA brewed locally that I think you'll enjoy."

"Why not, if you're having one."

He pushed a button on some handheld device, barked out a quick order and turned his attention back to me.

I needed to get my bearings. I felt awkward and out of place, as if transported back to Downton Abbey in the twenties and not understanding the protocol. League certainly wasn't overly formal, but the trappings and extravagant display of wealth were overwhelming. League had been married to the same woman since his college days, but the house bore no feminine touch that I could see.

"So you're probably wondering why I called you here this evening, why this couldn't wait until business hours."

"In my line of work, there are no business hours."

"Exactly. Men of importance do whatever it takes, whenever it takes. Ah, Marlowe just leave the tray on my desk. Mr. King and I will serve ourselves, thank you."

Marlowe must have run track at some point because I could swear no more than two minutes had elapsed since League had proffered the beer. Just to travel from one end of the house to the other could take at least that long, not to mention producing two chilled pilsner glasses and clear long necks.

"Cheers," League toasted, handing me the glass. I prefer wine to beer these days, but this was good. I doubted the local Shop Rite kept a supply in stock.

"So, this is obviously about Ted McCarver, Mr. League."

"Call me John. Of course. The reason I wanted to speak with you is that Ted respects you and I would like you to intervene with him on a matter that I can't seem to make headway on. In fact, he's fired me over it."

FIFTY SEVEN

"**W**hy the hell would he do that?" was my question. In such distinguished company, I would have liked to have phrased it more elegantly, but I was hoping we could speak plainly and avoid legal double talk.

"We have a disagreement as to tactics. Riley, if I may call you Riley. I made my reputation by never losing a big case. Now, no one wins them all, but I am very careful about the high profile clients I take on. Even in this day and age of social media, you can disguise the little setbacks, cases you appeal and then quietly drop for a plea bargain. But the headline grabbers, like this one, I can't afford to lose."

The beer was excellent. I sipped mine slowly as he spoke, figuring he'd filibuster or at least continue his lecture. But I couldn't resist jumping in at the apparent contradiction. "Wait a minute, counselor. You said he fired you, not that you quit."

"Fired might be too strong a word. A mutual parting of the ways, instigated by his intransigence might be more precise."

"Meaning you wanted to fight down and dirty and he disagreed?"

"You get right down to it, don't you, Riley? I don't consider my tactics dirty. I don't do anything illegal.

Sometimes, I have to resort to strategies that polite society might term disagreeable, but they are effective."

"And what does this have to do with me?"

"Again, so to the point. I invited you here to enlist your aid. Ted McCarver made it clear during our conversations that he trusts your judgment. He values your expertise in these matters. He realizes that you have doubts as to his guilt and that distresses him no end."

Ted's distress over my suspicions means nothing to me. Even though I had been chasing other leads, I hadn't found one that provided even a hint of reasonable doubt. "So let me guess. You want me to convince him to go along with your plan, whatever that is."

"Essentially, it distills down to that, yes."

"And of course for me to sell him on your plan, I need to know what that plan is."

I had no intention of selling Ted on anything. But knowing the game plan could be vital to unearthing the truth. I wasn't sure that League would trust me fully with intricate details of his master strategy, so I was prepared for the abridged version that a dolt like me could grasp. The musings of a genius of his magnitude would be beyond my limited comprehension, or so I hoped to lead him to believe.

"As you undoubtedly know, one of the best ways to sway a jury is to present an equally plausible scenario to the one the prosecution is presenting. You don't have to prove someone else did it like they do in the movies, merely sow enough seeds of doubt that the jury must acquit. And although the District Attorney will attempt to winnow the prospective jurors down to those who have never heard of the case, it's almost impossible to do in this age of instant access."

"I did work for the FBI for ten years, counselor."

"I'm well aware of that. My point is that I see a promising way to exonerate Mr. McCarver, and he won't let me pursue it."

"Exonerate? As to prove that he's innocent or just get him off?"

He raised an eyebrow. "Oh, my. An idealist. Here I thought I was dealing with a hardboiled P.I. who did what it took for his clients. Your resume led me to believe that was the case. Plus the word of a client of mine you had some dealings with."

"You're referring to Tony Gazza."

"You know I can't say. But I pray we aren't at cross purposes here. My job, hopefully our job, is to spare Mr. McCarver prison time. Your comment makes me question that you don't share that goal."

"My goal is to find the real killer."

"What if I told you that I believe that Theodore Chesterfield McCarver is innocent. He has sworn to me that he didn't do it, and it was important to him that I believe that. As I said, that little fact doesn't matter to me and actually I advise my clients not to tell me whether they're guilty or not."

I needed to drop the Batman routine if I wanted to learn anything from League. "I want Ted to be innocent, okay? What I've been doing the last couple of days is to develop alternate theories. So yes, we are on the same team."

This wasn't exactly true, but I needed to know where this was headed.

"That's reassuring. So you'll speak to Ted?"

"What's your alternate theory?"

He took a long pull on the IPA. He wiped the froth from his mouth with a linen napkin that Marlowe had thoughtfully provided.

"I want to leak something to the papers. I have developed numerous contacts in the media over the years. I can orchestrate a campaign that will pressure the police to chase down my idea, so much so that I can convince a jury that he had as much motive and opportunity as Ted to kill this woman."

I knew where he was going but let him continue.

"But Riley, McCarver wouldn't hear of it. He said it would be sullying the reputation of an innocent man and that rather than have that happen, he'd be willing to pay for a crime he didn't commit. Very noble of him but also very stupid. The police would have a hard time making a case against this other man, but all we're going for is reasonable doubt. McCarver shut me down before I could start."

"Why would he do that? Does he have some special relationship with this other guy?"

Of course I knew who he was talking about. And even though I might still have trepidations about Ted, this went a long way in my book to making me believe him.

League proceeded cautiously. "Someone he worked with for years. A man in the public eye who will attract publicity on his own, as he has in the past. A fellow by the name of Rick Stone. Friend of yours, I believe."

FIFTY EIGHT

It wasn't as if there was a whole line of folks waiting to visit Ted in prison. He looked awful. As fresh and vital as he had appeared when we first encountered him at Hilton Head, it now became clear that his porcelain good looks took more than routine maintenance. Whatever regime he practiced at home was not available to him in the Ocean County lockup. Combined with stress and lack of sleep, he looked old and worn out. Of course, it was possible that the cops had located and destroyed the portrait of himself that he keeps locked away in a closet, and the aging process was catching up.

"I thought you were done with me, King," he said quietly, in lieu of his normal hail and hardy greeting.

"I never said that, Ted. You doing okay?"

"It's not exactly the Four Seasons but it's not the Bastille either. What brings you here? Any news?"

"Your former lawyer sent me actually, although his agenda and mine don't exactly coincide."

"I know what his agenda is. What's yours?"

The interrogation room was otherwise empty. There was a guard posted at the soundproof glass door. I had been thoroughly searched for weapons and contraband --- no smuggling a shiv baked into a cake. If either one of us started choking the other, a TASER would be applied to the offending party.

I said, “League told me that you fired him because he wanted to develop an alternate scenario that Stone killed Stevie, is that right?”

“That’s it essentially. He wanted to leak things to the media that would blacken Rick’s reputation and I won’t allow that.”

“Why not? You’re sure he didn’t do it?” I was playing Devil’s Advocate.

“Yes.”

“Why? Because *you* did it?” I said.

Ted looked lost. His head bobbed back and forth a few times before he answered. “No, I didn’t do it. But I’d rather be convicted of it than besmirch Stone. He had nothing to do with this. I know the man.”

“For what it’s worth, he knows you too and believes you. But I have to ask: Rick sent you an email the night of the murder. Did you see it?”

“Not that night. But yes, I did see it on my phone the next day.”

“This is the phone you allegedly lost?”

“The very one.”

“And I don’t suppose you know of its whereabouts now that you’ve had time to think about it?”

He remained silent. League, as an officer of the court, couldn't instruct Ted to suppress evidence. But the veteran counselor had ways to communicate his desires without spelling it out. I was sure that both he and Ted knew where the phone was.

I said, "I suppose that you're aware that your non cooperation with the phone could be interpreted as you trying to cover up your motivation for killing Stevie. Easy dots for the cops to connect. You come in, enraged upon learning that your fiancée slept with your friend, and in a fit of anger, you shoot her."

"That would make sense if I hadn't known for weeks that Stone and Stevie had a brief encounter."

THAT was breaking news and it opened up a whole new set of questions. "How did you know that?"

Ted hesitated for a moment before replying. "I had hoped to keep everything that was between us private, but now that she's gone, I suppose it doesn't matter. That first weekend at Hilton Head, we made a pact. Let it all hang out was how she put it. I told her about Mary Chesterton. My ex-wife and her wish to avoid contact with me, even to this day. The fact I'd been seeing Doctor Mills for years. In turn, she told me about Rick. And a few others."

"Do you have anything to back that up?"

"No. We never exchanged letters about it or anything in writing. Unless she kept a diary and chronicled it, there's no proof."

I scratched my head. "So let me understand this: you knew that one of your best friends had slept with the love of your life and you never confronted him on it? And he was your first call when you found her body?"

Ted was placid, almost as if he was on some drug that took away his highs and lows. "She told me that she instigated the whole thing with Rick. Revenge against me mostly. But she felt lousy about it and broke it off. In a strange way, it made her realize that she still cared for me. She was there for the taking, all I had to do was reach out. Of course, I didn't know that. But I do know you're blaming yourself for what happened to her, that's why you're here now. You're conflating this with those other women that you feel responsible for. But you're blameless on this one. A heartfelt letter from me would have enticed her back."

Ted was offering me absolution that I hadn't asked for. My cynical side said that he thought by expunging my guilt, it would cause me to work harder to clear him. And by refusing to let League go after Stone, it sure made him look noble.

I said, "You know that the police have you pegged as the only logical suspect. They've asked Rick a few questions so that it looks like they didn't just center on you and ignore other possibilities. And at trial, any good defense attorney will go that route --- implicating Rick and anyone else who might have had motive and opportunity."

"Not if I forbid it."

"Then you're practically guaranteeing you'll be convicted."

"If that's the case, so be it. I want to find the real killer more than anything. If you need manpower, I'll hire others, however many you need. But I won't allow an innocent person to be dragged into this and his reputation destroyed, just to save my skin. Without Stevie in my life, what good is it anyway?"

It sounded like Ted had accepted his inevitable conviction. I brought up Jaime's idea. "Let's say hypothetically that you were the target, not Stevie. Does anyone have a reason to come after you?"

"I thought of that. I've been racking my brain. In business, I've fired a few folks over the years, but obviously none since I've been retired. And I always was pretty generous with the severance, even when I didn't have to be. And I never screwed anyone on a one-sided business deal. I always left something on the table for the other guy."

"Anything you picked up at distress prices, like WJOK? Could the sellers who sold it to you resent how well you did with it?"

"The old man died years ago. And if he invested the money he got from the sale wisely, his heirs would have made out well too."

This was turning into a blind alley. "I've been searching for Stevie's enemies the last couple of days. I can't find any. That's the problem. Nobody other than you had any reason at all to kill her. Police find the simplest solution is the right one almost all the time."

"*Almost* all the time. But not in this case. And I didn't have a reason to kill her. I wanted to spend the rest of my life with her."

I was leaving no more enlightened than when I arrived. I said, "Before I go, let me clear one other thing up. Did you send her that bottle of wine with a note that night? Or any other time?"

"No. Never. I brought wine with me a few times. She wasn't really appreciative of fine wine. She was just as happy with a ten dollar bottle. She thought that Silver Oak was no better than Fourteen Hands."

"Was there a particular wine store in Toms River you used to buy Silver Oak?"

"Not in the last few years. Lately I've gotten got my wine through the restaurant down on the island."

"I have Stone checking the places around here who sell it. There aren't many. If that wine wasn't from you, whoever bought it might be the killer."

Ted stood up. "I'm painfully aware that you still harbor suspicions that I did this. But King, I appreciate everything you're doing. I know that you won't take my money now, but if you can get justice for Stevie, there isn't anything of mine that won't also be yours."

"I'll exhaust all the other possibilities but like I've said all along, if the trail stops with you, that's where I'll go."

"That's all I can ask. Thank you for all you've done and all you're doing. I hope I can earn your trust and respect again."

He extended his hand and after a moment, I took it. One handshake didn't mean we were BFFs, although I was starting to believe more in his innocence. A guilty man who feared incarceration wouldn't shackle his lawyer's best line of defense.

That said, Rebecca's warnings still echoed in my mind. The man thought in three dimensions. He was a silver tongued devil who could convince you that the ocean isn't wet.

His words of gratitude were touching. Although I had to remind myself that the man who sold me the Audi had given me the same spiel.

FIFTY NINE

Stone had left a voicemail while I was in with Ted. I called him back. He'd visited the four wine merchants who stocked Silver Oak in the Toms River area and none of them had a record of sending a bottle to Ted's condo. Nobody recalled doing so off the books, either. The wad of twenties Stone flashed convinced him they were telling the truth.

Rick had been allied with Ted in the radio business for almost thirty years. He had never heard Ted refer to a jealous rival or a disgruntled employee. He allowed that most people were hesitant to speak ill of McCarver in his presence, given their friendship, but he knew the industry well enough that if Ted did have enemies, he'd at least be aware of them. No one came to mind.

Stone suggested I call Michael Harrison, a man who knows more about talk radio than anyone else on the planet. He publishes a daily magazine catering to that industry and is tuned in to all the dirt. After I used Stone's name as an introduction, he confirmed what Rick had told me. Harrison assured me that Ted's standing in the industry had been beyond reproach until now. Everyone he spoke to was pulling for his vindication.

I was near the end of the road. If McCarver wasn't guilty, who else had reason to kill Stevie Perry? Or who might have wanted *him* gone? He had no lethal enemies in his business career. The only misgivings he had in his life was the way he had treated women, three in particular.

Fictional detectives' credo: *When you have eliminated the possible, that which remains, however improbable, must hold the answer*. I think Arthur Conan Doyle had Sherlock Holmes saying something along those lines. Of the three women who Ted had wronged, Stevie was the victim and Mary was dead. That left only one --- Rebecca Hunter.

She was living a peaceful, quiet life on a Virginia farm. My visit had upset her greatly. Her world would be rocked if Ted McCarver were to become part of it again. Her husband worked for the government in an unknown capacity. Was it possible that he sought to protect his wife by eliminating Ted, and that Stevie just happened to be in the way? And wasn't it convenient that if convicted, Ted would likely spend the rest of his days locked away where he posed no threat to Rebecca/Gretchen?

It was a stretch but at this point, but it was all I had. I could see no reason to stay in New Jersey rummaging around. I needed a break and I needed to give Charlene some attention. By taking the western route back to Charlotte, I would pass within a few miles of Wintergreen and the Dew Drop Inn. I could spend time while driving thinking about exactly how to confront Rebecca. Was it possible that her hubby Douglas had acted on his own without her knowledge?

To give Rick something to do, I would ask him to widen his search of wine shops from a ten to a fifty mile radius of Toms River. He was on the air and I didn't want to distract him with a text or call, so I ran by his house, left a note, picked up my things and headed south.

Several times during the five hour ride, I changed my mind about even following through on this off-the-wall hunch. It would be incredibly proactive to kill someone who merely wanted to contact his ex-wife to apologize for his treatment of her. Rebecca was deathly afraid of the man, and fear could cause one to overreact to a perceived threat. And her husband was dangerous, according to Logan.

As I passed through lower Pennsylvania, I called my old FBI buddy. Logan had been guarded about Douglas in our original conversation, but now that I had a theory about the crime that had a modicum of credibility, he might be more forthcoming.

"Oh, Danny boy, the pipes, the pipes are calling." I approximated an Irish tenor admirably.

"Riley King. Twice in less than a month. You missing your old pal Logan? Want to come back to the bureau?"

"Don't worry, I'm not after your job. No, I just need to ask you about something you eluded to when last we spoke."

I filled him in on the McCarver case, which was on his distant radar screen but no more than that. A tabloid murder in Jersey might be of passing interest to him as a super Federal crime stopper, but he had larger matters of concern as agent-in-charge in New York.

"Sounds like they have a decent case on your boy," he said when I was finished. "It would help if they had the weapon. He was there, they argued and he discovered the body. All circumstantial. They'll try to build a psychological case against him, or at least I would. Find other instances of abuse of women. You said his father killed his mother by deliberately ramming their plane into a mountainside. They'll try like hell to make that admissible."

"I'll admit, a lot of things point in his direction. But as you said, circumstantial. Like the wine. They can't prove he spiked it. He can't prove he didn't. They can't prove he just found out about Stone's little fling with Stevie. He can't prove that he knew about it all along. Sounds like stalemate to me."

"Hey Riles, don't dismiss the politics of the thing. Imagine that you're a small county D.A.. McCarver would be a big pelt. You can't afford to look incompetent by not arresting somebody. Even if you lose in court, you can blame it on a tone deaf jury. But for a politico to be clueless as to who did it, that's unacceptable when you are up for reelection every few years."

I crossed the Mason-Dixon line into the ten mile sliver of Maryland I had to traverse before reaching the West Virginia border, followed by Virginia forty minutes later.

"That's why I washed out of the bureau. Couldn't stand the politics. No offense. You've learned how to play that game and bravo for you. But I've always hated it. Anyway, let me tell you why I called."

"Don't tell me you've written a Broadway musical based on my adventures. And Charlene will star in it."

"Someday, maybe. But the title *Broke Down Piece of Man* is already taken."

"What a quipster you are. Here, you're calling for a favor and you insult me. No wonder you stink at politics."

"Seriously, Dan. I'm now tracing people who might hate McCarver enough to harm him and I've narrowed it down to his ex-wife. It's a long shot, but you had warned me about steering clear of her husband. That he might be dangerous."

"Uh-huh."

"Dangerous how? Is he CIA? Does he do contract work of a terminal nature for them?"

"Riley, I love you, man. But do you realize what you're asking? You know that Scooter Libby needed a presidential pardon to avoid prison for exposing Valerie Plame as a covert op? And he had better connections than yours truly. You know I can't tell you that."

"I understand. But you did say dangerous. Would that danger would be physical or something that could affect my financial or mental well being? That vague enough?"

"Can't say that either." The line went quiet for a second. "Hey Riles, did hear that Olivia Newton-John is touring again? Brave woman, with that breast cancer and all. I loved her stuff back in the eighties. I hope she comes to New York and does some of her big hits from back then. Look, I got to go. Sorry I couldn't be of more help."

With that he was gone. Logan was a weird cat. He was into Broadway musicals big-time, but why bring up Olivia Newton-John out of nowhere? She was in the movie *Grease,* which I hated and he had once told me he liked. I admit to thinking she was hot in those tight leather pants but her music always left me flat. Except for that Peter Allen tune she did. *I Honestly Love You*. I kind of liked that one, but it was not on my personal playlist.

In any case, Logan had been of no help. That damn Peter Allen tune kept echoing around in my head and I couldn't shake it. What was it called, an earworm? Maybe if I heard it once, it would go away. I used the Audi's voice command to bring up *Spotify*, and told it to play some Olivia Newton-John. A miracle of modern technology, put to trivial purpose.

The first song it streamed told me all I needed to know.

Logan. No wonder he had risen in the bureau where I had stalled.

I hated the song but his message came through, loud and clear.

Let's Get Physical.

SIXTY

Douglas Hunter didn't fit the Hollywood profile of a CIA field agent tasked with wet work. James Bond he was not. He was bald, unattractive, and since Rebecca was nearing seventy, he had to be within striking distance of that vintage.

Logan didn't tell me if Douglas Hunter was active or had retired. He didn't say if the guy was the agency's go-to guy or just someone who had eliminated an annoyance once upon a time. All I had was a musical clue that Hunter was someone I had to be careful with, since he might be a paid government assassin. I knew nothing of his methods or temperament.

I arrived at Wintergreen in the early evening, just before dusk. Not wanting to telegraph my arrival, I parked off road and hiked the long winding drive to the main house. There were several cars in the unpaved lot in front of the building, guests who wanted to catch the last of the fall colors on the mountain before the trees were denuded for the winter. The old Ford Explorer that I had seen Douglas Hunter drive away in was there, so I assumed he was in residence.

I used the failing light as best I could to disguise my approach, ducking behind foliage as much as possible. The horses were still out in the meadow. Someone had to lead them to the stables for the night and I figured that someone might be Doug. I unlatched the gate that contained the stalls for the animals, and waited with the Beretta in my jacket pocket.

I didn't have to wait long. A figure emerged from the bed and breakfast and made his way toward the horses. With practiced boredom, he shooed them into their shelter. I held off until he had stabled the last one, a proud white Arabian that he called Aristotle. I'd confront him, gun in hand, before he could return to the house. That was my plan.

But my improvised strategy was disrupted by the sensation of cold steel pressed against my neck from behind. In the few seconds I had lost sight of Douglas Hunter, he had somehow maneuvered his way around me. He rid me of my weapon before shoving me around to face him.

"King, wasn't it? I could ask what you're doing here, but I already know."

"Do you, now? I've always been partial to horses. My dad promised me a pony once but I settled for a dog."

"Right. I suppose you were hoping my wife would be putting the horses down for the night so you could cap her and be on your way. Lucky for us it wasn't her night."

"Wait a minute. You think I'm here for your wife? You couldn't be more wrong. I'm here for you."

That seemed to throw him for a moment. "So your boss's plan was to eliminate the competition for Rebecca? As if that would endear him to her."

It was pretty clear that he thought I was here to kill one or both of them at Ted's behest. The Beretta reinforced the scenario. I'd find out soon enough if Doug was a cold blooded assassin or man capable of finding other solutions.

"I'm not working for Ted McCarver, if that's what you think. Are you aware that he's in jail now, accused of killing his fiancée?"

"Of course I'm aware. Ever since you were here the first time, I've been aware of his every movement. No doubt that's why he sent you to finish the job. He killed one of his women, and sent you to eliminate another. Or maybe you did the other one, as well."

"No, I was liking you for that one. Come off it, Hunter, I know what you do. I was FBI for ten years. We have some common background."

"I'd be very surprised if you know anything about me. It seems I have a couple of alternatives here. I could shoot you right now. You're trespassing on our land with a loaded weapon. I doubt anyone other than your boss knows you're here and he isn't likely to fess up to that fact. There's lots of acreage on this farm that's as cold and dark at night as it was two hundred years ago."

I said, "You said you have two alternatives. I'm not in love with the first one, what's the other choice?"

"Cut the wiseass PI chatter, King. I'm serious. My wife is the most important thing in my life and I'll do whatever it takes to defend her. I could just call the local authorities, have you arrested and tip them off that this is all tied to a murder case in New Jersey. Doing that would expose Rebecca to unwanted scrutiny and if somehow your boss beats the rap, he'd know where we live. So sadly for you, the first alternative might be the best."

All the while we were talking, I was calculating. Angles, velocity, anything that could disarm Douglas and give me a fighting chance out of this. He was older than I. Maybe he was a trained killer, but maybe I was a tad quicker. I couldn't envision coming out of this unscathed, but possibly I could emerge on the right side of the grass if my reflexes were up to it.

Or maybe this man wasn't impervious to reason and I could talk my way out. Worth a try. "I got involved in this because Ted McCarver was my best friend's boss and needed help. His plan was to give the three women in his life that he had wronged a million dollars each as a way of apologizing. The first was a woman on Long Island who had already died. The third was the woman that Ted is accused of killing. The second is your wife. As part of my deal with her, I promised not to tell Ted where you guys live and he accepted that without protest. I'm now working under the theory that whoever killed Stephanie Perry was really after Ted. The only person who might have the slightest motive for doing that is your wife. And when I learned what you did for a living, it made me think that you might be responsible. You're kind of proving that now."

"And if I *was* responsible, smart guy, you just signed your own death warrant. But I didn't kill this Perry woman. Up until ten minutes ago, I believed that Ted McCarver no longer posed a threat to Rebecca."

"Then why were you tracking his every move?"

"I wasn't about to let my instincts compromise her safety. In my line of work, you leave no stone unturned. You see, a few days after you came here the first time, I visited McCarver."

"He never told me that."

"That's because he didn't know. I flew down to Hilton Head and stalked him for a day or so. I did my research. Found out he was a fan of fine wine. Just so happens that I am a bit of an oenologist as well. So when he went to that restaurant that he has an interest in, I managed to sidle up to him at the bar and we started comparing our favorites. I found myself almost liking the guy, despite the things he did to my wife. Well, by the end of the evening, we were telling each other stories. Mine were fictional, I believe his were real. I managed to extract that he was sad his ex-wife hated him but that he respected her decision to remain hidden. I came home convinced that he posed no threat."

"What if he had posed a threat? What would you have done then?"

"Hard to say. I might have tried warning him that if he ever came near Rebecca, I'd kill him. Or worst case, make a preemptive strike."

I began to see a way out. "If what you've just told me is true, let me propose a bloodless solution. I can get someone in to see Ted tomorrow morning and if he backs up your story, I can cross you off the list."

He laughed off my suggestion. "You seem to forget who's holding the gun here, friend. If I let you go now, how can I be sure that you won't come back to do your business later?"

"The name Dan Logan mean anything to you?"

"The FBI guy who worked the terrorist case on the Jersey docks a few years back. Yeah, everybody in my line of work knows that story. He's a legend."

"His private number is on my speed dial. He'll back up everything I've been telling you."

"Call him."

I did. Dan answered right away. I handed the phone to Hunter. He asked a couple of questions to verify Dan's identity and then apprised him of the situation. Within two minutes, he lowered the gun and handed me the phone.

"King, I never want to see your face again. FYI, there are people in this world who know me by other names who would be very interested in paying me a visit. Be advised, I have cameras all around the perimeter. I saw you coming a mile away. I normally don't put the horses away with a gun in my pocket."

"So you're not the reincarnation of Hopalong Cassidy?"

"Get your ass out of here and thank your stars that your friend Logan backed up your story. And if you ever tell McCarver about Rebecca, I'll find out and we won't be having a conversation, unless it's your last words while bleeding out. Understood?"

"If your story checks out, we're done. But if not, you and I may meet again."

"Don't press your luck. Out. Now."

For once in my life, I took someone else's advice.

SIXTY ONE

As much as I dreaded driving six hours over mountainous terrain at night, especially through the treacherous parting in the Appalachians known as Fancy Gap, I needed to sleep in my own bed. Darkness had already descended when I pulled out of Wintergreen, and dense fog was a common companion after nightfall.

I called Logan to thank him and he shunted me off. He was headed to the theater with his fiancée, but said that we were in for a long conversation in the very near future. I wasn't looking forward to the lecture I'd be getting, but it was a small price to pay for his intervention with Hunter.

Next up was Stone, who was on his way to a Thursday Night Football club night for WJOK and no doubt a rendezvous with any winsome young filly who caught his fancy.

I said, "Hey Stone, what's up?"

"Where the hell are you? I came home expecting to see your ugly mug and all I get is a note? I feel jilted."

"I saw Ted this morning and it just didn't make sense for me to stay in Jersey spinning my wheels." I explained how I'd confronted Douglas Hunter, casually mentioning my close call with a log grinder. "So what I need you to do is visit Ted in the morning and see if the Hunter story checks out. See if he remembers talking wine, women and song with a stranger down in Hilton Head recently."

"I can do that."

"Great. One thing other you should know about Ted. He claims that he's known about your little affair with Stevie for some time now. He says that she told him about it that first weekend when they reunited. So whether he opened your email or not the night of the murder, he says that it wasn't an issue."

I could hear him breathing on the other end but he didn't say anything. "Rick?"

"I'm here. I'm just taking it all in. I mean, I talked to him several times after that weekend and he never said anything about it. I would have thought that he'd at least mention it, even if it was to say that he understood and was cool with it. But he never said a word."

"That's the problem with so much of his story. It's 'he said, she said' and she's not around to tell her side. I know, it's not like many guys are marrying virgins these days. You have to put it out of your mind that your woman has been around the block a few times. Leave the past in the past. God knows women have had to do that with men for centuries."

I didn't expect that Stone would notice the reproach in my tone and he didn't disappoint. And I certainly was conscious that my little spiel applied to my current live-in, big time.

Stone said, "Yeah, but it's one thing to accept that your bride-to-be has been with a few faceless lovers, but another when one of them is a good friend. If I found out you were porking Lisa Tillman after we broke up, I'd be pretty pissed at you."

"Now that you mention it.... No actually, no worries on that score. It's weird, kind of like Stevie and Ted had an EST session that weekend the way he describes it. They both laid all their cards on the table, confessed all their sins to each other. Swore that there would be no secrets between them. Good luck with that. I'm trying to get there with Charlene, but it's hard. I can't help but thinking there are some things that she's better off not knowing."

"You headed home tonight?"

"Hopefully, if I don't run over the guardrail at Fancy Gap. That area scares the hell out of me. There's a sheer drop off of a thousand feet just off the highway."

"Driven it many times visiting you. Take it slow. I'll call you after I talk to Ted."

"Remember, he called you right after he found the body. So either he'd already forgiven you like he says and still considers you a good friend, or he hadn't opened the email and still didn't know."

"I'll try to get a read on that. So it sounds like you still think he may have done it."

"Well, something else happened that I haven't told you about that may be a game changer. I was out before you and your little friend were up this morning."

"Oh, I was up. Early and often, with my little friend."

"Good for you, Hef. Here's something to chew on. Ted fired John League because League wanted to leak stuff to the media about you and Stevie. Ted wouldn't let him. League asked me to convince Ted otherwise. Of course I wouldn't do that. But Ted was willing to throw away a credible line of defense to protect your reputation."

"Whew. I know you think that he's some kind of mad genius but that clears away any doubt in my book. He'd be willing to take the rap for something he didn't do to protect me."

"That or he did kill her in a fit of anger and didn't want to cause any more harm to people he cared about. He's a great one for making amends. That's what started this in the first place."

"You believe what you want. I *don't stop believing*. I'm going to do whatever I can to help him."

"I'd expect nothing less. But don't forget, I came close to becoming horse feed tonight trying to find an alternative killer. I just have to admit, there's no one else with motive and opportunity. So unless this was some random act or Stevie had some secret enemy that no one knows about, everything points to Ted."

He sniffed. "I know that. I just can't believe it and I never will, even if they find a smoking gun. The guy just doesn't have it in him."

We said our goodbyes and I drove on down I-81 toward home. So far the night was clear and cool --- the fog wouldn't set in until morning. Passing Roanoke, I switched from the Classic Vinyl channel on Sirius to the football game, involving two AFC South teams I had little interest in. It was just white noise to distract me from my trepidation.

The game was tedious and there were more commercial breaks than action, or so it seemed. The ads seemed misdirected --- lots of them were aimed at women who I wouldn't think were the target audience. I'd mentioned this once to Stone and he told me that a lot of the spots were leftover network ads or make-goods that were thrown in when they couldn't sell out availabilities to specific sponsors. There was a particularly annoying one for a national flower delivery service that ran in almost every break. I guess it was aimed at the average schmuck who wanted to make up for creating a football widow Sunday, Monday and now Thursday nights.

Something in the ad triggered an idea. The flowers came with a free personalized gift card.

The wine that had been delivered to Stevie had come with a card. McCullough had told me what the card had said, but not if they tied the handwriting to Ted. I knew from my time with the feds that even though television makes testimony from handwriting experts seem unimpeachable, it rarely is. I dialed McCullough's cell and he picked up right away.

"Hey Flint, it's Riley King."

"Hey King, not a good time. I'm at a sports bar with some friends. We're unwinding, watching the game."

"No problem, just a quick question. Was the note card that came with the wine handwritten?"

"No. Computer printed and signed. Lucida Handwriting was the font. No prints if that's your next question."

"Would it be possible to email me a picture of that card?"

"I really shouldn't but it'll be available in discovery anyway. Why?"

I could barely hear him over the noise in the bar. I wondered if it was the same one Rick was at. "Just a thought."

"Look I can't talk now. I'll send you a jpeg of the card. I guess it can't hurt. Just don't tell anyone where you got it or my ass is grass. Look, I gotta go. You'll have it in the morning."

Wine stores that stocked Silver Oak 1991 were rare. Stores in New Jersey that also carried that particular gift card, perhaps even rarer. Straws like this were all I had to grasp.

SIXTY TWO

It was after one when I arrived home. Charlene was sound asleep and I knew she wouldn't be alone. I was a little surprised that her bedmate didn't get up to greet me, but the steady thump, thump, thump of his tail on the mattress assured me that he was happy his master had returned. Although I wasn't sure who was the master in this case, since I attended to his every need whenever and wherever he chose.

I slipped beneath the covers, gently easing Bosco aside. Charlene issued a sigh to acknowledge my presence. Probably had popped a Benadryl or something stronger. Although worn out from the trip, I didn't doze off until two.

I usually beat Char to the breakfast table by a good half hour. This morning, I found her fully dressed and deep into the Observer by the time I rolled out. When she looked up from the newspaper, her face was streaked with tears.

"What's wrong, honey? Did somebody you know die?"

"Not somebody. Just my career."

She pointed to a headline in the entertainment section. It announced a Christmas Tour, sponsored by the Cirrus Radio group, and her name was not among the artists slated to perform. Instead, a twenty year old named

Joanna Black was listed as the opening act, singing her soon-to-be hit rendition of an old holiday classic by The Band.

"What happened? I thought this was a done deal," I said.

"So did I. But when Harrison Mitchell didn't return my calls, I suspected there was a problem. I just wish the bastard had the balls to tell me."

Dirty business. I hated the idea that Charlene had to subject herself to these piranha infested waters. I learned early on in private practice that when a potential client doesn't book you after the initial pitch, you might extend the courtesy of one attempt to reach them and if that fails, assume that they've 'decided to go in another direction.' Even the most polite people hate to say no. They draw matters out, hoping that you'll get the message without them having to be the bearer of bad news.

The trick is separating the tire-kickers from the serious buyers early enough so that you don't waste each others' time. Deadlines help. Car dealers are loath to let you walk out the door without a signed contract and a deposit. If someone balks at turning over a modest retainer, even when they are assured that it will be refunded if the deal falls through, I run the other way.

This was not the time to remind Charlene of my business rules. She needed support and sympathy.

"Bastards. Well, babe, there will be other tours, ones that might actually pay you something. You want me to talk to this Mitchell guy?"

"Why? So you can muscle me back onto the tour? I want it on my terms or not at all. I would have thought you knew that about me by now."

I let her flare of anger pass. I tried to double up without piling on. "I understand. If there is anything I can do, let me know. Even if you just need to vent."

"This morning I'll just return the clothes I bought for the tour. Even if there is another one someday, it won't be until late spring at the earliest."

"Up to you. Although I hope you'll keep that Catholic schoolgirl outfit. I can think of other places you can wear it."

She punched my arm, hard enough to hurt and went back to the bedroom to change.

With the day off to a lousy start, I took coffee into my home office and booted up the computer. McCullough had been in at 5:30 a.m. and had dutifully sent me a hi-res jpeg of the note card, including a quick précis on the watermark, weight of the stock and brightness level. Using his parameters, it took me less than ten minutes to find the distributor. A couple of phone calls and another search narrowed it down to ten wine shops within a fifty mile radius that used that particular card. Several more calls, weaning out the ones that didn't stock Silver Oak 1991, narrowed it down to one.

Mulligan's on Long Beach Island.

God, I'm good. Or lucky. Or both. I caught Stone right before he went on the air.

"Hey, Ricky boy, did you see Ted this morning?"

"Yeah, I did. Where are you?"

I said, "Back home. What did he say? Did he remember the wine rap with the stranger?"

"He did. He couldn't recall specifics, because he drank much more than normal that night. He really hit it off with the guy."

Douglas Hunter was a real pro. He'd disguised the contempt he must have felt for Ted, knowing what he did about the spousal abuse. He maintained discipline to get the information he sought. He probably drank less than half of what Ted did, staying sober so he could steer the conversation toward his objective. The potted plant next to him must still be soused.

"You didn't tell him who the guy was, did you?"

"Of course not. I learned my lesson after I sent that email you told me not to. I'm working hard at making up for it. I'll hit all those wine shops after work."

"Well, I come bearing good news about how hard you'll need to work. After you get done with that cush job knocking the Jets. There's only one you need to visit today." I told him about my search and how a visit to Long Beach Island was in the cards.

"An hour and change round trip. Not bad. Today's actually pretty mild up here. Maybe still a few bikinis on the beach in Surf City. You know, where there are *two girls for every boy.*"

"Bored with Cindy, already?"

"Variety. The spice of life."

"Uh huh. Well, since you brought up your licentious habits, did Ted say anything about you and Stevie?"

"Not a word. He didn't bring it up and he had plenty of openings. He did want to know why I was asking about the guy he met at Hilton Head. I told him that you were just casting a wide net and wanted to know anyone else who knew about his wine preferences."

"Anyone of the millions with access to the station's Facebook page. I warned you guys about putting too much private information up. Even something that seems innocuous like his favorite wine, might be something used against him."

"Check. But Riley, I did I bring up my fling with Stevie. I was pretty tense but I was amazed at how cool he was. More than ever, makes me think he didn't kill her. Look, I'm on the air in a few. I'll call you from Mulligan's if I find anything."

"Call either way. Thanks."

My next call was one I had said I wouldn't make. I called Darius Rucker and explained what had happened with Charlene. Although he wasn't on the Christmas tour, he knew the agent Harrison Mitchell and told me to sit tight for a few minutes. True to his word, he called back and gave me Mitchell's private number and said that he'd be expecting my call. I thanked him and made a note to send a little something his way, although I didn't think the usual Wolferman's basket would suffice.

"Harrison Mitchell. Riley King."

"Hey, King. You have some pretty heavy pals, don't you?"

"Black guy making it in the country music biz has to have some solid connections, in addition to a ton of talent."

"I wasn't referring to Hootie. I meant the big shots at Cirrus radio. They could buy and sell him."

I came prepared. "Blowfish had the sixteenth bestselling album of all time, FYI. But this isn't about me and my friends. This is about Charlene. She was convinced that you were booking her on that Christmas tour and today she reads in the paper that you're using someone else."

"That's right. Joanna Black is hot now. Kids love her too, so she crosses over."

"I'm not going to argue talent with you. I just want to know why you told Charlene she was in and then bounced her without so much as a phone call. Pretty low. Is that the way you do business?"

I knew why he didn't call. I wasn't going to change the way he conducted his affairs. He'd been at it for decades and had made a good living at it. The best I could hope for was to guilt him into booking Charlene for something else.

"I'm taking this call as a courtesy. You get abusive and I don't give a flying fuck who you know, I'm hanging up. You want the truth I'll give it to you, but I'm telling you upfront, you ain't gonna like it."

"I didn't call for some bullshit story. I want to know what happened."

He said, "Fair enough, chump. This ain't like the old days when you could break a new artist because you had a deejay friend who would spread the word if he liked the beat. Them days is gone. Now these big radio companies see the writing on the wall --- they know they're dying, so they're milking it for every last dollar. You want airplay, you pay for it."

I'd worked some payola cases with the bureau ages ago. I knew that play for pay wasn't illegal like most people think. It is only against the law if it isn't divulged. Big radio groups now are lobbying to allow them to accept money if they disclose it on their website. That way they can bury the language in some boilerplate that nobody actually reads. A lot more snarky than confessing on the air, even if the disclosures are buried in commercial clusters late at night.

"I know that. So why did you book Charlene in the first place and then withdraw it?"

"You see, a man named Ted McCarver paid Cirrus beaucoup bucks to get her on this tour. But the aforementioned McCarver is currently cooling his heels in the clink for offing his girlfriend. The radio folks didn't need the heat and asked out. Black's people jumped right in with even more. You really want me to tell your girlfriend that's how it worked?"

That explained why Ted was so angry with me when I told him Charlene wouldn't play his wedding. I had no idea how much money "beaucoup bucks" constituted, but a minimum of six figures sounded right. Gone were the days when talent ruled. Now, you needed to convince a wealthy patron that you have what it takes to make it and that's how you get on the radio. Was it any different than when Charlene had to sleep with record execs to get airplay? Just different currency, I suppose.

Leveraging Mitchell to make things right wasn't going to work. Maybe I could appeal to whatever humanity he had left and get his honest assessment of Charlene's talents, as if it mattered to anyone else. It did to me.

I asked and he answered. "She's not bad looking for an older woman. Still got the pins to carry it off. Her pipes aren't bad, but nothing a few dozen others can't match. This Broadway idea of hers would only appeal to ancient drag queens. Demos skew too old on that shit. I suppose with the right material, she could open for somebody. Problem is, the hot writers are going to give their shit to someone younger and already established. She needs to come up with great tunes of her own You wanted my take, asshole. You got it."

I hung up. And took a shower to wash away the stench.

SIXTY THREE

I spent some time on the computer, answering emails, accepting a couple of small jobs, turning down a few more. Charlene was gone, returning her outfits. As much as I wanted to be there for her, she opted to deal with her disappointment alone. Eventually, the pain of losing the tour would come out and she'd vent her frustration, but she wasn't ready for that yet.

All I could do was encourage her to work on new original material, which she was finding difficult. They say that happy artists are the least productive, that one needs a certain amount of angst to inspire great work. I don't know --- Keith Urban seems pretty happy to me.

I made some lunch and spent a couple of hours reading the papers and professional journals online. The phone was quiet until Stone called at four.

"Hey, Riles, we finally caught a break."

"Mulligan's panned out?"

"In a major way. The guy who runs it, the owner I guess, is this big, tall handsome galoot, reminds me of Bubba Watson."

"How nice for him. Was he wearing a green jacket?"

Stone could barely contain his excitement. “Har har. The day before the murder, someone came in and bought Silver Oak 1991. The proprietor remembered it because he doesn’t sell much of it, and the person who bought it hardly looked like a wine connoisseur.”

“Please tell me he used a credit card.”

“No such luck. Paid cash, which was odd considering they were charging a hundred eighty bucks a bottle. Free gift card, of course.”

“That’s steep even for Silver Oak but once you go over that causeway to Long Beach Island, prices have a way of going up. Did the owner at least give you a good description?”

“Better than that. Mulligan’s has been around thirty years and they’ve had a couple of robberies. Generally happens during the high season, when tourists are on the island. Anyway, after the last one, they installed a high end video surveillance system. Software to isolate time and location and instantly provide stills.”

“That is a break. So you’ve got an actual picture of the guy who bought the wine?”

“Yep. Pretty hi-res, too. I have it on my phone, and the Mulligan dude is emailing it to you directly soon as he gets a chance. He’s the only one in the store now so it might be a little while. I could send it on my phone, but it won’t be as sharp.”

I thought about it. As much as I didn’t want to wait, it was a cleaner chain of evidence coming directly from the store. Also, if I needed to ask Logan to run facial recognition on it, the more pixels the better.

"Rick, did the guy remember anything unusual about the person who bought the wine? Like why he didn't want it delivered?"

"Mulligan's is a small shop. They don't have a regular delivery service. They farm it out and only on the island. But the dude didn't want it delivered and said he wanted to fill out the gift card by himself. Wanted a personal message, maybe a little too personal, the Mulligan guy thought."

I said, "Anything else that struck him?"

"Just that the guy was really effeminate. I had to coax it out of him, but he thought the guy was gay. Wore wire rims. Dressed in a sweatshirt, jeans, very short hair. Kind of like a kid trying to sound like a grownup. But it wasn't a kid. Guy had to be in his forties at least, maybe older."

"Good work, Ricky. There might be a job in sleuthing for you yet. After your miserable sports talk career is over, that is."

"This is how you reward your friends for doing your legwork?"

"You'll get half my fee. How's that?"

"I thought you were doing this gratis."

"Exactly. Talk later." I dropped the call.

I couldn't wait to tell McCullough what we had uncovered. By-the-book ramrod that he was, I didn't expect him to be jumping for joy that this little fillip was added to his investigation.

"Yeah, King, whatcha got?"

I told him and as expected, he wasn't moved.

"That's interesting but doesn't get your boy off the hook. McCarver could have hired this person to buy and deliver the wine. And just because someone buys a bottle of Silver Tree or whatever the hell it's called, doesn't mean they're the killer."

"But don't you think it's more than a coincidence? Silver Oak 1991, the same gift card. There was only one store within fifty miles of Toms River that carries both."

"It's interesting but it's a small world these days, King. Who's to say some place in, oh I don't know, Hilton Head, South Carolina, doesn't stock the same two? You got to bring me more than that if you want me to take this seriously."

"How about I forward the picture to you and you run it through your facial recognition software. At least get me a name and then I'll track it down."

"Us little local peons don't have that capability. You're talking Homeland Security, FBI. I can't ask any of them to do this on a hunch. Even one of yours. Sorry."

He was being his stubborn self, but no more than a District Attorney or Circuit Court Judge might be, presented with the same evidence. "Thanks for nothing, Flint. I thought you wanted to catch the real killer."

"I do. But far as we're concerned we have him in custody already. If you can prove otherwise, you have my number." He hung up.

I'd succeeded in pissing an ally off, never a good thing. It was clear that Stone and I were on our own. The Ocean County authorities were satisfied that they had their man.

SIXTY FOUR

The JPEG from Mulligan's arrived a few hours later, in the early evening. Charlene still wasn't home yet.

Despite what you see on television, there is no way to instantly sharpen blurry pictures taken with cheap cameras. There is software that will help somewhat, but the images will still be grainy and those magic facial recognition programs need decent quality to be effective.

Fortunately, the photo I got was taken with a hi-res camera and the second I saw the picture, no further boost from technology was necessary. My primitive brain and sharp eyed sleuthing skills told me all I needed to know.

Mark Chesterton had bought the wine. Mary and Mark either had to be twins or they'd been born no more than a couple of years apart. The family resemblance was that strong. I conjured up the old photos I had copied from Stonewall, Rogers and the internet. After comparing the images, there was no doubt in my mind. The McCulloughs of the world wouldn't be swayed by my impressions, though. I needed more.

If Mark had bought and delivered the wine, it still didn't prove that he was responsible for Stevie's murder. I could hear McCullough's words before he spoke them.

Why go to Long Beach Island to buy the wine? Why not just have it delivered from wherever Chesterton lived? Where was that exactly? Could it be Long Beach Island?

Stonewall Jackson would know but he would likely be protective and tip Chesterton off that I was suspicious. Contacting him was an option, but not my first choice. I called Stone and ran it by him.

"So Riles, what's your working theory on this?" he asked after I'd explained my findings.

"Obviously, this could be revenge for something that happened forty years ago. I probably kicked the hornet's nest when he talked to Mark about Mary. Maybe McCarver and what happened was a repressed memory that resurfaced when I started digging. All the bile over that incident came flooding back, and with social media being what it is, Ted's condo and wine choices weren't hard to find. This doesn't get Ted off the hook, though."

"Why not? If we can prove Chesterton spiked the wine?"

"Spiking wine and killing someone? That's a big step. It might have just made it easier for Ted to do it if Stevie was incapacitated, even by someone else. That's what McCullough will say. Regardless, what we need to do next is find Chesterton."

"But you don't trust Jackson, so how do you plan to go about this?"

"Are you up for another trip to LBI?"

"Always. What do you have in mind?"

"I canvassed some realtors down there when I was investigating Paige White's murder. It's like Hilton Head in that it's a small island and everybody knows everybody else's business. Especially realtors, who need to know who's divorcing or who's in financial trouble or who's dying so they can get listings. If you show that photo to some of them, I'm sure somebody will know an address if Chesterton lives down there or if it was a rental. It's off season so rents wouldn't be crazy high like they are in the summer. Might even be cheaper than a motel."

"Worth a shot."

"If you can get an address, I'll run up and take it from there."

"All of this work for half of your fee?" Stone asked.

"Tell you what. Sixty per cent and not a penny more."

"Good deal. I'll start tomorrow, right after I get off the air. Wait a minute, it's the weekend. I'm not on."

Sixty five

It was nine p.m. when Charlene pulled her BMW Z4 into the garage. The little sportster was overloaded with clothing. I offered to help her carry things into the house but she shooed me away. Her breath was strong with drink, and had I been a cop, I would have insisted on a sobriety test. I held off comment until she appeared in the kitchen, flustered and obviously high.

"So what happened? The stores wouldn't take the stuff back?" I asked.

"I decided to have lunch and a couple of drinks first with some girlfriends and we had a good talk, lasted until dinner. Then we ate, had a few more cocktails and by the time we were finished, the stores were closed."

This was an obvious lie. Most stores in Charlotte close at nine Friday nights, and here she was. Rather than challenge her directly, I asked, "I guess you could just go back in the morning."

"We have any Amaretto? Grand Marnier?"

"Maybe. Haven't checked lately. Charlene, what's going on? You lit out this morning, never called, never let me know if I should eat without you or what."

"I'm supposed to report my every movement to you? Is that our little arrangement, King?"

This wasn't the time to pick a fight. She was out of her gourd, but sometimes the false courage of drink brings things to the surface that have been bubbling under. Things had been really chafing her lately Between her anger at me for sticking with the McCarver case and her angst at being dropped by Cirrus, these were not good times for Charlene.

"I was just worried, that's all," I said, backing off.

"What, you don't think I can look after myself? Well, for your information, I was doing fine before I met you and I can do fine now."

I was tempted to say that if doing fine meant being married to a criminal who was murdered in their bathroom by a Russian mobster, then have at it.

"I'm sure you can, babe. Let's go to bed and we can talk in the morning."

"So that's your answer to everything. Fuck me silly and it'll be all right. Show me who's boss in the feathers."

I'd never heard that expression but it didn't take an advanced literary degree to figure out what she meant. "You look tired. I just thought that you had a long day and needed some sleep, that's all."

"Not like your little sexy Catholic schoolgirl fantasy? There's Sacred Heart Girls' Academy just a few miles away. I'm sure a big hunk like yourself wouldn't have a problem finding a teenager willing to give it up."

Where was all this coming from? What had happened today to turn Charlene into this venom spewing hydra?

"Let's not go there. I'm turning in," was my last attempt at civility.

"That's it, King. Walk away. Don't engage. That's your way of avoiding the truth."

"That's it." I had tried to ignore the brickbats, but she had pushed too far. "What the hell happened today? You come home plastered. Pissed off at the world, and me in particular. What's going on?"

"You let me walk out this morning, ready to abandon my career. That's what you wanted all along, wasn't it? You be the big breadwinner and 'lil ole Charlene will stay at home cooking and cleaning. You couldn't have been happier when the tour fell through. Admit it."

"I never said that."

"You didn't have to. You're out gallivanting in New Jersey with your whoremaster friend Stone trying to vindicate a wife beater pal and I have to stay home and take care of your damn dog."

Bosco was asleep on the bed when last I saw him and I was surprised that all of Charlene's shouting didn't bring him out to see what was going on. I tried to keep from raising my voice, but I failed. "You are being totally irrational. I never stopped you from going on tour all summer and I took care of the dog, even when it interfered with my work. And if you can remember back to this morning, I said you should keep the outfits and that there would be another tour soon."

"Yeah, right. A weak little protest, designed to make me think you care about my career when you'd really like to see it go up in flames. Admit it."

“Who called Darius Rucker’s people to get you started again? Did you forget that?”

“You think you did me a favor? His manager said that you approached him very timidly and said if he didn’t think I was right for the tour, to let it drop. You really undersold me big time, King.”

It was true that I hadn’t pressured Rucker’s people. I didn’t want to make it just a favor to me if she couldn’t deliver the goods. That’s why I low-keyed it. But it had worked and she had been given a chance that thousands would kill for.

“I don’t know what you’ve heard and from who, but the call I made for you helped. You got the gig.”

“The only reason you volunteered to help was that you were afraid I’d try to fuck my way into a job, like I did before.”

Some things said in anger, can be forgiven. Some things are the result of long buried emotions that come pouring out when the brain’s governor is chemically removed. But there are certain things you just can’t un-hear. I was about to say things that I thought needed to be said at the time. I felt Charlene needed a big dose of reality. Things had gone so far that my irate brain’s governor was off, as well.

“You want to know why your Christmas tour was cancelled, Charlene? It was Ted McCarver. He paid for you to be on it. That’s how it works these days. When he got arrested, the radio people wanted to distance themselves from him and returned the money. Then they hired this Joanna Black, the girl that they wanted all along.

The only way you got this in the first place was my *wife beating pal*."

If I had slapped her across the face, I couldn't have hurt her more. She sunk back into herself for a moment, then rushed into the garage and started the car. I waited a beat to simmer down a little, then went after her. She was already patching out of the driveway when I got there.

I didn't know how we could recover from this. I could blame her for goading me into telling her the truth about Harrison Mitchell, something I'd resolved not to do less than twelve hours earlier. She was right that I had reservations about committing to someone who would be away a large part of the time. But the months we had lived together were great when both of us were home, so I was willing to try.

Maybe her explosion saved us both a lot of pain. I'll never know. The next morning, three large men arrived at my house and told me Charlene had sent them to gather up her belongings. They showed me a note, in her handwriting, granting them permission. She worked fast.

Maybe I should have just walked away when she started in on me. She might have had a nightcap, retreated to the guest room to sleep it off and apologized the next morning for her alcohol induced paranoia.

It hurt like hell. I really believed that she was someone I might spend the rest of my life with. I'd called it quits with Jaime over this woman. I searched my soul for my part in this failure. Maybe a Doctor Mills could show me how I went wrong.

Why someone as beautiful, talented and smart as Charlene couldn't make a go of it with someone other than a sordid mobster was something I've never understood. There was a void within her that must have sabotaged other relationships along the way. I felt awful that a woman with so much to offer had a hollow spot inside that could never be filled.

As it was, I had no idea where she would stay now that she had left me. She had a lot of girlfriends. But I wasn't really worried about the physical welfare of Charlene Jones.

She'd land on her feet. She always did.

SIXTY SIX

I was lucky that Mrs. Keegish loved dogs, especially Goldens. I was running out of ways to thank her for taking Bosco on the spur of the moment. She never accepted the cash I tried to press on her, and I was running out of ideas for cute tokens of gratitude.

I felt guilty about how I was treating my canine buddy. Although you can never know for sure what's going through a dog's mind, he seemed confused and more than a little hurt that Charlene was gone and her things had been whisked away by the hands of strangers. On top of that, his dad was off again, leaving him with the old lady down the street. Although by now, he must be used to his play dates with Mrs. Keegish, who probably spoiled him more than I ever did. Nonetheless, I resolved that once this case was over, I'd spend a lot of quality time with Bosco; a road trip to a park where he could run free.

I felt little trepidation leaving my home unguarded. Charlene still had a key, although it would be out of character for her to try to inflict any damage or take anything she wasn't entitled to. The men she had sent to take her belongings had left several items behind that weren't in plain sight or in her closet. If she came back for them while I was away, I couldn't stop her. Wouldn't want to, either --- cleaner that way.

I would spend the next hours heading north filled with misgivings about the last year. My association with Ted had played a large part in losing Charlene. He represented everything she hated and feared. Given what she had been through, I should have been more sympathetic. She'd experienced this terror firsthand. She saw him as a rapist and abuser and I had chosen him over her. It now was apparent to me that had been more egregious than my qualms about her career.

A mid morning phone call from Stone had spurred my decision to return to New Jersey --- that and a quick online search of Long Beach Township's municipal records. Technology afforded me the ability to do both simultaneously. I still marvel at how effortless it is.

"Riles, got a great lead. It was easy. You actually take money for this?"

"A ten per cent bonus is headed your way, pal. What do you have?"

He laughed. "I'm thinking I'll hold out for twenty. Call me back if you agree to my terms."

"Funny. Okay, out with it."

"The first realtor I canvassed in Harvey Cedars. A woman named Joanne. Been working the island forever and she's grooming her daughter for when she retires. Broad's got a photographic memory, I think. Anyway, when I showed her the picture, she said that she remembered this person had come into their office, like a year ago, looking for a deal on a fixer-upper. Didn't have a lot of money to put down and this Joanne suggested he look for a foreclosure but there weren't any she knew of that fit the bill at that time."

"That's your lead? Slim pickings there. Did she get a name?"

"No, the guy came and went pretty quickly, just talked to her at the counter, wouldn't sit down at her cubicle even. But Joanne says she ran into him at the hardware store a few weeks back. Asked how the search was going. Dude acted like they'd never met before so Joanne backed off. But she said he was buying electrical items, switches, Romex and such. She figured that he had found a fixer-upper on his own."

"She didn't get an address?"

"Said she planned to look through some foreclosures out of curiosity and see which one the guy had bought but got busy with paying customers and never followed through. She kept calling the guy a kid and when I asked her about it, she said that she was seventy five so anyone under sixty was a kid to her. But she did say the guy had a boyish quality. Looked young like he didn't even shave yet but had lines, like someone with some age on him. Short hair, like military."

"Sounds like Mark Chesterton. Where are you now?"

"Still on the island. Thinking of having lunch here."

"Do that. Afterwards, I want you to check out a place. Just cruise by it. Don't look into any windows or snoop conspicuously." I gave him an address.

"Why? You think you know where Chesterton lives."

"I do. I'm flying up today. Call me after you check this place out. I'll likely be well on my way by then."

"Charlene won't like that. You've barely been home and you're taking off again."

"Charlene isn't a factor anymore."

"What?"

"I'll tell you when I see you. Enjoy your lunch."

I left him hanging. Before talking to him, my search had revealed no purchases in the last year to a Chesterton on Long Beach Island. But there was a sale that had to be a foreclosure, given the location and the price. The property had been snapped up for a figure barely above the value of the land. I was a bit surprised that an investor or a syndicate of real estate speculators hadn't grabbed it first.

Or maybe they had. The name on the deed was Jackson, Robert Wynn. Known to pop music fans as "Stonewall."

SIXTY SEVEN

I had landed at Newark and rented a car. Next order of business, call Stone.

Stone said, "Black Eye Susan's in Harvey Cedars. I'm telling you Riles, they know how to make a burger sing."

"Thanks for the review. Maybe when your sports gig at JOK is over, you can work for the Food Network as the Grand Gourmand."

"I guess it's a long slog. Next time why don't you drive and bring Bosco along. You'll have someone on your level to talk to, at least."

"Have you had a chance to scope out that house or were you too busy looking for a custard stand?"

"The restaurant had a nice dessert menu. Strawberry cheesecake, yummy. Then I hit the beach for a bit, but it's too chilly for bikinis. But yeah, I drove by that address you gave me. Great location, not so great house. Someone's doing some work on the place. There was a chunky old white guy in a tie-dye tee shirt and a ponytail painting some trim and a skinny guy working on the deck. Skinny guy looked like the picture, best as I could tell from a distance. A truck and a beat up Toyota in the driveway."

"You got plans for tonight?"

"I do, but nothing I can't get out of. Why?"

"Book us a room at that motel on the island, the one just over the causeway. They shouldn't be full this time of year."

"Us a room? Or two rooms?"

"I don't mind sharing. We've done it before. Just make sure there are two beds if you do. And get some nasal strips for your snoring."

"Two rooms it is. Should I use our own names? *Secret Agent Man. They've given you a number and taken 'way your name.*"

"No reason not to use our real identities, or you can sign in as Bruce Wayne if you like. I should be there by seven or so. Go ahead and eat. I'll grab something on the way down."

"Roadkill. Delish. You've assimilated to Southern Cuisine really well."

"See you later."

Next call was McCullough. As usual, he answered after two rings.

"Yeah, King. What do you want?"

"You working tomorrow?"

"I'm always working. But it's Sunday and I'm not going *in* to work if that's what you're asking. Got some buttoning up to do around the house, getting ready for winter."

"I've got a lead I'm following up on tomorrow. I might need you."

"What kind of lead?"

"I don't want to say yet in case it doesn't pan out. But you're what, about a half hour from Long Beach Island?"

"I am."

"Great. I may call you tomorrow morning. But I promise, only if an arrest is imminent. I won't waste your time."

"And you won't enlighten me further? You expect me to just drop everything on a Sunday morning and come to your rescue."

"I do. Because that's the kind of guy you are."

The rest of the drive down was uneventful. Played some Joni Mitchell, tried to focus on tomorrow. Tried not to think about Charlene but every so often, Joni hit me with a line that brought back the pain.

SIXTY EIGHT

The motel room smelled musty and I had no doubt that there were roaches and mold hiding behind the walls of the spartan bathroom. Even in the off season, weekend rates were high given the quality of the accommodations, but location is everything. With the windows open and the wind blowing from the east, you could hear the surf pounding against the dunes. It didn't help me sleep but nothing would.

After filling Stone in on my plan, we re-tested the equipment I brought with me, second generation stuff I hadn't used in a while. The technology was basic and worked as it should.

Stone had bought a six pack that we killed while some uninteresting college football played on the television. I gave him the Cliff Notes version of what had happened with Charlene. He tried to be consoling and said that he never really liked her that much anyway, that Jaime was a much better match. During my drive I had become convinced of that but I'd blown it with Jaime and it was too late to go back. Stone tried to change the subject to lighten things up, raving on about how one of the quarterbacks in the game we were watching might be a Jet next season. I feigned attention but he sensed I wasn't into it and retreated to his room to turn in early.

The good old US of A had switched from Daylight Savings to Standard time so the sun came up early over the

Atlantic. We found a breakfast place a few blocks away. I ate light, just coffee and an English muffin. Stone didn't know the meaning of eating light, so I had to watch as he devoured a stack of syrup drenched hotcakes with a double side of sausage and home fries.

Rick had noticed that the house next to Jackson's was closed down for the season. It was shielded by a tall row of arborvitae, which made perfect cover for us. As we pulled up, there was only one vehicle at the Jackson house, a late model pickup truck, looked like a Dodge Ram.

"All set. The record function is activated. You have my cell with McCullough on speed dial. Wait for my signal to call him. We may need his help down the road and I don't want to piss him off with false leads."

"Gotcha. You think I'll need this?" He raised his .38 Sig Sauer.

"Doubtful. But it's good to know you have it. Don't forget, honk twice if anyone else pulls in."

"All set."

"And Ricky, no heroics this time. No charging in, guns blazing. You almost bought the farm once for me. I don't see this situation getting out of hand. If my little plan works, we'll hand it off to McCullough."

Stone nodded and I walked across the gravel yard to the house next door. It was small, probably not more than twelve hundred square feet. It stood tall on pilings to protect it from flooding, and was outfitted with hurricane shutters and an aluminum shake roof. After Superstorm Sandy ravaged the Jersey shore, there were a lot of second home owners who were willing to let their places go at a loss, just to get out of harm's way. Even though Long Beach Island was spared the brunt of the storm's wrath, values were way down from their peak. Since this appeared to be an unattractive foreclosure that needed work, a handy flipper willing to do work on it himself might have picked it up cheap.

I tucked the Beretta into the small of my back, hidden by my Panthers windbreaker. It was just a precaution but the FBI and Boy Scouts taught me to always be prepared.

I rang the doorbell. Not functioning, so I knocked.

"Hold on, hold on. Did you forget your keys?"

Jackson flung open the door and couldn't stifle his shocked expression.

"What in blazes? Riley King. What are you doing here?"

"I think you can figure that out, Stonewall. We need to talk."

"About what?"

"May I come in? Can we handle this like gentlemen?"

His eyes darted around the porch to see if there was anyone behind me. "Come in, laddie."

The place had potential. It was tiny and a work in progress but what had already been done was done well. The kitchen was miniscule but open to the main room with an island large enough for four barstools. The floors throughout were some sort of hand scraped engineered wood. There were a couple of open doors which I assumed led to bedrooms, one of which looked finished, the other still showing joints with tape and compound.

"So, you bought this for Mark?"

"The funds were his but he hadn't established credit so I bought it in my name. I gave him a little help which he's paying off. Look, if you came here to talk to him, please leave him alone. I told you when you first came around that I want to respect his privacy. He wasn't interested in any pot of gold from this sod McCarver, so just leave him be."

"If that's all this was, I wouldn't be here. You must know that Ted's in jail, accused of killing his fiancée."

"From what Mark told me of the cheeky bastard, I wasn't surprised when I heard. After what he did to Mary."

Jackson was far from the avuncular welcoming presence he had been the first time we met. He was clearly jumpy about something.

"Let me lay it out for you. We have video of Mark buying wine and a gift card. The same vintage and same card that was found at the place where McCarver's woman was killed."

He shook his head rapidly, as if on a spring. "So?"

"So, the wine is pretty rare. And the specific note card and wine combination are only sold at the one shop."

"I'm not sure what you think this means. If Mark bought some bleeding wine as a gift for someone, so what?"

"And Mark is wealthy enough to spend almost two hundred bucks on a bottle of wine as a gift and pay in cash?"

I could see I needed more to convince him to tell me what he knew. So I made something up. "And some of the wine spilled and the cops got a partial print and also a shoe impression. It didn't match anyone already in the system but I'll bet dollars to doughnuts that it will match Mark's."

His face turned ashen. "They have no right to demand fingerprints."

"Oh, but they do. The wine purchase. The history of Mark's sister with McCarver. The wine spiked with the same date rape drug that McCarver allegedly used on her. That gives them probable cause."

"So why are you here and not them?"

"Because there's no official record of a Mark Chesterton anywhere. No driver's license. No credit cards. They don't have time to chase down a ghost. I do. And now that I've found him, I'll turn it over to them."

Jackson paced the small room. I touched the Beretta for reassurance.

"Listen, King. I'm going to appeal to you as a man. You know what a barmy life his sister had. She blamed McCarver. Maybe he didn't start the ball rolling with her problems, but he chivvied along the process. So maybe Mark wanted a little revenge. Maybe he wanted to show McCarver what it was like to be drugged with that stuff. But murder? Bugger off."

"So you admit he bought the wine, spiked it, and delivered it to McCarver's place?"

"It's not up to me to admit it. King, what's the point of this? That woman was killed. Does it really matter if she was bladdered? Isn't that small potatoes compared to what happened to her? Why put my mate through this when the police have the bloke that done it locked up?"

I heard a horn beep twice. Someone was here. I didn't let on to Jackson that this was Stone's signal to me that we were about to have company. I wanted Jackson to think that I could be reasoned with and that his scenario was feasible. "You have a point. Even though the police could view person drugging the wine as an accessory to the murder, that was not the intent. I get that."

The door opened. It was Chesterton, clearly recognizable from the pictures.

"Oh, Bob, I didn't know you had company," Chesterton said. "An old friend? You didn't tell me."

Video, photos, and sound recordings all have their purpose. Talking to someone on Skype is almost like the real thing. But all our digital devices can't perfectly replicate the experience of *being there*.

There was no twin brother or closely born sibling. There was no *Mark* Chesterton. The person who walked through the door was Mary Chesterton.

SIXTY NINE

Mary/Mark was wearing a sweatshirt and baggy cargo shorts. Her hair was still dark, clipped short, military style. Despite her attempts to look hard and masculine, her face retained a femininity that was impossible to disguise. She seemed smaller than she appeared in the pictures I'd seen --- no more than five and a half feet and barely over a hundred twenty pounds. I'm not versed enough in transgender matters to guess if she was getting hormone treatments or had had some kind of surgery. To my eye, she was still a woman masquerading as a man, as insensitive as that may sound.

"My name is Riley King. I was working recently on behalf of Ted McCullough, er McCarver. You remember, it was about his desire to make amends for some of the things he did when he was young. Stonewall told me he'd broached the subject with you and you declined."

I'd deliberately botched the name. That was my signal to Stone to call McCullough and get him down here.

She said, "I remember. And I do remember telling Mr. Jackson to tell you that I wasn't interested in soothing the old man's conscience."

"Well, talking to your friend Mr. Jackson here, I have to applaud your ability to forgive someone who did you wrong. Delivering a bottle of expensive wine as a wedding gift was very thoughtful."

Her eyes shot daggers at Stonewall. “I don’t know what you’re talking about.”

“The police have video of you buying a bottle of Silver Oak 1991 along with a gift card and they’ve matched that to the one found in Ted’s condo. Along with the dead body of his fiancée. Now do you know what I’m talking about?”

Jackson had been quiet until now. “Mark, I told Mr. King the truth. You told me that you wanted McCarver to see that you held no grudges, so you sent him a bottle of wine.”

Mary played outrage convincingly. “What are you saying? Are you crazy, old man?”

I had come prepared with a stratagem to have them turn on each other, but they were doing a great job of it on their own. I just watched.

Stonewall said, “King here is just faffing about. Come on now, don’t be shy. You did a kindness. Take the credit.”

Jackson was doing a poor job of acting. His tone was that of a father admonishing his child for misunderstanding his orders and over trimming the hedges.

Mary seemed confused but she finally pieced it together at around the same time I did. She lurched toward the old man and pounded her fists against his chest. He grabbed them and pulled her into a close embrace, which she struggled to break.

“My God, what did you do? Stonewall, what did you do?” she said, spitting the words out.

All the while my phone was transmitting their words to the recording device in Stone's possession a few dozen yards away. I'd keep the two of them from harming each other, but there was no reason to break the momentum.

"I did it for you, child. I did it for you."

Mary crumpled into a heap on the floor, dumbstruck. "Not for me. How could you? How could you?"

She curled into a fetal position, sobbing. Jackson looked at me and tried to explain.

"Mark was dodgy about McCarver after you called. Oh, why the hell are we pretending, it's Mary, all right. You know that don't you, King?"

I nodded.

"She hacked into his email account. It's all she talked about when we spoke, how Ted did this and Ted did that. The bloody bastard. The bloke was getting married and going to live happily ever after. She'd call me, day and night. It always started with, *Can you believe what McCarver is doing now?*"

Mary now lay motionless on the floor.

"I had to do something with this dog's dinner. Mary had tracked his movements so I knew that he was flying up that day. I had Mary buy the wine the day before. I spiked it and delivered it meself. I rang and left it on the doorstep. I thought that they'd both drink it and it would fark them up. Then I'd let Mary know that she'd gotten a wee bit of payback for what he did to her."

"So you're saying you did this all for her? Kill them both for what he did to Mary?" I said.

"No, not kill them. I just wanted them to feel helpless, like what Mary felt all those years ago. I even waited on a roof where I could see into their window. But then I saw the chuffed bugger storm out, didn't even drink the wine."

Mary didn't even stir now, her eyes were blank.

The old man was distraught. "I started to worry. After the bastard left, she started guzzling straight from the bottle. She might have drank the whole lot herself. You see, I know all about dosing from my days with the lads in the band. Half a bottle will make ya sleep, the whole thing could kill ya. So I knocked on the door. She must have thought it was him."

The words ran together as he related his story. "I told her about what her man had done to Mary. I thought when she heard what a shite her intended really was, she might be having second thoughts."

I said, "If you were so worried about her safety, why didn't you just take the bottle and pour it down the drain?"

"I wanted her to hear the truth. But then she went and defended the pommy bastard. She said he had told her all about Mary and she believed him. She said Mary was a weak little crybaby who blamed her troubles on others. A pathetic loser."

He shivered convulsively, as if he had stepped into icy water. "I lost my temper. I did it for you, Mary."

Mary was still on the floor motionless, catatonic. The door to the beach house creaked open. Standing there, handcuffs at the ready, was Flint McCullough.

SEVENTY

Noon the next day, at the Starlight. Even though there was a big press event scheduled for two o' clock, Flint's lunch break was inviolate.

McCullough barely looked up. I was used to it.

He said, "Thought I'd see you here, King. Ordered you a BLT. Held the fries, keeping with the new, trimmer you."

"Gee thanks, detective. You're so good to me."

"If you only knew. Sorry we had to move you out so quick yesterday, but can't have civilians hanging around a big arrest. Wouldn't look right." He took a big gulp of water and gave me what passed for a grin.

I said, "Yeah, I did have a couple of questions. Like how you got there so fast. It couldn't have been ten minutes after I signaled Stone to call you."

"Huh. It was *that* long. Truth be told, I heard about this great breakfast joint on the island and I was dying to try it. Wife and kids went to Mass, so I was at loose ends."

"Right. Even though I told you I didn't want to waste your time on a false lead."

"Guess I've learned to trust your hunches when I'm on my own time. So sue me."

The waitress brought our food. “Don’t you ever order anything else?” I asked.

“Egg white and greens. Keeps me regular and I’m a regular guy. Dig in.”

I took a bite of the perfect BLT. It’s hard to go wrong with a BLT.

I said, “So, I suppose you’ve already talked to the powers that be. What are the charges going to be?”

“Jackson --- Second degree. Might bump it down to man one given his age and the circumstances. Some of the ADAs were pressing for murder one given that he planned it with the wine and all, but I don’t think that will fly. The girl or guy, take your pick. Psych ward for now, she was pretty much catatonic, all day yesterday. They may charge her as an accessory later. She did buy the wine, and probably spiked it. It led to a murder, regardless of whether she intended it to. McCarver’s out today after they process paperwork. They wanted him at the press conference announcing the arrests but he declined.”

“I know. Stone’s picking him up out the back door after he gets off the air. Trying to avoid the media.”

“Bravo for him. He could have rubbed our noses in it. Still could, but somehow I don’t think so.”

He went back to eating. It was strange. Here we were, sharing diner food as if we were two old chums at an accounting firm on our lunch break. Just happened to be talking clinically about life and death matters.

McCullough said, “I know Stone saw McCarver yesterday afternoon. Anything you want to share?”

"Nothing you won't find out on your own eventually. He's giving John League a retainer to handle Mary's case. And money for the shrink she needs if it's not too late for that. He'll cover Stonewall, too."

"Hate to say it, but your guy has a few bolts missing. The man did kill his lover. In a way, I feel bad for the old coot, though. Devoted his days to saving what others deemed unsalvageable. Old houses, damaged women."

"How poetic. I didn't think you had it in you."

"It's the Irish in me, lad. Take it a step further. In his mind, he wanted to spare Stevie from Ted. But you met Stevie. She was plain spoken to a fault, at least the Stevie Perry I knew. Didn't waste time with bullshit. If she had just graciously sent him on his way and thanked him for his concern, none of this would have happened."

I said, "I suppose so. Although who knows how the drug affected her judgment? If she was straight, she might have been a tad more diplomatic. You knew her better than I did."

"There was some concern about how we got onto him, since some liberal judge might throw out your recording and everything thereafter as fruit of the poison tree. But he hadn't disposed of his weapon. Had some sentimental value to him. Ballistics will match it to the slug they took out of Stevie and that should seal it. It'll be months, maybe a year before a trial. Guy's got clogged up arteries, according to him. Who knows if he'll last that long."

I finished my sandwich and took a sip of my Diet Dr. Pepper. "Poor old fool thought the pistol was one of

General Patton's. Worthless replica that should be sitting at the bottom of Barnegat Bay now. As for Mary, I don't know."

McCullough nodded. "I'm with Stevie on this one. You gotta get over the shit that happened when you were a kid. Can't blame your parents forever. And I'm lost when it comes to this gender confusion. I guess some people's wiring is just messed up. I suppose the docs will know if she had shots or surgery or whatever. I really don't want to know the gory details unless I absolutely have to. Call me backwards if you want, but that's me."

I said, "The brain's a curious organ. There's so much we don't understand. I guess we just have to accept people's differences and let them be who they are."

"Well, I've got to get back for the press conference."

"Are you going to be a hero or villain on this one?"

"I suppose the DA will portray me as a dogged old veteran who wouldn't settle for easy answers. I'll come out okay, mayhaps even a promotion. Hey, I've got to get back. Thanks, King. After all you've done, lunch is on me."

Who said mine is a thankless job?

SEVENTY ONE

Stone had texted me that an intimate dinner had been arranged for Ted in a private room at one of our old haunts, a place we frequented when I worked at the Jersey Shore. *Wind on the Water* was under new management, and I heard that they had undertaken a much needed updating of both the atmosphere and menu. As long as they had a decent wine list, I was fine with the choice. Silver Oak, anyone?

When I walked into the cozy paneled room, Stone was sitting alone at a small table with place settings for three. I assumed Ted had been delayed.

Stone cleared his throat, theatrically. "I have a couple of things to tell you that I didn't want to mention by text or on the phone. First thing is, Ted won't be joining us tonight."

Clearing the man of murder charges warranted at least a heartfelt thank you. Not that I needed one, but it seemed out of character for the genteel McCarver to duck the obligation.

"Knock me over with a feather. Do I get any further explanation?"

"You remember *Band on the Run*?"

"McCartney? Sure, why?"

He said, "*If I ever get out of here, gonna give it all away, to a Registered Charity.*"

"Thanks for not singing it. So what, Ted's going to become a monk?"

"How did you know?"

"I was kidding."

Stone said, "I'm not. It seems that after Stevie died, Ted was going that way. He hired a lawyer while he was in stir. He's donating a good chunk of his assets to a home for battered women in Hilton Head and some of the rest to the Monks of New Skete. They're the ones who train service dogs. He's on his way to join them now. They're non denominational, don't care who you pray to. He wants to live a life of service. Without Stevie, he can't see getting involved with another woman, so he says he's going to live and I quote --- *a celibate life of quiet contemplation and sacrifice in upstate New York.*"

I was glad for the alcohol in front of me and I drank deeply from it. All I could say was, "You tried to talk him out of it, I hope. These aren't the kind of decisions to be made in his emotional state."

"I did. But the time in jail gave him time to reevaluate things, *again.* You know Ted, he's no fool. He gave himself a hedge. He'll keep a good piece of money in trust accounts. He'll hold onto the plane. Still has a share in the restaurants. If he does change his mind someday, he says he'll have enough to get by, although not in the style he did before. He did mention that he wired a little something into your account to say thanks, and that he even had a little gift for me, but wouldn't say what it was. And he set aside some funds for a sick friend, as he put it."

"Mary Chesterton's psychiatric care. Well, I would have like to have seen him one more time, at least. Since it turns out he was the genuine article all along. I guess we raise our glasses, in absentia. To Ted."

We clinked and downed the fine wine. I still couldn't tell the difference between it and my current favorite that sold for ten bucks. "So who's the third setting for?"

"Someone who I thought should share your moment of triumph."

"Hey, it's not my moment. We all pitched in. And I'm giving, what is it now, sixty per cent of my fee to you?"

"That and a couple hundred bucks will pay for this dinner, except Ted took care of it in advance."

"Of course."

"I'll be right back. Hold the fort."

The third setting had me thinking. This place wasn't McCullough's style. Was Stone going to announce that he and Cindy were ... no, not that.

Imagine my surprise when Jaime Johansen walked through the door.

SEVENTY TWO

Through some paranormal gifts or maybe just based on our long friendship --- Rick believed that Charlene was not going to be more than a brief chapter in my life. I was unaware that he had been lobbying Jaime all along, with occasional lunches and dinners when business brought him to New York. Upon hearing the news that Charlene had moved out, he persuaded her that she should fight for the man she was still in love with. He'd convinced her that when she asked for a time-out in our relationship, she maintained silence for too long. She admitted that the surge in her agency's film activity had caused her to put her personal life on the back burner, which in turn gave Charlene the opportunity to fill the void.

Rick also had been working Jaime on the business front, emphasizing that he had been able to do his New Jersey radio program from North Carolina and there was no reason she couldn't do the same with her agency.

Rick vanished when Jaime appeared at Ted's farewell dinner, leaving us to sort things out. The biggest obstacle was still distance: I wasn't about to leave Charlotte and she spent most of her time in New Jersey.

She said she was now willing to try to conduct as much of her work as she could from North Carolina, traveling to New York or Los Angeles as needed, which she stipulated would be frequently. She had worries that her staff might lose its edge without her daily supervision, but she would entrust her top lieutenants with more responsibility and monitor them from afar.

She needed a few weeks to make the necessary arrangements. She planned to keep her apartment in New Jersey, and not move the bulk of her personal items south until we were both sure that it was working. If we wanted to be together, this represented a decent compromise, mostly on her part.

I wondered how Bosco would react to being reunited with his old mistress, or if he'd even notice the difference. Maybe he'd think Jaime was a better fit, too, although he seemed to cotton to anyone who would feed him. That evening, Jaime drove home after a chaste kiss goodnight. I stayed at Stone's and booked an early afternoon flight back to the Carolinas.

Rick and I talked in the morning before I shoved off. I thanked him for his stealthy intervention with Jaime. He was happy that we were going to try to make a go of it. I told him to come down over the holidays, and I said if Cindy or a reasonable facsimile thereof was necessary to make the trip more enjoyable, I wouldn't object.

There was one more item I needed to address before leaving. After a little digging online, I confirmed my suspicions. What I discovered gave me no joy.

So I made a stop at the Ocean County lockup and was granted an audience with Robert Wynn Jackson.

Unlike Ted, Jackson showed no deleterious effects from his incarceration. He looked as robust as the day we first met. His voice was almost mirthful as he said, "I hope you haven't come to gloat, King. I'm here eating porridge at Her Majesties' Pleasure. No more need be said."

"Always the lyricist. But I need to say a couple of things before we part. I want you to know that I'm aware of what you're doing."

He shifted uneasily in his too tight orange coveralls. "I thought that would be obvious after Sunday. I did what I did. I'm not cracking proud of it, but I can't take it back."

"You could, actually. I have access to E-Z Pass records, don't ask how. Just for the hell of it, I ran your plates. Turns out your truck was on the Triboro Bridge at the time Stevie was murdered."

"And are you so sure I was driving?"

He was determined to play out his role to the bitter end. But I held all the aces.

I said, "If you really want to persist in this charade, I can alert McCullough and he can probably get security cam photos at the toll plaza. I don't think you want me to do that, do you?"

He knew his bluff had been called and threw in his cards. "No, I don't. King, I'm old and used up. I've had a great life. Done things others could only dream of. Opened for the Beatles. Jammed with Dylan." He mopped his brow with his sleeve. "There's no death penalty in this state. My wife died last year. Mary is the child we never had. Do you blame me for trying to help her?"

"How did she get your gun?"

"I lent it to her. I only come down here weekends to work on the house with her. She's alone during the week so I gave it to her for protection from these Jersey shore blokes."

"She killed an innocent woman with it."

"And I'm willing to pay the penalty for bodging that up. She's undergoing a psychiatric evaluation. After what that poor lass has been through in her life, I don't know lies ahead. If they can fix her, maybe she can have some semblance of a proper life."

"That wasn't a convincing act you two pulled on Sunday. If McCullough hadn't come in when he did, I might have burst your bubble then and there. There was no rooftop where you could see into their condo. But you couldn't know that because you were never there. You were eighty miles away when it happened. I doubt the police will investigate that little wrinkle, since you confessed."

"I didn't think Mary would ever act out her revenge fantasies. I thought it was all bollocks. She told me about the wine and I thought that whatever she used to cock it up would be the extent of it. A good dosing would've served the bugger right. I found out what she did later. I was still processing the whole shirty mess when you barged in."

"So why not just let her take the rap and plead mental incompetence? Why condemn yourself to this?"

"And make her re-live every last detail of her abuse as the barristers try to prove that she was responsible for her actions? And what if that Inspector Morse clone McCullough keeps at it and she's locked away for good? This way, if they just see her as an unwitting mug, she has a chance. Maybe not a great one, given all the damage she's suffered, but a chance."

If she was charged as an accessory, League could easily avoid a trial that by accepting a lenient plea bargain. It is a lot easier to strike a deal for an unwitting accessory as opposed to a premeditated murderer. Either way, Chesterton would pay some kind of price for Stevie.

I said, "*Stonewall* Jackson. An artist who spent his autumn years restoring neglected houses to their former glory. A champion of lost causes."

"I've always tilted at windmills, laddie. Poets believe in redemption, in one form or another. I pray Mary isn't beyond repair but I doubt I live long enough to see that I was right. I told the bobbies about my heart disease, but never mentioned the cancer."

"As I said, Ted McCarver will pay for the best therapy available for her and an attorney for both of you. Should I ask that he add a good oncologist?"

Jackson shook his head, in sad recognition of his fate. "Too late for that, my boy. I'll be accepting of whatever comes to pass. I'm supposing with my advanced years it will be minimum security. Books, poetry, music --- a wee bit of work around where I can use my carpentry skills. It's not the road I would have chosen for meself, but there are worse endings for the likes of me. Don't be thinking I'm asking for your pity, King. My bucket list was filled long ago."

I wasn't going to argue. "Take care, Stonewall. You sure are true to your nickname." I'm not a hugger, but this time, I made an exception.

I left for the airport. As I drove north, I thought about how my good intentions had again resulted in someone's death. Had I refused the case as my initial instincts told me, Ted and Stevie might still have found a way to get together. Maybe Mary wouldn't have discovered their liaison; maybe she would have. I can't change what happened. I have to live with it.

I did my job and found three women. The third is dead at the hand of the first, whose fate rests in the hands of authorities who have no idea of the real extent of her crime. The second, the luckiest of the three, still lives in fear, but is married to a professional assassin who will devote his life to keeping her safe.

And there are two old men, both choosing to live out their days confined to prisons of their own making.

And then there is me, Riley King, caged in by what I do and who I am. If Stone was around, he'd echo what Don Henley once sang: *We are all just prisoners here. Of our own device.*

Acknowledgements

All my radio friends and colleagues were great inspirations for this book. Mark Chernoff and Mike Francesa of WFAN have been particularly supportive. A nod to Mark Mason and Bob Gelb at CBS as well.

Reed Farrel Coleman has been a constant mentor and my many conversations with friends like Michael Harrison and Peter Larkin helped flesh out the characters. I borrowed the name Robert Wynn Jackson from an old college buddy, who was one of the most talented musicians I ever met and who was indirectly responsible for my start in professional radio at WLIR.

As always, my wife Vicky has been my biggest supporter and has done a masterful job designing the graphics and handling the business end of publishing. Duncan, our English Style Golden Retriever, insists that Bosco is based on him, and I have a hard time dissuading him.

About the Author

Richard Neer has had significant roles on and off air at three legendary New York radio stations. He has been a program director and morning show host during his almost thirty year stint at WNEW FM, the groundbreaking progressive rocker. Along with Michael Harrison, he started WLIR as a rock station in 1970.

He has worked as a sports talk host at WFAN since 1988, the first full time sports station in the country.

His work of nonfiction, *FM, the Rise and Fall of Rock Radio*, is the story of how bottom line oriented interests killed a form of radio that was loved by millions.

His Riley King series began with *Something of the Night*, followed by *The Master Builders* and now *Indian Summer*. The next installment, *The Last Resort* will be released next year.